WHISPER OF TREASON

Action: a secret underground forward Soviet military intelligence headquarters in Poland; a chance encounter in Zagreb airport where the American traveler Ben Cornelius gets caught in the web of the Yugoslav Secret Police; the mountains of Roumania from whence the most important Soviet defector since Penkovsky is to be spirited away; and Belgrade itself, where Ben matches his wits and pits his life against the KGB, UDBA, and hidden opposition within the CIA itself. Only a lovely Yugoslav girl and a wise old spy are there to help him. Treason's whisper is everywhere.

A first journey to the Balkans is Ben's initiation into the violent and treacherous world of spies. He emerges, as will the reader, an insider—stronger, tougher, forever changed by what he has seen and done.

Nowhere else in the literature of espionage are the inner workings of the Soviet apparatus, the CIA and UDBA stations, or indeed the mind of a defector, set forth with more realistic drama.

Realistic? It could not be otherwise, for Hartshorne is an intelligence professional, the KGB his beat. No wonder the reader will experience with Ben Cornelius the adventures of involvement in this world of spies from which, although it is invisible, there is no escape for any of us.

WHISPER OF TREASON

HARTSHORNE

Reprinted by arrangement with Robert Hale, Ltd.

ISBN: 1-55547-191-9

ONE

The Balkans, mothers to War, sisters to Injustice, nieces of Treachery, godmothers to Chaos; a lovely family to be sure, but misleading to strangers, for though their smiles are charming, they are not without their wiles. This September day at the Zagreb airport only shrill Chaos was evident, but with the whole of her fateful family in the background, indeed present today by proxy.

Proxies may be unaware of the purpose to which they will be put. Such was the case for the well-dressed American waiting impatiently on the wooden bench for his airplane to Split, that airplane now five hours delayed. The American was Benjamin Cornelius, 37, an Oregonian generally blessed by life but now in transition. It would prove more transition than he could guess.

The Balkans have earned their image of conflict and cunning, Europe having enjoyed there, with and without the help of Russian, Austrian, Turk, and German, a pretty series of wars as well as massacres, assassinations, and pious and monumental betrayals. In fact, Balkan history leads to the conclusion not simply that humans are, by nature, prone to violent discord, but that man not understood in the context of murder is not understood at all.

Benjamin Cornelius had no such understanding, but the man waiting irritably across from him comprehended it all

very well. Blagoje Savic had surpassing Balkan understanding, as befitted the Deputy Minister of the Interior
and Administrative Head of the UDBA, the Yugoslav
Secret Police. That he was, just then, irritable was natural
enough—the bench was hard, his plane, too, was late, he
was tired, and so much of this discomfort could have been
avoided were he not traveling with false papers as Arso
Pijade, the shabby "guest worker" from Karlsruhe. For
Savic as himself, there would be a private airplane and no
plebeian nonsense in public waiting rooms. But one burden
of intelligence work, even for the chief of spies, is business
travel. In this case Savic had been attending a murder. To
be exact, he had been supervising two murders, "simplifying cases" in the Belgrade jargon.

Intelligence chiefs avoid being present on news-
worthy occasions, but that natural reluctance was counter-
ed by the responsibility for seeing that things went right.
Under his predecessor there had been several embarrassing
mishaps. In 1973 UDBA officer Slobodan Mitric had not
only been arrested after killing three "nationalist"
Croatians in Amsterdam, but had had the poor taste to
confess to the Dutch police. He had confessed not only to
the murders, but admitted he was an UDBA officer whose
further assignment had been to kill Dapcevic, a pro-Soviet
former Montenegrin resident in Brussels. Given the
campaign against Yugoslav separatists, there had been a
number of "simplifications" on the books, but Mitric had
thrown the whole schedule out of synchrony.

Then there had been the Blagojevic affair. When the
simplification program moved forward again, Boara
Blagojevic, a Serb, was slated for removal during his visit to
the United States, but Blagojevic had a natural understanding of his situation and asked the FBI for protection.
The FBI had been helpful. And why? Because another

Yugoslav agent, code name Twilight, had recently defected. A delicate touch, that name. Savic, then in charge of logistics in such affairs, had assigned it himself. Gentle twilight, the time just before a man enters the darkness, the time the assassin stalks and the bullet speeds from the gun.

Only a hired agent, Twilight's balls had shriveled and he'd turned himself in to the FBI before earning his killing keep. He also handed over his weapon, an old 7.62 Tokarev TT-33 automatic. UDBA had a supply of these work-horses and so it was no surprise that when Blagojevic was killed in Brussels the following year, it was by another Tokarev TT-33. Unfortunately, the Belgian police had found the pistol, compared notes with the FBI, and had little difficulty concluding that UDBA had been "simplifying" its cases again. Bad publicity, and no help for Savic, for whom discretion was the highest virtue.

Savic, with four days' beard, revolted by his own guest-worker smell after hours without washing, his eyes rheumy and red, preferred not to dwell on these troubles, but he couldn't help ruminating. He and his country—he genuinely loved Yugoslavia—were besieged, by the Soviets foremost. Savic's world was a mosaic of Soviet Cominform pieces; spies political movements, provocations, weapons depots, propaganda.

Yugoslavia was besieged too, Savic felt, by the separatists, worst among them Croatians who, based and supported abroad, had become blatant terrorists. Their goal was a "free" Croatia. Free indeed. Savic shook his head thinking about the contradiction of a free terrorist state.

Savic loathed liberals. His own perspective had been shaped in the bloody savagery of World War II. There he had learned that there would be no society without hierarchy, no hierarchy without power, no power without authority. For authority to be sustained, there must be ideology. Yugoslavia must have authority, strong authority, and an uncontaminated ideology.

All of this, the traitors Mitric and Twilight, the Soviets, the terrorists, and the overriding need for order, for authority, for ideology to maintain this beloved and fissiparous state, were the reasons why Savic had been in Paris and Munich. In Paris, well alibied by a visit to the Intergovernmental Commission on Migration, he had chatted with a social worker through a timely bombing of a Croatian cell leader's car. The bomb, the car and the Croatian went off together, and Savic, traveling that moment as the Bulgarian academician-tourist Traicho Chervenko, had departed Paris on the Trans Europe Express to Munich. In Munich, following his tradecraft rituals of contact, pass, callback, feint, call and eventual safe-house meeting, Savic had seen to the dismissal of another case. This time his men, as much to avoid laying too neat a pattern for INTERPOL as to avoid the noise, were told to use a quieting needle.

The execution—of his plan and the victim—had been easy. This Croatian frequented a beer tavern whose talkative patrons were not always *gemutlich*. During an ordinary shouting match one of Savic's men escalated matters to a shoving match. Behind their Croatian, seated several tables away, another shove occurred; this one needle into buttocks. It hurt, but by the time their victim turned, his area too had erupted into shouts and shoves. As the patrons became vociferous, the UDBA team glided away, for they were peaceful fellows with no interest in a Munich brawl. The Croatian with the needle-sore ass went home with a splitting headache, and conveniently died that night. The miracle of chemistry. Savic had been delighted as he stepped on the Munich-to-Karlsruhe train. In Karlsruhe he had laid over for four days before taking the Munich-

Zagreb flight. From Zagreb, where he sat now, his destination, Belgrade, was only an hour away if anyone in the Yugoslav Airlines, JAL, ever came up with a plane to go there. Savic was no fan of JAL.

Anna Oposevic sat on the same bench, down at the end near the ladies' room, for she liked tea and had a small bladder and a bad case of nerves. A woman of sixty-five, gray-haired, plump, with good features and very blue eyes, Anna had once been beautiful and was still handsome, poised and tall. Dalmatian neighbors in Split, that lovely seacoast town, considered her one of them. That was kind, for not all Europeans are as tolerant of strangers, even after decades, and Anna had been born Russian.

She'd met her husband, Edvard, during the war, as Soviet troops had moved into Yugoslavia, raping and pillaging in support, Stalin had said, of the Communist Partisans. Anna, a nurse with the Soviet forces, had been appalled, but had kept her mouth shut and tended the wounded. In one of those incidents that beset the plans of commanders, her hospital unit had been caught in a German counterattack. The Russian flank turned and, its back to the mountains, had no place to go. Their commander sacrificed the hospital units as the rest of his division made its escape through a mountain chasm.

Neither the Germans nor the now terrified Russian patients and medical staff had counted on so near a Partisan presence. A Partisan regiment under cover of darkness had sliced down off the mountains on the advancing German flank, taking them by surprise. By night the Partisans had blown a dam at the valley's head, whose waters came rushing down on the German troops, drowning them as they lay encamped.

The confident Partisans had time to attend to their

Russian allies' hospital. In the hours of darkness before the dam blew, they had moved the patients and staff to high ground. Partisan lieutenant Edvard Oposevic met Russian nurse Anna Myagkov, heroically saving her patients and her lovely self. As romance decreed, Anna and Edvard fell in love.

The politics of their marriage were difficult. By dint of patience, applications in quadruplicate, payment of bribes *(blat)* to the division clerk, and catching her commander after a romp with the nurses, Anna managed permission to remain in Yugoslavia. She and Edvard moved to Split, his family home, where he, good artisan, good Communist, and by no means stupid, climbed upward in the ranks of his local fish cannery, becoming a member of the workers' council, then council chairman, and finally, elected manager of the factory at a salary five times higher than his ever-so-equal co-workers and not far below that of the mayor and the local Party chairman. They enjoyed money. Anna used it for travel, sometimes for vacations and for trips as often as possible to see her brother.

"Urgent." The letter had come, containing special visas to Poland.

"I've a letter from Pyotr," she'd told Edvard immediately. "It worries me."

"Your brother?" Edvard raised an eyebrow. That his brother-in-law was a Soviet general was Edvard's bad luck. To have a Russian general in the family was like being a chef whose mother was a known typhoid carrier. Edvard's mail was always of interest to UDBA, although the secret police personally understood and forgave him the accident of his marital choice. Since he knew several of them from the war, there was hardly much secrecy about either the general, the mail cover, Edvard's annoyed embarrassment, or the tolerance of UDBA.

"What does he have to say?" Edvard hardly cared; at least he could be sure it was not political. Compared to what happened to a Russian general's mail outside of Yugoslavia, Edvard knew the UDBA surveillance was nursery school stuff.

"He says he's still in Poland," Anna replied.

"Good. At least he's liberating Poles, not Chinese."

"Oh, Edik, be more sympathetic. You know my brother's no imperialist." Anna's tone was aggrieved.

"Oh sure, the Russians are everybody's friend. That affectionate big bear hugging Estonia, Bulgaria, Poland, Germany. And your brother is a very sharp claw on that bear." Edvard avoided a sneer; it wasn't worth having another fight with Anna about it.

"You don't know that for sure, Edik. I think he is what he's always told us he was, a supply officer."

"Supplies, Anya? You think munitions are harmless?"

"I don't care, and I'm not going to have another brawl with you."

"Not going to have another brawl" meant one was just around the corner. Edvard knew a diversionary tack was called for.

"What else is in the letter? So far I don't hear anything to be worried about."

"That's because you don't give me time to tell you."

She was still bristling; Edvard retreated further. Remarkable, he thought, how one wins a battle and a maiden and returns home with a war and a wife.

"Go ahead, tell me." Edvard was resigned.

"He says he's nearing retirement, hopes to settle near Yalta where it's warm, and wants to know what to do with our parents' things in his Moscow apartment. He reminds me many of the pieces are mine and thinks I ought to help him divide them before he moves. Victor and Natasha apparently don't want them, Raya is willing to part with them."

"His kids and his wife don't want them? Are you kidding? When you visited them all in Moscow, you said the kids were as calculating a batch of greedy bastards as you ever saw. And Raya's no darling either. Let me think." Edvard paused, counting. "Those kids will be thirty-seven and thirty-nine now. Don't tell me they aren't interested in silver plate, old samovars, ikons, and whatever else your family saved from the revolution, not that I expected they'd have saved enough to squabble over."

"That's just it, Edik. They didn't save anything, just the photographs, a little silverware and two old ikons. I'm sure of it. After all, I was there too and I've seen Pyotr's apartment. It's fancy but there's almost nothing in it that belonged to our folks, nothing I have a call on except maybe the ikons. After all, nobody on Pyotr's side is religious."

"But you're different, right?" Edvard, a conventional atheist, would never get used to his wife's Orthodoxy. Church every Sunday and all that, as if there'd never been Communism. Edvard considered it nonsense.

But he had more sense than to push it further. "Now what's all this fuss of Pyotr's about dividing an inheritance you don't have?" he said. "Has he gone crazy?"

"No." Anna was serious. "What he does say is that he wants me to join him in Poland so we can have a family discussion about it. It's rather sad, really. Here, listen to this. 'Anya, we're both getting old and we should see each other while we can. There won't be too many more times; Yalta is far from Split and you never know what will happen.' There! Doesn't that sound ominous to you?"

This time Edvard was listening. In the Eastern bloc such letters are written for two audiences: the secret police who read them first, and then the family. The family's task is to deduce the meaning. A whole language evolves of mystification for strangers and revelation for intimates, each language peculiar and private to each family. Edvard wasn't sure what Pyotr was saying, but when the alarm went off, as it had done now, Edvard knew that the family encrypting was in use. He answered her seriously.

"I agree, Anya, something is on his mind. He's worried about the future."

"And he wants me to come see him about it. He wouldn't say that unless it were urgent; otherwise he'd simply say he's looking forward to a vacation visit by me."

"True," Edvard nodded. That had been the style preceding Anna's earlier visits to Russia.

"And it has something to do with the family," Anna went on, "or he wouldn't have put it in terms of the heirlooms and his children."

"Makes sense," Edvard agreed. "I guess the family is on his mind."

"It always has been," Anna affirmed. "He's been very close to me all these years, and I know he's terribly disappointed in his children. They've turned out to be such materialists, so ambitious, so ruthless."

"The new Soviet man," Edvard said sarcastically. "Just what the Russians wanted and just what they deserve."

"Pyotr doesn't deserve it, Edik, he's a good man." Anna loved her brother; she nodded gently as she spoke.

Edvard had stopped feeling irritable. When things were serious he and Anna—and their family—stood together. Nor, except on principle, did Edvard have reason to dislike his brother-in-law. Everything he knew about him—except that he was a Russian general—was to the good.

"I don't know what it's about, Anya, but I think you should go to him as soon as you can."

"It's good of you to understand. You're awfully good to

me, you know." She walked over to his chair and kissed him. He took her hand.

"You're good to me, Anya. I'll miss you. You say he enclosed a Polish visa?"

"That's right, a special entry. It would have taken weeks to have gotten that from here. That's why I'm so sure something is wrong."

"Do you think he's ill?" Edvard asked.

"That's what worries me most," Anna said, pressing her lips hard.

"It could hardly be anything else," Edvard continued, "certainly nothing political or . . ." He let his voice trail off. Even to think there might be something wrong that was "political" was bad luck. Pyotr would be better off with heart disease or cancer. "Yes Anya," Edvard spoke more emphatically now, "Yes, you'd best make plans to leave as soon as you can."

Anna, child of fate, sat at the end of the hard bench in Zagreb airport, the letter, visas, money and small gifts in her purse. She had noticed the seedy, stubble-faced worker across from her, but paid him no heed. The American nearby could not be ignored; a good-looking young man, she thought, obviously a Yankee. Americans had that optimistic shine on their faces, the quality in their clothes, and the good ones a naive readiness to be friendly, as though they did not know about the world. This was such in American.

But Benjamin Cornelius would soon learn.

TWO

The JAL departure for Split was by now five-and-one-half hours delayed. The delay had occurred, so a sullen information clerk had told Ben, because the incoming flight from Paris was delayed. The clerk had no intention of saying more. As if he knew. If the fool American did not yet comprehend that explanations were irrelevant, that was not his problem.

"You'll let us know when the flight is to leave?" Ben was tired. It was his first trip beyond the coddling efficiency of Western European airlines.

"Departures are announced and posted." The clerk pointed to the departure board above the waiting room exit.

"I see, yes, thank you," said Ben. The clerk ignored the courtesy. Ben walked to the luncheon counter for a cheese and sausage sandwich. It was braced with the first good local experience Ben had had: a giant beer, excellent, for twenty-five cents.

At 7:45, another beer later, he glanced again at the departure board. Where Split flight 704 had been only five minutes before posted as "delayed," there was nothing. Nor had there been an announcement, at least not in English. Even seasoned travelers panic in moments like this. Ben's pulse went fast.

"Good God!" He rushed to the information desk about which, by now, several dozen people milled.

"The plane is gone," the clerk said officiously, glaring accusingly at his questioners, a fat Frenchman and his wife. "Why aren't you on it?"

"Because it wasn't called," screamed the Frenchman.

"It left, therefore it must have been called," replied the clerk.

"It didn't, it wasn't, you've . . ." the Frenchman was popping. To his shouts and those of several dozen other passengers, the clerk remained indifferent. He picked up his newspaper, opened his kiosk door, and walked casually away, leaving tourists and Yugoslavs alike cursing his retreating, disdainful backside.

The JAL girl remaining at the counter tried to explain that since the first Belgrade plane had been late the second had been early and a third one unscheduled because it didn't go to Fiume but had left taking the passengers on the second and fourth Belgrade planes because the fourth should have been late when it was in fact not coming at all but that didn't matter except for those with reservations who should have known to change them because later a fifth Belgrade plane was scheduled. "You see?" she asked sweetly.

They didn't.

She agreed it was regrettable, a breakdown in the departure board and the speaker system, a short in the circuits somewhere.

"But we *heard* announcements," insisted a Swiss, an observation with which everyone, Ben included, agreed.

"You did?" asked the girl.

"Yes. All through the day."

"Odd," said the girl. "Someone told me the system was broken."

Pandemonium then broke loose.

The seedy man who stank, whose eyes were red and whose small chin bristled with uneven black whiskers, stared at the JAL girl. This, Savic reminded himself, this is what it's like to travel with the mobs. Praise be privilege. As for JAL, he dearly hoped he would find some reason to send its staff, all of them, to Pozaravac prison on capital charges.

Ben, sick of sitting, walked out into the small park in front of the Zagreb airport, warm with the last green of autumn. He sat on a bench watching the children. Workmen passed by and an old woman, kerchief on her head, wearing a long peasant skirt, ambled toward him.

"Ingles?" she asked.

"American," said Ben.

"Oh yes," she grinned. "I'm Romani. Shall I tell the gentleman's fortune? Only one dollar. Please, one dollar for the palm." She reached for his hand.

"I don't believe in fortunes," said Ben, not deciding whether to be amused or put out.

"The Sir will enjoy it. Perhaps I will see love. Surely there will be a girl."

Ben let her take his hand. The old woman, her gold-capped teeth gleaming, bent to the lines, beginning to talk even before she looked.

"You will . . ." she paused, for now she saw the lines: fate, life, Mars, Venus, Mars again. "You . . ." her voice faltered, "no, I think perhaps . . . perhaps some other time."

"Oh? Something wrong?" Ben enjoyed her theater of mystery. These gypsies, he'd heard, were actresses.

"The Sir will be with other gypsies soon. The palm tells that the Sir will learn his fate from them."

"You expect a dollar for that?" Ben was teasing, but

anger was near.

"No money. The Sir has dark lines. The bird wings close to him, the two-headed bird."

The woman dropped his hand nervously. She was studying him, a witch frightened by her own omens.

"No money?" asked Ben in surprise. "Well that is something." She had piqued his interest. Bless her, he thought, she'd earned her fee for the play. "Just forecast one thing and I'll give you a dollar."

"No money from the Sir." She was adamant. "The thing you want to know, I will tell you. Melalo is coming to ride on your shoulder. Yes, Melalo, child of Anna, he comes to whisper in your ear." The woman actually shuddered.

"Who's Melalo?" Ben asked.

Shaking her head, muttering, refusing the dollar he held out toward her, the gypsy woman hurried off down the path.

Ben, disturbed in spite of himself, walked the few feet back to the waiting room. Just what, he asked himself, was that all about?

Some time later he noticed a departure door open and an agent standing to gather boarding cards. There were no boarders, since this time there was no announcement and no posting on the board. Ben, sick of it all, walked over to the agent. Savic saw her too and shuffled behind the American.

"Where to?" Ben asked.

"Belgrade," she said.

"No Split?"

"Yes, Split too. Take doorway ten. That plane will load in ten minutes."

Savic, boarding card and ticket in hand, hesitated a moment as he stared at the back of the American's neck. A long scar curved around from behind the ear to the nape, a scimitar-shaped keloid. Above it, Ben's rust-red hair glistened, well washed and barbered, a condition that Savic, his own dirty head itching furiously, envied.

A scimitar scar on the neck . . . Savic searched his tired mind. Something somewhere rang a bell. But no recollection emerged. Tomorrow Savic would remind himself to remember. Savic made a mental note that the man with the interesting scar was traveling as an American, was about five feet eleven, between thirty-five and forty, stockily built, with green eyes, a straight nose, good teeth, and a pleasant face with an easy smile. There was a slight cleft in his chin. He carried himself well, walked briskly, and had no apparent mannerisms or injuries. His clothes—a single-breasted, dark-blue summer suit set off by a white-flowered necktie—were singularly different from those of most foreign travelers, who generally wore sport shirts. The American also wore expensive casual shoes in need of polishing and carried a thick briefcase. In that, Savic knew, there were at least some books, for during those long hours on the bench Savic had watched his fellow passengers out of policeman's habit.

The American in no way aroused his suspicion; in fact, Savic rather liked him because he alone had retained his good humor, smiling at the boarding agent girl. An ugly bitch, Savic thought to himself, his own narrow face wrinkling with bitter disgust. The American wastes his charm.

The unannounced Geneva-Zurich-Zagreb-Split Swissair flight was nearly full. Ben sat down in one of those miserable middle seats, inserting himself between a plump lady in a bright green dress and a short, chunky fellow wearing expensive velveteen jeans. Both glared at him as he took *their* seat, for so are strangers received in much of Europe.

When Ben offered them macadamia nuts left over from a prior flight, both turned amiable. The green woman, he learned, was Swiss and was on her way to the island of Braj off Split to meet her married son and his family in a resort hotel. The fellow with the velveteen jeans was also off on vacation.

His companions learned from Ben that he had just opened a small art-and-antiquities store in Portland, that his assistant's aunt and uncle were Yugoslavs living in Split, and that Ben was on his way, thanks to his assistant's family, to look at some art objects in a collection coming up for sale in Split. However new he was to the art business, Ben had a feeling that one was wise not to give everything away in conversations with strangers. He was, therefore, vague about the collection.

When they arrived at Split, Edvard Oposevic, whom Ben recognised from the photo that Valeria, his assistant, had shown him, met him at the airport. Oposevic was unconcerned about the plane's being six hours late, saying that it happened all the time. He had telephoned a friend who worked for JAL to find out when it was really arriving, and so he himself had not been inconvenienced at all.

Valeria's uncle was a black-haired, dark-eyed man about five feet ten, strong featured, with dark jowls and a pot belly bisected by the tight belt of his trousers. He smiled hesitantly, halfway between the trusting greeting a Yugoslav reserves for his family and the suspicious restraint with which the rest of the world must be met. As his niece's boss—and from her letter Oposevic suspected there was more to her feelings for the American than just that—Ben was a family friend and therefore genuinely welcome; yet, as a stranger and a potential customer, the American was an outsider. In the Balkans one does not fully trust outsiders. Not ever.

"I'm sorry, Mr. Cornelius, but my wife isn't here. She had to leave this morning suddenly, some family matter, so I fear you'll not be able to enjoy her cooking this week. We both apologize." Edvard meant it. He missed Anna already.

Ben was concerned. "Oh, I hope it's nothing serious. What an inconvenience for me to arrive just now. I am sorry."

"Oh no, please, I'm glad you're here and Anna will be too as soon as she gets back. Her brother wrote to her, some business about his moving and wanting her to come get some family things, that's all." Edvard, reflecting on that letter from Pyotr, wondered what Anna would find when she arrived in Poland. Nothing good, his nose could smell that. One doesn't discuss that sort of thing with visitors.

"Oh well, that doesn't sound so bad. Where did she go?" Ben asked.

Oposevic picked up Ben's suitcase over Ben's polite protest. The parking area for the Split airport proved to be just a few feet from the front door of the small, modern airport building. The car, a new, deeply-cushioned Citroen, got up off its haunches and purred along the narrow road amid the shadows of vineyards and vegetable gardens of the Dalmatian countryside, the gray and black Karst massif rising dramatically in the half-moon's light a few miles to the east.

Edvard had taken some time to measure his reply about Anna's journey.

"Not too far," Edvard finally answered, and then, shifting, "You see over there?" He pointed westward, "Near the Adriatic Sea, the high smokestacks? Those are cement plants. Our fish cannery is near the farthest one."

"Oh yes, I see." Since the smokestacks were invisible in the night, Ben realized that Anna's trip was not to be discussed further.

"Valeria sends you both her love," he said, "and she gave me some things for you as well, California goodies. They're in my bag."

His host grinned. "That Valeria, one fine young woman, don't you think?"

Ben agreed. "Beautiful, and good natured."

"Yes." Both men summoned her image.

"You're not married then?" Edvard asked.

"I was, but not now."

"Children?" asked his host.

"None. My wife didn't want any."

"In America women decide things like that?" Edvard had heard much of America, some of it from Valeria on her visits, but this shocking business of not having children had never come up.

"Yes, marriage is very democratic there."

"You mean the women rule?"

"Sometimes." Ben was embarrassed. He'd never thought of Constance as king.

"Anna and I have three children," Oposevic said, intending no insult, "two boys and a girl, all grown."

"You're a lucky man," said Ben.

"I am, you're right about that."

His host had booked a room for Ben at a small hotel on a narrow street just behind Diocletian's Palace.

The palace, with a broad avenue between it and the sea, was, by streetlights and moon, all heavy walls, towers and tiny lighted windows, with a rush of people in and out.

Oposevic explained that most of old Split used to live inside it, and even now perhaps 9,000 citizens still did. His own apartment was inside, near the old Temple of Aesculapius, the directions to which, given to Ben, were labyrinthine.

"I'm sure you're tired," he said. "Have you eaten? Do you want to sleep now? Or a drink? There's a pleasant place right there." Oposevic pointed to the street which led under a portico into the palace, where Ben could see tables set in front of several cafes, now at 10.00 p.m. alive with drinking, gesturing, laughing crowds. The old palace, his host explained, was a city rather than a single structure, and the accretion of almost two millennia. It was bursting with people in the warm September night, its marble worn smooth with seventeen centuries of use.

"I'd like something to eat, and a drink here," Ben agreed. After all the trouble getting here, he thought, why not enjoy it?

It was the next morning before Edvard and Ben got down to business. Ben was here because of Valeria. He had hired her a few months before as he prepared to open his shop, as he prepared, in fact, for a new kind of life, without knowing exactly what that life would be.

He had been in advertising, directing market research for a major firm's northwest offices, but had become tired of being the man in charge of measuring just how gullible consumers were.

Years before he inherited from his bachelor uncle some lovely things; a large and remarkably varied collection of art. Ikons foremost, and prints: Durer, Piranesi, Cranach. There was ancient glass, too: Roman, Phoenician, Egyptian. He lived with it, loved it, but thought little of it except to know that being with beautiful objects was immensely satisfying. Constance had never given a damn for any of it. If she couldn't wear it to the opening night of the opera, use it to set herself off, or faintly mock it to show how clever she was, she had no use for it. That measure of value came to include husbands.

Valeria, thank God, came along just when he needed

her. An art history major with three years' experience in an Eastern museum, with a father who had actually been in the business and, unlike Ben, knew how to make a cash register ring and keep a set of books, she had been recommended to him by a friend. Valeria was a gem; a gem with a Yugoslav uncle to whom she'd written, once Ben's store had opened, without telling Ben, for when Valeria had visited Dalmatia the year before she had learned something of interest.

And now Ben and Oposevic were at last talking about it together.

"That's right," the uncle was saying, "when we were expanding our plant, as you know I'm manager for the big cannery here, we acquired a block of old buildings. One of them was a church. These days here in Yugoslavia we don't have much need for churches. Oh, some of the women still go and there's freedom of religion, but it's all nonsense and most of us pay no attention. In any event, when we were tearing down the church we found a vault deep underground. It must have been covered for two centuries, no doubt against invaders. In it were these ikons Valeria told you about, and some stone sculpture, twelfth, thirteenth, fourteenth century. Small things, heads of angels, figures of saints, the Archangel Michael, that sort of thing."

"That old? That long in a vault and in good condition?" Ben asked.

"Amazingly so. The paintings were sealed in lead, airtight. Those old priests knew what they were doing. You can imagine what it was to find buried treasure."

"But I can't understand why you haven't sold it all before now."

Oposevic's jaw muscles tightened.

"Mr. Cornelius, you touch the heart of the difficulty. I won't try to explain how Yugoslavian Communism works, except that each industry is quite independent, each run by a workers' council. In my industry, the cannery, the workers' council selects and supervises all of us who act as managers, and the council approves all policy decisions. I used to be on the council, but for ten years I've been their director. It's not easy for men who are very good at canning fish to know how to sell statues and ikons. The easiest thing that comes to mind is to sell them here, but consider. Perhaps if the man from the regional museum in Zagreb were to come to help us to sell, he'd declare our find a national treasure. Then he would expropriate it all to put in his Zagreb museum. Or, if he didn't do that and did allow us to sell them after all, regulations require that we sell them through the state export agency. That's their specialty. It happens that that agency has an embargo on national treasures and even if Zagreb says they're not that, the export agency—which is in Belgrade and run by one of those cunning Serbs—might say these nice Croatian beauties go to the Belgrade museum. Even if that didn't happen, the state export agency has the right to buy them from us, since we are not licensed to sell anything but canned fish, and then they would sell them. They would give us a very low price, you can count on Serbs for that, to cheat a Croat when they can.

"Now, my job as director is to be sure our factory makes a maximum profit; after all, profits are distributed to become salaries to all of us factory workers, and our workers' council, whatever it doesn't know about art, does know that it wants a profit from these items if we can manage it."

"Why not invite some Swiss or German dealer down, or sell them at auction in England, say Christie's or Sotheby's, on consignment?"

"Very good ideas, Mr. Cornelius, and my ignorant

workers and I thought of them too. So let's say these big dealers offer us a good price and then find they can't get an export license from the state agency. The deal is off, the agency comes to Split and takes the art away. What if we do write to your Mr. Sotheby? Maybe we pack them up, exporting them out as a consignment of fish. Then someone at Sotheby's lets it be known that these canned fish, very expensive fish, came from our vault, not the sea. Where would we be then?"

Now Ben knew why the correspondence between Valeria and her uncle about this trip of his, which she had planned and insisted he take without giving him this background, had made no reference either to Ben's actual business or to anything else except possible "imports" to America. For the censors, that had meant "fish." Ben had come to Split thinking, thanks to Valeria, that there was a small family collection of ikons for sale, and here he was, invited in as a conspirator for smuggling what might be a major collection.

"None of us in the workers' council knows anyone at all who deals in art," Oposevic went on, "and we dare not ask. Everything is a risk. We let the museum know and we may lose. We let the export agency know and we lose. We try it ourselves and . . ." Oposevic's voice trailed off.

Ben concluded for him. "And the same thing happens, or you get blackmailed, or you are accused and everybody goes to jail. Is that it?"

Edvard met Ben's eyes. "That is it, Mr. Cornelius, and that is why when Valeria was here last year we asked her to find someone we could trust to advise us. She found you and I'm very grateful to you for coming here. Now, tell us what to do."

Ben shook his head. Two months in the art business and he was faced with this. He wondered how he'd like a

Yugoslavian prison? He was also facing the surprise of learning that his darling Valeria—calculating Valeria—had been appraising him from the first, setting him up as her Yugoslav family counselor in contraband.

"I don't know," Ben said. "I don't think you appreciate how very little I know about things like this, certainly nothing of licenses, smuggling, the darker markets. I'm as naive as anyone."

"Valeria said you were modest, and we fully understand that you are not experienced in these international dealings. Nevertheless, we have no one else to turn to. Valeria told me in her letter, 'Benjamin can tell you what to do.' Valeria is my niece. She is a wise as well as a lovely young lady. Come, we shall have another coffee and then I'll show you the factory. Later you'll meet some of the workers on the council and tonight we'll show you our treasure. Tomorrow you start thinking about what to do. There's no hurry. If you decide the objects are as valuable as we hope, maybe you can take your time in Switzerland or England on the way home to find out what to do. Or take them with you now. You and Valeria sell them in America. If you need another trip back here, bring Valeria along. If I were your age that's what I would do." Oposevic paused. "You know, she seems to think a great deal of you, Mr. Cornelius."

He leaned across the table where they were seated over the second coffee and clasped Ben's shoulder. It was a strong hand that gripped him. It said clearly, "I've decided to trust you."

Ben could only take another sip of his rubber-bitter espresso. Here was a frank conspirator to introduce a fellow to the Balkans. Still and all, he seemed a good heart, and if his planning was a bit kinky in the service of profits, that at least made Communism look very much like an animal he knew well: business for a buck.

"I'll think about it, Mr. Oposevic, and if I can help I will, but I'm not your smuggler, not even if you pack the whole of your art in barrels labeled 'herring'."

"Call me Edvard," interposed the older man.

"All right, thank you," said Ben, "and I'm Ben, of course."

"Good, Ben. Well now, let's go to my office and after that, well, we shall see what we shall see."

THREE

The road from Krakow is narrow as it moves west. The first checkpoint is hardly beyond Krakow's borders, a routine stop, if a concrete pillbox and a machine gun sniffing the traveler can ever be routine. One's papers had best be in order and evidence strong that one resides along the coming way, Skawina, say, or Zator, Oswiecim, or the rich farms that lie about these villages.

The miners on their way to pits of coal, lead, copper or zinc ride the road in buses or crammed in trucks. There are some who have yet ever to ride in a private auto. The peasants walk or, with their women—those wearing full skirts with nine petticoats—ride in wooden carts pulled by oxen or horses. Some push old wooden wheelbarrows upon which, along with a sack of rice and salt and a new hoe, sits a child or two. Women hereabouts come down easily with pregnancy, for there are two pleasures, sex and children, which the state does not ration.

There is another checkpoint between Skawina and Zator as the road winds along the upper Vistula, here called the Wisla. Routine again, for machine guns can be routine on roads in the Pact countries. Again one had best have proofs: identity, residence, and permits. Their absence will lead to more routine events: arrest, interrogation, perhaps a routine beating or even a routine incarceration, and for a few, a routine firing squad.

Zator itself, like Skawina, has a town square, about which hover the three- to five-storey medieval houses, the lower floors of which once housed guildsmen's shops and are still used for trade. There will be food shops for such edibles as are local agricultural surplus and a few goods that the state canning enterprise has managed to move down the chain as far as these outlying squares. There will certainly be taverns on the square. The school is more likely new and on the outskirts. The old Catholic church is there, for in spite of Marx, Lenin and Gomulka, church will be full on Sunday.

Communism promises bread and equality, the Church love and heaven. The failure of the first is evident, there being only some bread and no equality. The second fails too, but the evidence is less compelling; everyone has known love and no one still in the congregation has proved the lie in heaven. On balance then, the Poles hereabouts rightly prefer the Church. Yet since Communism can deliver more than it initially promised, restrictions for example, or prison—or other punishments more extreme —no Pole is fool enough to advocate the one against the other. At best there is a balance.

In times of trouble one deceives, and since there is always trouble, deception is as good a rule to follow as any. The troubles are not without humor, however—best taken black. Bruno Schulz came from Drogobych, a town much like Zator. *The Street of Crocodiles* he called his fantastic stories. Bruno Schulz, Jew, was killed one day by an SS man for simply walking downtown. Today Communist Zator proudly boasts that there are no SS men. While the guards on the Krakow-Zator-Oswiecim road also tend to be anti-Semitic, as are many Poles, their machine guns point without prejudice at everyone.

Outside of Zator, southward along one of the Wisla's tributary streams, one might come across a pine forest bordering a large, abandoned pit, an old mine perhaps, or a quarry, with yet some desultory earth-moving activity. There is a large shack there. Actually, very few will come this far, for there is a checkpoint on the Zator road where the lane to this secluded place turns off. Unlike its predecessors, this checkpoint is not "routine." Passes, photos, stamps, orders, a card with an electronic key—the whole paraphernalia of Soviet military security is brought to bear.

Major General Pyotr Myagkov sat glumly in the general staff conference room, an expensively appointed chamber, windowless, one hundred and fifty feet underground. He was, he realized, in a morbid frame of mind. For one thing he had a hangover, for another his girlfriend, a young Pole in Krakow, had been making eyes at a Georgian colonel at the party last night, for a third, Myagkov was scheduled to brief a contingent of newly arrived officers.

Myagkov groaned and held his head in his hands. The hum of the air-circulating system grew noisier. How he hated these mornings after, and that lousy circulating system. Nothing could make this tomb less fusty; sweat, stale vodka, dank earth, ozone and boredom, hangovers and bad nerves, that's what was circulating here. This, his command. Was this what he'd struggled for?

"Comrade General? Perhaps I could bring you something for your headache? Aspirin? Orange juice? Vodka?" His aide, Lieutenant Zemskov, was trying to be helpful. He was attending, Myagkov felt irritably, like a mosquito around the ears.

"No thank you, Zemskov, nothing." Unlike most of his colleagues who'd been reared in pigpens, he would be courteous to his aides no matter what. He grit his teeth against the urge to squash the mosquito. Poor Zemskov.

Myagkov knew the bumbler meant well.

"Comrade General, the newly arrived officers are assembled in briefing room B. Shall I tell them you're on your way?" How delicately Zemskov put it, thought Myagkov, mosquitoes leading elephants to their duty.

"Yes Zemskov, my dear Leon, tell them I'm on my way." The general heaved his bulk up from the leather armchair in which he'd been seated morosely these last two hours.

There were eleven new officers waiting respectfully for him when he arrived, lieutenants through majors. Colonels and generals were always briefed individually. The Soviet Army, however muddled it otherwise was, Myagkov reflected, at least was clear about rank and privilege. As under the czars, so was it now. Myagkov had pondered Russian history. Power meant privilege. Privilege invoked disdain. Disdain generated resentment, and resentment, dissidence. And dissidence? Myagkov, completely absorbed in his own thoughts as he walked to the lectern, considered just what dissidence could generate. It was a fundamental question.

"Comrades," he began his talk, "you are now posted to the forward high command. As commander of the Central Sector Strategic Planning and Intelligence Staff, we abbreviate here as CPS, I welcome you. Your duties will be explained to you in detail over the coming days by your superiors." General Myagkov paused. He must now go into the obligatory nonsense, the "roof," that ritual glorification of the Party. To utter it was ridiculous, to listen stupid, to believe it insane, yet to fail to provide the "roof" was suicide.

"Our Party and our Government have given us a very important task. They believe in us, our goal is critical in the achievement of socialism. We are surrounded by imperialistic NATO forces. Even when asleep they dream about a new war. All Soviet peoples are as one in the defense of the homeland. The people are all as one in implementing the decisions of the last Party Congress. The Soviet Army, in harmony with workers and peasants, is in the forefront of those who sacrifice for Communism and Russia."

It was time for the "bridge"; the transition from these stupidities to the task at hand.

"It is my task to impress upon you the overriding importance of your assignment here, to provide you with an overview, and to remind you that only the most highly selected and qualified personnel are seconded to this post. In consequence, I have the highest expectations for your performance. Any deviation from an exacting standard will not be tolerated; any slacking will result in your immediate reassignment and appropriate entries in your file with respect to those failures." Myagkov paused to let that welcome sink in.

Chalk-white faces stared at him impassively from under the blue fluorescence of the overhead lights. Myagkov looked sourly at those expressionless eggs. Nevertheless he knew what was going on in their respectful minds. Fear. He had pressed the button on which was written "Your careers are at stake here. I am a tough commander." After fear, there was always that retreat into some space in the mind where he, Myagkov, no longer existed for them. The men had disembodied him already; he knew the reaction. What other defense in the heritage of serfs?

The general continued, "This unit is responsible for co-ordinating and integrating forward military intelligence into the battle plans for the ground forces of the Soviet and Pact armies." Myagkov paused to let the few satellite officers in the group know where they stood. The politicians spoke of the Pact armies "including" the Soviet forces. But one day when war came, it would be, Myagkov knew, Soviets against *them* as the inevitably dissident Poles, Czechs, Germans, Hungarians, Romanians, and the rest of them made their bids. Get it out in the open now. Myagkov challenged them silently, one by one. "You there!" He had his eyes on a captain wearing a Hungarian uniform. "You there!" Myagkov's eyes demanded, "Stand up and bleat if you can." The Hungarian's eyes fluttered under Myagkov's unrelentingly hostile stare. The general's unfriendly eyes moved to and lingered on the Poles. He guessed them as no different from the peasants here in Zator. Their heavy farmer's thumb would be on the scale giving short weight. He knew how they would tilt when left to their own devices. Churls, Myagkov reflected, none of you will get near our central operations as long as you're posted here.

The two Poles and the Hungarian in the group had received the message. Each knew he was to be isolated, denied an integral role, always suspect beneath a veneer of vodka camaraderie. And Myagkov, in turn, knew what they were thinking, "Ah, these stinking Russian imperialists, we'll get you one day." In a pig's ass they would.

Myagkov went on speaking.

"In time of crisis, this unit has the responsibility to monitor standby readiness for each of the operational field armies in the Central Sector, and to insure that its posture is in conformity with plans based on day-to-day intelligence updates as that data, forwarded by Moscow, is translated strategically and tactically. Using our computers, and ours is a select unit equipped with the latest electronics for modeling and gaming total field unit performances, we advise army and divisional commanders as to their readiness and needed modifications, as we advise Moscow of these same analytic conclusions.

"In time of war . . ." Myagkov let his voice rise a bit and project further, for after all this was what it was all about, the bottom line, ". . . in time of war we serve an autonomous field intelligence coordinating and planning function with . . ." again he paused, "a readiness for direct command responsibilities for the Central Sector should there be any breakdown in normal-channel command communications. To that end we maintain separate communications systems with each and every forward land army and division. Our location is of prime importance to this mission, for in the coming nuclear war both forward and rear line headquarter units may expect some traumatic nuclear assaults. We, on the other hand, out of any expected line of march or battle configuration and . . ." again a pause, "and, comrades, this is essential, completely unknown to NATO either by function, identification or location, we may anticipate optimal communications and functioning. That is why we are here, behind the Tatra, hidden underground in a wood, concealed from photographic reconnaissance. That is why we use farm trucks on our roads, go out infrequently, and maintain the heaviest security. Do you understand?"

Did they really understand? Myagkov wondered. One could only hope they did. The general walked over to the blackboard and sketched a geocommand chain model.

"Conceive of us this way, comrades. We are a separate, insulated, and particularly high-powered brain. We receive, as headquarters do, field intelligence. We receive, as armies do, plans based on intelligence. We do, as others do, strategic and tactical planning down to the divisional level, but we do it autonomously and we do it with the most advanced computers available in the Soviet forces. Ordinarily our output, to Moscow and the Western armies, is used as a test of both field readiness—or performance—and headquarter plans. If there is a dissonance, it is the obligation of line commanders and their intelligence staffs to consider those discrepancies and to revise their own postures if they so see fit. As a staff unit we do no more except apply this continual computer matching to base data and such posture modifications as line commands make. That is our basic function except in time of war. Then, should line command be disabled, we take over the Central Sector using our models as command masters. This concept, comrades, of an autonomous forward brain, computer warfare at its most innovative, is unique to the Soviet and Pact forces. When war comes, it will be a decisive advantage. That is why, in Moscow, comrades, this unit is known as the Forward God. Were any of your Christian grandmothers here that would be blasphemy, but as it is . . ." Myagkov let himself smile for the first time, "it is a compliment. Now comrades, are there any questions?"

To his surprise there was one. A Soviet major, from his face and complexion a Tartar, rose. Not many of those darkies get this far. What will this special case, Myagkov asked himself, be like?

"Comrade General," the major said, "it's a privilege to be here, to serve under you. My own training is computer intelligence and so I ask you, Comrade General, if the computer capacity allows the input for the whole Sector of multiple contingencies?"

"What sort of contingencies, Major? Give an example."

"Each requiring quite different postures, Comrade General. Say, for example, one, an aggressive NATO nuclear strike against us without warning; two, one with warning; three, a limited non-nuclear warned strike by us against NATO; four, a no-warning conventional strike; or five and six, nuclear strikes under warning and no-warning conditions. Can we daily update storage file data for these separate models, Comrade General?"

Myagkov lowered his bald head, gleaming under the lights. He looked out from under bushy red eyebrows. "No, Major," he replied, "we do not have such a computer capacity. We run consecutive models for each contingency, but we cannot do daily concurrent updating. Each model is, of course, on file. During any crisis we must select the contingency which has the highest priority."

"There is, then, Comrade General, because of intrinsic delay, an element of judgment in selection of priorities for any one run?"

Myagkov nodded. "As in all wars, Major, judgment must rule the computer, not the reverse."

"Yes, Comrade General, of course. Can you tell us, if you will allow me a further question, Comrade General, what our current status is, that is, which contingency has the highest priority at present? I assume, Comrade General, that for any one epoch—I use the conventional term 'epoch' to refer to one gaming cycle—that we stand on a priority daily until the run is complete."

Myagkov found it difficult to believe what he was hearing. This cheeky Tartar bastard actually knew how the system worked. Moscow must have made a mistake. They'd sent someone intelligent. Myagkov nodded vigorously, replying, "Exactly, Major. I'm delighted at your comprehension. Now, let me test you, just as an exercise, what would you guess to be the answer to that question?"

The Tartar spoke confidently. "Am I to assume, Comrade General, no special status for the computer today —for example no down time, program debugging runs, or test games for in-war conditions?"

"That's right, Major, no tricks or alien programs."

"Well, Comrade General, it must be one of the four major contingencies. It is September so the crops are in, SALT talks are underway, NATO is militarily ineffective, the West is relaxed, our African and Central Asian policies are progressing, and the Americans are vacillating and appeasing, so I would estimate, Comrade General, that the present run or next priority will be a Soviet no-warning conventional strike, my number four. Obviously, it's the opportunity for it."

Myagkov grinned, gold-capped teeth shining as he thrust his great bull neck forward. This was his kind of meat.

"And if I say 'no,' Major?" He waited for his opponent's move. No matter what, it would be check in less than five moves.

"In order of choice, Comrade General, my numbers six, five, and one. I exclude as impossible number two, a NATO nuclear strike with prior warning, given the Western posture at this time."

Myagkov beamed. Cats smile like that when the mouse is in the claw. "No, Major, wrong on all counts."

The Tartar was astonished, his voice rising with excitement. "You mean, Comrade General, that we are running a priority number two? That we have knowledge of an impending NATO nuclear strike?" The Tartar's voice went a register higher.

"Major, I can see you are intelligent, but you have failed to examine your assumptions. No chess player wins by unnecessarily restricting either his own actions or by assuming an opponent will do so. I remind you, Major, that the Russian national game is chess." Inclining his head forward slightly in a feint of a bow, General Myagkov, a virtuoso acknowledging the acclaim of an audience, raised his hands, palms outward, quieting what he knew was their silent applause. Combat between others was safe enough to watch; they would relish any other's defeat.

"Thank you, Major, you may be seated. Are there any further questions?"

There were none, except for the puzzled Tartar who was wondering what about Soviet strategic policy they had failed to tell him in his just-completed War College. Myagkov ambled away from the lectern, his hangover and his lethargy vanished. It was time for a hearty lunch.

At three the same afternoon a dirty, wide-bodied pick-up truck arrived at the dilapidated building at the edge of the old pit. Four men in work clothes, brand new and unsoiled, entered the construction hut. The driver stayed in the anteroom. Saluting hands passed three of them through to the inner room where they took off their overalls. The three boarded the elevator for the descent, passed through several nuclear-shielded doors, sat in the forward seat of the electric tram, sped the quarter mile of horizontal shaft, and emerged in the spacious ants' nest that was CPS. General of the Armies Alexei Aleksevich Strizhenko entered, accompanied by Major General Mitrofan Vevlaineevich Sazanov and an aide.

General of the Armies Strizhenko was in a good mood. Krakow was a fine town, the girl he'd had last night had bounced around under him as though she'd had her ass in a thornbush, the drive along the Vistula was lovely this hot September day, and he was almost boyishly thrilled by the cloak-and-dagger approach to CPS, a prize facility. It was only the second time he'd been here.

Something more substantial than Cuban adventures, Ethiopian forays, Afghan coups was in the offing. The Forward God was critical to its evolution.

Strizhenko lost no time. The CPS staff would be ready for him in the conference room. Myagkov and his crew saluted snappily as the visitors entered. As a "nomenclature" officer, the top brass of the CC and the CPSU, Strizhenko was accustomed to complete deference.

"All right then," barked Strizhenko, "let's have it, your own computer match with our General Staff's evaluation. Remember, no holds barred; this is the first time you've run a command plan against your computer using that fancy new statistical program of Comrade Academician Lavrukhin's over there."

Professor Lavrukhin bowed his head, pride dominating modesty in the way it cocked sideways. He was the only civilian in the room. One of Russia's outstanding mathematical statisticians, he'd been assigned here for the last six months. If the honor hadn't been so great, he would have preferred it otherwise. In this instance the honor carried the sharp axe of the Party Secretary's own order behind it. Lavrukhin's task here was to come out with a mathematically sound probability calculation of success in the Central Sector should the contingency plan currently being mulled by the Brain—his word for the Forward God since he was a genuine atheist—be put into effect. Today was the day when the harvest was inspected.

Lavrukhin cleared his throat nervously. "Perhaps if I give you the mathematical background first, so that you can see our postulates, follow me in the derivation of the new statistic, then you can see for yourselves if . . ."

Strizhenko cut him off. "Academician Lavrukhin, the mathematics are your responsibility; the product is General Myagkov's. My responsibility is to decide whether the plan will work. Now just short circuit, if you will be so kind, the stuff we don't understand for that which we do."

"Yes, Comrade General, it is not that simple but I shall do my best. You see it is an exceedingly complicated problem which, basically, is an econometric theorem of replacement utilities, values loss . . ."

"In a nutshell if you please, Professor, just tell us what will happen if we put the plan into effect." Strizhenko was capable of patience, no one achieved nomenclature status without that. Even so, he was about to blow a gasket. Academicians were all asses, he thought to himself.

"Yes, General." Academician Lavrukhin's palm was so wet that a paper clung to it as he lifted his hand from the stack in front of him.

"Yes?"

Everyone in the room was waiting nervously.

"If the data provided to us are correct, if the non-mathematical assumptions you have made about the enemy's response are correct, your plan will have a success probability expressed as P=less than .03." The professor let out a deep breath and waited for the reaction. He was premature.

General Strizhenko tapped the table vigorously. "And just what does that mean, Academician Lavrukhin?"

The professor looked at him in surprise. "Why it means that there are less than three chances out of one hundred, as I said, given a number of constraints about the parameters in which we are working, that there will be an adverse outcome. That is to say, General, that using the ordinary canons of statistical inference, you are to assume the plan will work."

"Ahhhh. Thank you, Professor, thank you very much." Strizhenko nodded happily. Three years of staff work, his own dream child, all vindicated. His own boss, Chief of the General Staff Kulikov, would now have to agree. "That is all, comrades, except for you, General Myagkov. I'd like to discuss this further with you in your quarters."

"There aren't any questions?" Lavrukhin asked. "No questions at all?" He sat there, alone now, his hands shaking with the enormity of the situation, of their acceptance of the plan at P=less than .03.

Strizhenko, already striding out of the room behind Myagkov, turned back to the mathematician with a shake of his head.

"Now we have answers, not questions, and it's about time. Good day, Professor."

"More champagne, Alexei Aleksevich?" Myagkov inquired. Neither would call the other by a diminutive. No room for friendly names.

Five in the afternoon was too early for Myagkov, but obviously not for the other. Strizhenko was on his second bottle by way of celebrating Lavrukhin's statistics.

"By all means, Pyotr Stepanovich, and help yourself. Now that I'm a bit relaxed I want your opinion."

Strizhenko disliked Myagkov intensely, and distrusted him, for he was one of those technicians who had risen in the Army and the Party more on the basis of brains than through the loyal, grunting sweat that Strizhenko had poured out on his uphill climb. Dog eat dog it had been for Strizhenko and for most of his kind, but Myagkov had come the alternative route, even though he was older and in many ways more traditional. Myagkov was topnotch in electrical engineering and, more embracingly, in analytic strategic conceptualizing. An independent, aggressive SOB, Strizhenko considered him. He had the kind of mind that, had Myagkov been one bit political, would have put him in Siberia years before.

"Yes?" Myagkov poured himself some champagne, waiting to hear what opinion of his was to be ignored.

Strizhenko went on. "Listen, the plan—well, let me use the key word I've coined for it just now, WALTZ. Do you like it Pyotr Stepanovich, eh?"

"Yes," the other lied.

"Good. Yet, to make sure Moscow doesn't retract, having gone this far, we must be sure—all of the General Staff and our very best men like you—that our ideological arguments are in order. Right?"

"Yes, that's right."

"Now then, the catechism, Pyotr Stepanovich."

"All right." The other was on his third bottle. Myagkov could see that anything would be okay—for a while.

"Now, then," Strizhenko went on, "is it true the danger of war exists as long as capitalist imperialism exists and that, therefore, the way to prevent war is to destroy imperialism, if not by cold methods then by others?"

"True. The Official History says as much."

"Good. Now, is it true that Marxist theory requires triumph over capitalism, and that theory and practice must not tolerate discrepancies over time?"

"Yes, Alexei Aleksevich, that's doctrine."

"Good." Strizhenko had scooped up some caviar with his fingers, talking now with his mouth full. "Now, is it true that we hold a military advantage over the West?"

"So we believe." Myagkov was cautious.

"Right, and it's intolerable for the West to allow that imbalance to continue, as it was for us, because that alone assures their destruction."

"No question about it."

"So they will eventually, if we don't act, restore the balance of mutually assured destruction. Right!" Strizhenko, agreeing with himself, no longer waited for Myagkov. "And so we are compelled to act in the interim if we are to act at all. Exactly. Further, we act from mastery. Wasn't it Bismarck who said that the master of Bohemia is master of Europe, Pyotr Stepanovich?"

"I've heard that."

"And here we are, a few miles from Bohemia, which is

already ruled by Russia. Furthermore, Lenin said, didn't he, that the Soviet Union's task is the 'ascent of an unexplored and hitherto difficult mountain,' that is, achieving world supremacy not just in the victory of Communism but for the Russian national interest. What do you think? Isn't it so?"

"Perhaps. As I see it, pure Marxist-Leninist ideology and the national interest may not coincide."

Strizhenko stopped in the middle of chewing. "My God, Pyotr Stepanovich, you're a revisionist. God bless us that no one else knows. You must be drunk."

"Yes, that must be it." Myagkov was too bored to argue beyond noting wryly, "We are all of us revisionists."

"My mother would have crossed herself if she'd heard me say a thing like that, Pyotr Stepanovich."

"She wouldn't have heard it, Alexei Aleksevich," said Myagkov confidently.

"Agreed," said Strizhenko in drunken solemnity. "May God bless her in her grave."

"To your mother." Pyotr raised his glass in a toast.

"To Mother." Strizhenko's glass waved about in his hand. "I miss her so." Tears formed in his eyes. "I forgot my ideological conclusion. What was the argument again?"

"Succinctly, Alexei Aleksevich, you want us to strike now while the iron is hot, based on Marxist-Leninist ideological grounds, knowing thereby that the national interest of holy Mother Russia is served. We also pray that it works."

"Exactly." Strizhenko leaned forward. "It must be that way."

"What way, Alexei Aleksevich?"

"War, Pyotr Stepanovich, war. Remember? Bulganin had it in his notes from the 1944 meeting with Tito. 'The war shall soon be over,' Stalin said, 'we shall recover in fifteen or twenty years, and then we'll have another go at it.' That's what he said, just like that. 'We'll have another go at it.' Russia is recovered, Pyotr Stepanovich. The West is weak. It's time to strike."

"You mean it then, don't you? You *really* mean it."

"God yes, I mean it. We've waited long enough. Now we *will* have another go at it." Tears streamed down Strizhenko's face.

FOUR

Noblesse oblige, the commander was to be present at the reception for the new officers. No gala with young noblemen in Czarist dress uniforms, but nevertheless Russia is not without continuity. This elite bunch in fresh grays, collar tabs and epaulette stripes in scarlet, were drunk as ever noblemen could be and were served by messmen as oppressed as any of those of the St. Petersburg Imperial Guards.

General Myagkov himself was fried to the eyeballs. Zemskov, his aide, watched him nervously. The general was crawling on the floor, the Tartar major beside him.

"You gotta consider the variations, Major, gotta be sneaky. 'Stratagems' we call 'em. Tomorrow you'll find out."

"Thanks, Comrade General, I appreciate that. Sneaky computer, huh? Sneaky plan I bet. I'll remember what you say."

He would, nor would the Tartar ever be so drunk as not to be surprised by a general officer socializing with field graders. As for his commandant here—was it the floor? It was all too blurred to be sure, but all amazing.

"Never seen anything like it," the major averred.

"Like what?" The general's head butted a chair out of the line of crawl.

"This place. Different, that's all. Real nice. You know what, Comrade General?"

"What's that?"

"Last station, before War College, Magdeburg, we had desertions all the time. They just ran away."

"Yeah?"

"Yeah. Soldiers didn't like the 'earnings method', not at all. We rented them out on the economy, us officers got what the Germans paid for the work. One paving job I made eight hundred rubles myself, but the bastards died."

Puzzlement crept into the general's bleary eyes. "Died?"

"Yeah, kind of. Three killed themselves and we shot four. Out of only one battalion. Imagine."

"Bad." Myagkov wagged his bald head.

"Bad." The Tartar nodded. "Yeah, bad. Have to fill out reports. Hate writing reports." The black hair fell over his face.

"That 'earnings method' I mean," said the general. "Soldiers are slaves; officers take the money. All wrong."

"Yeah. Do it all the time. Not here though, I can see that. More democratic here. Comradely friendship. Real Communism." The major's words were slurred.

"All wrong, whole thing wrong." The general's arm fell off the other's back. "All wrong," he said again. With effort, the general tried to stand up. Zemskov came over to help him.

"Let's go, Zemskov. I can't stand this."

"Yes, Comrade General."

His arm draped over his aide's shoulder, Zemskov guiding him, the general left the party.

"I'm disgusted with myself. I was drunk last night, I disgraced myself fraternizing with subordinates. I cannot go on much longer." Pyotr Myagkov looked at the words he had just written. He was sitting at the table in the bedroom of his private quarters, where he wrote his diary. It was, he knew, worse than foolhardy to keep a journal —an entry ticket, should it be found out, to one of the KGB "psychiatric" hospitals, or Siberia. Yet, he must speak out or go insane. Since there was no one among his colleagues here, nor his wife or children in Moscow, nor his mistress in Krakow, the journal was his conversation. There were army friends elsewhere with whom he could share the disillusionment, the despair, with what Mother Russia had become and how the dream had been betrayed. After he'd written a page he would read it, nod, and then burn it. So much for his thoughts.

His friends were far away. Kostya, for instance, now a divisional commander in Vladivostok, or young Dimitri, chief of the Belogorsk military district in that tinderbox of the upper Amur, the China border, he could talk to them. But would he tell anyone else? That was the question. Russians were only talkers, whispering windbags, coffee-shop radicals. Or like Oblomov who lay abed endlessly talking, decrying the state of affairs, frozen by constitutional indecision. Here he was, likewise impotent, high priest to the Forward God. Myagkov clenched his fist. Hell, he was just a goddamn nursemaid to a rustbucket copper-wired rat's-nest abacus. He wrote on.

"The meeting yesterday with Strizhenko was what I feared it would be. The man's a fanatic. He has an ikon of his holy mother in one hand—mother or Mother Russia, what does it matter?—and an axe in the other. The old Russian axe, bloody as Ivan. It's Stalin's axe that Strizhenko carries, Axing Alex, the General Staff, the Politburo, all of them hacks hacking away.

"Blood doesn't bother me. I bathed in it in Stalingrad, let it like a butcher myself in Poznan, stomped on Budapest. I welcomed spring in 1968 in Prague, but crushed the city in August with the tank corps." There was a joke among Russians that the tank is the only transportation an ordinary man can expect to use for tourism outside of Russia. How true. Myagkov paused, then wrote again. "Until this job I've never met the men who *made* wars happen. Here he is, that little SOB who'd be Genghis Khan, wanting to make war to make history. Fancy, it's my computer that told him to do it.

"Lavrukhin, that simpering fathead, believes in the damn thing. Yet the whole engineering staff knows that the electric mongoloid can't handle the load. Breakdowns, blackouts, it's got more bugs than a Bulgar's blanket. What if Lavrukhin's program is wrong? Just as bad, what if it's right? Something's got to give. I just can't stand much more. Thank God Anna will be here soon."

When he finished writing, he read and reread his words. Then he got out his matches and watched the pages burn.

Nothing held him any more; his wife, Raya, was status-hungry, sharp, and loveless, her life the up escalator of politics in the Communications Ministry, slinging newsprint and bullshit for the greater glory of the Slavs. His title and connections were helpful to her, as was his absence, for Raya's lovers were sure to be useful people whose little cockdipping forays into Raya's purposeful pussy were fair trade items. Her career flourished. He himself had not touched her for years.

His children, Victor and Natasha, were chips off her icy block. He realized they had been spoiled rotten, enjoying every privilege that came with the uppercrust of Moscow's political elite; the special stores, special restaurants, special schools, and now, the special careers. As a child Victor had been a charming and artful liar, clever about money. Now in the Ministry of Heavy Industry, Victor had put his talents together. He had become cunning, self-satisfied, dissipated, dipping with his high official cronies into other people's money. Natasha? Like her mother; a pretty carbon copy well placed, thanks to Raya, as economics editor at Pravda.

Myagkov had been for some time obsessed with his failure as a father. What rot in him had begotten such rot? There was no shortage of excuses. When the children were tiny he'd been fighting at the front, glad that Raya and the children were safe in Magnitogorsk in the Urals. After the war he'd been transferred so often that it was not only convenient to leave them in Moscow, but Raya insisted on staying there anyway. He had, that he must face, abandoned the children to her. The cult of the mother was strong in him for his own mother had been so dear. He had also been afraid of her. He preferred the bloody battles that men fought in contrast to Raya's ball-breaking onslaughts. The fact was that he enjoyed manly battles, but with women he was a coward.

When CPS had been on the drawing boards, there had been a vicious battle as to its command between line commanders on the General Staff and the Chief Intelligence Directorate (GRU) of that staff. The GRU argued that since CPS was receiving, analyzing and transmitting intelligence, GRU should be in charge. The line generals insisted that since the main function was strategic planning, with intelligence as input data not product, the facility was rightly the planning staff's own. The GRU is a subordinate arm, and in this instance was subordinated. For consolation prize it was given command responsibility over communication links in and out of CPS. As a result, the GRU presence at CPS was large. Since part of the GRU responsibility was overall security, of which counter-intelligence is part, that function, with its expansive potential, was vigorously exercised by the GRU commander of the CPS, Colonel Shibunko.

Shibunko was seated in front of Myagkov; they eyed each other with hostility. It had been necessary for Myagkov to summon the GRU man. All contacts planned with civilians, let alone foreigners, must be reported in advance to the GRU when one is at an ultra-clearance installation like CPS. After contact, another report must be submitted. And during contact, Myagkov knew, the GRU would likely be watching—indeed, eating an expensive meal at the next table if they had the chance. Myagkov had always accommodated to the routine, and so, naturally, his letter to Anna, with its special visa, had been cleared through Shibunko.

These intrusions were galling only if one first conceived of privacy itself. The nearest Russian word, *vedinenie*, really means solitude or retirement. Sociable in any event, ordinarily immersed in family and joined with friends, their lives crowded by choice every bit as much as circumstances, most Russians do not think in terms of "privacy," even though they might well resent or fear the constant threat that surveillance presents.

Myagkov, who read French and English, had only slowly learned the Western meaning of privacy as a desirable state, a right to be protected. He had become chronically irritated that his own life, his own meetings with his sister, were inevitably defined and degraded by the presence of these nosey, self-important, petty, paranoid secret police hacks. His reactions were, he knew, a bad sign. He had become un-Russian, an alien in his own land. Different and therefore dangerous, and thus in danger.

"Well, Comrade General? I am at your service." Shibunko took no pleasure in waiting for the commandant to speak, and yet as subordinate he could but burn quietly.

"As you know, Colonel," Myagkov spoke slowly, "my sister Anna arrives from Yugoslavia this weekend. I shall meet her at the airport and spend two days with her. She will be my guest at the military staff house in Krakow."

"Thank you, Comrade General, everything is in order I'm sure. It's been some time since you've seen your family, hasn't it?"

Myagkov felt his lips tighten. The bastard was digging him. Everyone knew that he and Raya were hostile, that he'd written off the children except for an occasional perfunctory letter exchanged. The price to him of that rejection was not seeing the grandchildren. Both Natasha and Victor had children Myagkov would dote on had he but the chance.

"That's true, Colonel, as you know." Myagkov gave nothing away as he answered.

"Well, still, one has other satisfactions I suppose . . ." Shibunko let his voice hang idly in the air.

He was referring to Polish Adela of course. No one in CPS had a mistress not approved by GRU. Adela was easily cleared; her brother a Communist Party local functionary, her father certifiably proletarian, herself pleasingly, aimlessly non-political. That was to say she didn't give a damn as long as life went smoothly. She was, at least, good-natured and affectionate, someone to whom he could turn for warm companionship even if there could never be any sharing of his reading, his work, or his secret life; his dissent, his forebodings. Good company, a good lay, and a warm pillow on weekends, that was Adela.

"Yes, Colonel, we all must take such pleasures as we may." He replied casually, for under no circumstances was Myagkov going to let Shibunko, who was always on the edge of impertinence, get to him.

"Indeed, Comrade General, as long as it doesn't affect

our work, eh?"

Now what was the bastard driving at? Myagkov had a flicker of anxiety. Face him now, skewer the innuendo, skewer him if you can.

"All right, Colonel, what is it exactly that you're driving at?"

"Nothing serious, Comrade General, but you know my duty here requires that I be observant, as you yourself would want it."

"Yes, Colonel, exactly," Myagkov nodded.

"You did show a rather exceptional camaraderie to the new junior officers at the reception the other night, did you not?"

Myagkov nodded again. So that was it. Worse, Shibunko was right. Face the dragon, don't hide from the truth.

"You are correct in your insinuation, Colonel, quite correct. I did not distinguish myself. I was drunk, stupidly drunk! I was an ass."

Shibunko preferred the torture to the confession. What satisfaction as shrivener, when one enjoyed only the foreplay of thumbscrews? Shibunko gave it up as a bad job. "Ah well," he said, "down here in this hole, what can we do? I myself get drunk."

"Indeed one does, Colonel, all of us, and no surprise, that."

Both men nodded, each a bit sadder for the truth exchanged. For Myagkov, who foresaw his world growing with lies, this shared understanding of boredom and sorrow fought by bottles was as close as he would ever dare come to the bloodhound Shibunko. Sup with the devil and bring a long spoon.

Myagkov met his sister Anna that Saturday at the dilapidated Krakow airport. Her plane from Warsaw was reliably late. His staff car took them to the Soviet residential compound on the northwest outskirts of the city. Dismissing the chauffeur, settling her in, finally he could sit down with Anna in the luxury restaurant. He ordered tea, and for the first time in months was happy.

"It's so good to see you Petya, you're looking quite well." Anna was beaming.

"And you, Anya, I can't tell you how glad I am to see you. It's lonely here. One needs family."

She reached over to cover his hand with hers. "I can imagine, Petya, I can imagine. Well, we'll have a good visit and that will cheer you up."

He smiled back at her, his red eyebrows rising in a crescent of pleasure. His bald pate wrinkled itself as in a grin. "I'm already cheered, Anya."

"That's better." She was quite motherly; he'd forgotten how much she resembled their mother.

"We do have serious things to talk about, Anya."

"Yes, Petya, I know. You wrote about it. Your retirement, our parents' things . . ."

She carried it off beautifully, not a hint of a question. Pyotr knew she was aware it was no inconsequential ruse being staged.

"Quite so. But no family talk yet. Let's wait until later when you've had a chance to relax. It's a lovely day. We can take a walk and talk then about the family."

Their eyes calculated the room. The bar was typically pretentious, aping the West; Scotch and bourbon bottles filled with colored water, a row of Czechoslovakian beer cans, a large discolored mirror. A few army wives were taking tea; a waiter busied himself setting tables while another polished silver. None were suspicious looking, each of them no less suspicious for that. He would not talk to her here.

Outside the compound were country lanes. Pyotr took Anna walking. No cars followed, no reflecting parabolic sensors gleamed from windows to read their lips.

"I imagine they'll wait 'til dinner," Pyotr said.

"Who, Petya?" Anna was enjoying the walk.

"The bloodhounds, you know. They've got their reports to fill in too. Why not, after enjoying a fat chicken and good wine?"

Anna nodded. She could never be so far from Russia as to forget the bloodhounds. Had they not knocked at the door one night in the thirties to take their father away? Their father, who had never been seen again? She waited for Pyotr to speak.

"I had to talk to you, Anya. I want to put a great burden upon you, my own. I want to ask your advice."

"If I can help, I will. You know that."

"Depending, Anya, on what you say, it will be a very dangerous burden. You're happily married, you have three fine children, you've escaped our Soviet paradise. Can I ask you to risk any of that?"

"It's that serious then?" Her expression was grave and tender.

"Yes, even more serious than that."

"Oh." She was not surprised by his remark any more than the face of the ikon, Our Lady of Kazan, shows surprise. Anna kept that ikon in her room. Anna and the Lady understood that it was a world of sorrow; neither Our Lady nor Anna could alter that, except as love might.

"You know I love you, Petya. I will do what must be done."

"I'm not certain what that is yet, for it depends on what you think. I'm too much alone. I've no one to test my judgment against."

"Not Raya, certainly." Anna said firmly.

"No, not Raya," Pyotr affirmed.

"Nor your Adela?"

"Adela is like an English roominghouse, bed and breakfast, but no friend to trust."

"I see."

"As for Kostya, Dimitri, my real army friends, we're separated by whole countries. They stay quiet as I do, and they suffer their dissent like Trappists."

"Yes, I can imagine."

"Anya." Pyotr stopped in the road. In the distant field a farmer was piling hay bales on a horse-drawn wagon. Near them a squirrel ran across the road. Crickets sawed in the hot afternoon. "I'm in bad shape. I think too much, I drink too much, and I work too hard."

"There could be a worse fate than that." Anna felt her spirits rise. Perhaps his complaint was not more than that, being sad and lonely. It would not be the death-dealing sorrow he'd intimated. Russians were so exaggeratedly melancholic.

"I don't know where being sorry for myself leaves off and being worried about the world begins." Pyotr was awkward. These were thoughts written earlier to his diary; on his tongue they stumbled. He went on, "For myself I'm indifferent; after all, vodka, Adela, and some weasel like Shibunko to hate are cures enough . . ."

Anna interrupted. "Shibunko?"

"Sorry, it's just that he's on my mind. He's my GRU colonel. He's the one who'll have my head if I get careless. He's chief bloodhound at CPS."

"Oh." Anna understood.

"The fact is, if I face it, perhaps it's only me that I can't stand, maybe the rest is dramatics."

"Like what, Petya?"

"Anya, Russia is a cesspool, the Party leadership are

bandits, we haven't risen a step morally from where we were when the princes of Moscow were carrying axes for the Mongol hordes."

"I haven't thought politically in a long time, Petya," she said, beginning slowly. "My own life is too busy, too good, and Russia is out of my mind. As an adopted Yugoslav I suppose I think like my neighbors, and that means I distrust the Soviet Union, distrust it intensely. The Russian in me tells me I have every reason to do so, even though I love my motherland. As for bandits and morals, I can understand how one would come to that. Every time I think of how they killed our father, how our grandparents lost everything, suffered humiliation, indignity, poverty in their old age—of course you're right. I've read Solzhenytsin. He agrees completely. Sakharov, Amalrik, Marchenko, all our sad exiles and sadder prisoners—who could disagree?"

"You've read those authors, Anya?" Pyotr was amazed.

"Of course. I know how to read."

"You can get those books in Yugoslavia?"

"Certainly. We can have books as long as they don't denounce the state. And so I read."

"What a blessing it must be to have freedom."

"We're not free there, but we're more free, free enough for some things. I'm not unhappy. You know how it is, Petya. All the barracks in the socialist camp are the same, but outside of Russia they're merrier. Yugoslavia is by far the best."

"I know that, and I'm glad for you."

"But," she said, "you've lived with these Russian sins a long, long time. You've prospered. Look at you, a major general and the apple of the Kremlin's eye. Why curse the wolf who suckles you? Isn't that hypocritical?"

He looked at her and then away. He stared at the rich plain and green trees, at the farmer baling hay. "I think not hypocritical, for I've never talked in favor of these Communist plutocrats. I've kept my silence, done my work, risen on my merits. But I may be ungrateful, and maybe a wolf shouldn't turn on his pack. That does worry me."

"I'd think so. The Army's been good to you. You live well. You have power, lots of power. With your power you've sent men to their deaths, haven't you?"

"Only in battle, Anya, only as a soldier. Never have I wronged my men. Punishment yes, but only because of violations of military discipline. I'm not party to any of the Gulag Archipelago, not any of it, nor am I corrupt." His voice quivered between righteousness and self-defense. His big head thrust aggressively toward her.

"I never imagined that you were." It was her turn to be defensive. "But what's so different in sending half a million men to die defending the Party that you knew was the very one that killed your own father? Isn't that hypocritical?"

"War is different, Anya, we were fighting the Nazis, defending our homeland against invaders. Surely you remember fighting in that war too? After all, you were a nurse in the same army."

"Yes," she said, after a pause. "I agree, that was different. It was the homeland to be defended. It was the filthy Germans to be fought. But surely when you commanded tanks in Prague you couldn't claim you weren't part of a rotten business."

"That's exactly it, it was rotten. So was Finland earlier, or Hungary, so is being here in Poland for that matter. You think the Poles want us? Like rabbits want foxes! That's what began to bother me as a soldier, it was Prague. After that, well, I've been watching and thinking."

"Everyone sees how bad it is, Petya, but if you live in a marsh can you be anything but a muskrat? What can you do about Russia?"

"That's the question that every Russian since Bakunin —Doestoyevsky, Gogol, even Lenin—has been asking."

"Lenin was the one with the solution, wasn't he?" She was sarcastic.

"And it didn't work," he answered. "Why does no Russian solution for Russia ever work?"

"But you seem to think you can change something. Will your solution be any better?" She gazed at him thoughtfully as she asked him; weighed him, it seemed to him, as objectively as a scientist a pebble. "When all is said and done, will you have done anything except make trouble for yourself?"

Lenin's mother, he suspected, had bruised her son with the same question. He pleaded with Anna. "But don't you see, I don't propose a solution for Russia, not even for myself. Mine is a modest goal."

"And what is that?" She looked at him just as his mother might have when he tried to explain, at age ten, his idea for a perpetual-motion machine.

He grinned. "I want to save the world."

"Thank God it's something modest like that. For a moment you had me worried." They both laughed. She was relieved. It was typical talk of men.

"Now tell me," she asked, "what is it that you do want to do? Write a book?"

"No, just what I said. I want to save the world."

"Petya, are you out of your mind? Go write a book, no *samizdat* of course, but don't pursue revolutionary nonsense. You must be joking."

"Anything as monumentally crazy as this is a joke, but nevertheless I'm serious."

"Before you tell me just what it is you'll save the world from, my dear, tell me how you propose to do it."

"I want to defect," he said. "I must go to the West."

She was stunned.

"Oh my God! Dear, dear Petya, is that what you've been talking about? Is that what you want to do? Oh my God!"

"If you're willing to risk everything to help me."

"Dear God." Anna broke into tears. "That's what you want?"

"No, not at all. I don't want it and I won't think of it unless one overriding condition is met."

"And what's that condition?" Her voice was tremulous. Why, she asked herself, when a Russian makes a decision after such soul-searching must it always be the most painful one?

"The condition is that after I tell you why I should defect, you not only agree with me but you, yourself, ask me to do it. Now understand, I can't tell you the details, that would put you in double jeopardy should anything go wrong. I can only tell you in a general way, but you'll understand enough to make a decision. I guarantee you that the decision you make will be one I abide by, I have to. You're my pass to the West. But beyond that, I'll obey because I trust your judgment more than my own. If you tell me to stay here and mind my business, I'll do just that. If I stay, I might be a full general, for that matter. More power, as you say. The decision will be up to you."

"Dear Mother of Sorrows." She dropped to the side of the road, legs too wobbly to support herself, facing upward at him as he stood looking at her from the dirt road.

"All right," she said. "Sit down beside me, Petya, and tell me why you must leave."

Succinctly, he told her about the Forward God and WALTZ. When he had finished, he waited silently while she pulled out the soft inner stems of wild oats and sucked them between her teeth. Finally she turned toward him, handing him a succulent stem, just as they had done when they were children.

"I am not a woman who imagines herself to have a historical moment," she said. "I don't pretend to care much, at least no more than any normally decent Christian does, for anyone outside my family. My children, my husband, and you, Petya, that's the circle of my love. Frankly I don't care if the rest of the world burns. But if it burns, my family burns, and so I have no choice." She looked at her brother, her face heavy with pain. "And you have no choice. You must come West. I ask you to, I insist that you try. I shall do everything I can, everything no matter what that brings. It is my responsibility too. I recognize that. Do you understand what I'm saying? Do you understand?"

They both had understood.

FIVE

The muted thunder of jets was background for Anna's passage. For eighteen hours she waited, was pushed, squeezed into too-tight seats of rattling Russian-built planes, pushed, waited, was pushed again. These people and noises were impositions. The world had become an imposition. She remembered wartime when she was a nurse, the bombs which should not frighten her, mutilations that should not make her ill, and cries of soldiers in pain that she should grow used to, herself, whose weakness should not shout at her in her nightmares.

What was she going to do? Pyotr had reminded her of a code system by which they would write. They had used it before. He had prepared copies for each of them. Recipes from her to him; perfectly normal ones from a French cookbook he'd found. The choice of recipe signified topics and themes, the ingredients were the words to be used against her decrypting list like a foreign language dictionary. Numbers and dates were concealed as weights and measures, with any change from the master recipe significant. He was going to write to her about Pushkin, a poet he admired enormously. Pyotr had listed fifteen poems; their inclusion in a letter his theme, a work list of his commentary, "don't you think it is a *perfumed* sentence," for example, carried meaning. It was like games they had played as children. That was better, he had said, for her and for the censors, than a more elaborate cryptographic system that depended upon formulas and counting.

They had agreed she had to find someone to be her intermediary, someone absolutely trustworthy, who had freedom of movement and who could, without suspicion, work with the Americans. Why the Americans? she had asked. Why not West Germans, whose presence in Yugoslavia was ubiquitous and whose commitment to NATO was certain? Because, he had told her, the West German intelligence system was so badly compromised that no one in it could be trusted. He reminded her of the Chancellor's personal secretary, of an assistant secretary in the defense ministry, of a thousand other known arrests. These were, he said, like counting cockroaches. For every one you see there are a hundred undiscovered in the cracks.

The English? Philby's master remained undiscovered, perhaps still at work. Who could Anna trust—granting that the English service could be superb—knowing that one of their spymasters still worked for Moscow? The French? Pyotr had smiled. That old whoremaster, the French Communist Party, was still wily, he had told her, in enticing vain and innocent recruits. No, he'd insisted, it had to be the Americans, faulty as they were, if for no other reason than that were he to defect successfully, he wanted to live as far away as possible from the KGB assassins. For Trotsky, Mexico City had been too close. "And think of it, Anya," he asked her, "how can they hide a big bald head with red eyebrows anywhere but someplace as big as America?"

"Anya, I'm so glad you're home." Edvard embraced her with a great hug, flesh rippling in waves as her plumpness met his paunch. "Here, meet our American." Edvard, with one arm around Anna, pulled Ben toward her with his free hand.

"I'm pleased to meet you, Mrs. Oposevic," said Ben, talking loudly over the din in the small room that was the Split airport terminal. Neither realized they'd shared a bench in the Zagreb airport the week before. Ben saw before him a tired, worried-looking woman, well featured and gentle, whose eyes were strikingly like those of Valeria.

"And I you, Mr. Cornelius. So you're Valeria's American? I apologize for not being here when you arrived. I'm sure my husband told you I had to go to Poland to see my brother; a family matter."

Ben wondered why Edvard had seen fit to hide the place, Poland. He replied, "I do hope things worked out for you both."

She sighed. "Yes, it was good to see him. I'm sure things will work out." It was said without conviction.

Edvard looked sharply at her. One wasn't married for all those years without knowing when something was very wrong.

Edvard insisted that Ben come to dinner that night. While Anna had been gone they'd been out eating together in little cafes, for Edvard neither knew how to cook nor intended to learn. No matter how tired or depressed his wife, it was her duty to cook for him when she was home and to entertain any family guest. Ben had heard Edvard boast of equality in modern Yugoslavia. He now knew what "equality" meant. The women could hold two jobs; one at home doing all the work and one in a factory where, more than likely, they had lesser status and pay than men.

Anna seemed to think no more about it than Edvard did. In the small kitchen of their brightly decorated apartment in this ancient and amusing rabbit warren, she bustled about dutifully.

"I do wish Valeria had come with you, Ben."

They had come to a first-name basis quickly; the assumption of a close family tie was a bit unsettling to Ben, as though they had already decided he was a relative.

Would it surprise them that he'd never as much as held hands with their niece? With a woman as thoroughly attractive as Valeria, he had held himself in check. A quick fling with someone from a singles bar was one thing; becoming involved with a woman who really attracted you—and who worked for you to boot—was a weighty decision.

"I wish she had come, but someone had to look after the store and quite frankly, she's a whole lot better at it than I am."

"We'll expect to see you with her here one day." It was Edvard the Balkan matchmaker speaking. Ben didn't need to know the custom to detect the signs.

The dinner was excellent, but Anna clearly was in a troubled mood. Ben left early, after agreeing to join them for lunch in the apartment the next day. It was Anna who particularly insisted. Edvard seemed surprised.

Lunch—it would have been dinner if Ben had eaten everything set out for him—was over and they sat in the living room. The stone floors were worn with a thousand years of walking. The stone block walls, never painted, were peppered with holes from generations of residents hanging their artwork to suit their fancy. The Oposevics' taste ran to weavings, family pictures, a silvered ikon, old photographs of men in uniform with backdrops of mountain and valley, and some lively, well-executed watercolors of Dalmatian villages and fishing boats on the sea.

"Valeria painted those," Edvard said of the watercolors.

"I had no idea," replied Ben, surprised.

"What have you and Edvard decided to do about the

things they found in the vault?" Anna asked, surprising Ben with her directness.

Ben glanced at Edvard. There was no question that it was a stunning collection, and Ben had been trying to answer Anna's question himself. He visited the local export people, Customs, and the library where, thanks to the Oposevic son working there, a few helpful volumes in French and English had been located. Ben had been able to place the sculpture (fifteenth century, local, perhaps a German as master) and the ikons (Bulgarian, Serbian, and as Edvard had guessed, sixteenth through eighteenth century). At Customs and the export agency he had learned, without revealing particulars, that there might be a regulation that allowed export purchases of redundant, obsolete, or extraneous goods directly from a workers' council. Local Customs could handle it entirely if it were not an embargoed or special-class item. Who decided these classifications? That, the two bored, unhelpful, and incompetent clerks had allowed, was not their concern. As long as the "competent authority" provided Customs with the proper export permissions, the local office would process them. Who was the authority? It depended on the commodity. Who had the papers? The competent authority. Who decided which was that authority? The industry making the export. Was there a master list of special-class and embargoed items each industry had available? The clerk could not say. The local Customs office only had a criminal commodities list: drugs, guns, currency, that sort of thing. Had they ever seen a list? No, it was not their job to look for lists. Did they have any further advice for him? Both shrugged, gave him a lemon-sucking stare, and said nothing.

"Okay," he'd said, "I'm going to shop for locally produced arts and crafts to ship to my shop back in the States.

I'll buy them where I can from whom I can. Is there anything wrong with that?"

One clerk, sweating profusely in the hot day, his sport-shirt wet and his glasses smeared with droplets, snarled at him, "How can anything be wrong with that? Buy it, fill out the forms, find a shipper, pass it through the authorities, ship it."

"Which authority for handcrafted items privately sold?" Ben asked.

"If it's special class, then the export agency. If not, us."

"And you can't tell me which it is?"

"Certainly not. How are we supposed to know?"

"Okay, give me the papers I need for ordinary arts and crafts items to be processed by you." Ben was ceasing to be exasperated; the damn thing might work just because it was so colossally snarled.

"There are no special papers, just the regular forms."

"Okay, give me the forms."

"That's irregular; we deal with agencies, not tourists."

"I'm an agency, not a tourist."

The clerks seemed perfectly satisfied with that.

"All right," one said, "here are the blanks." He reached into his desk drawer and, without giving them a glance, hurled on the counter a rubber-band-bound sheaf of dogeared printed papers. "When you're ready, have your agency authorities authorize shipment and the goods can be processed."

"I'm the authorizing agent," said Ben coolly, seeing just how far Alice could push the Hatter.

"Well, why didn't you say so?" said the clerk, even more irritably. He pushed the worn bundle of papers at Ben. "Come back when your papers are completed and stamped."

"Stamped?" Ben asked. "By whom?"

"By the authorized purchaser, of course."

"What stamp?"

"How should we know?" screamed the clerk, suddenly losing his temper. "Every company has rubber stamps. Don't you know anything about your job?" Hissing like a steam pot, the fellow turned his back and walked away.

"Jesus!" Ben swore to himself as he walked out the door, "this is what they mean by the Balkans."

It was this encounter that Ben related to Anna and Edvard. The papers, all in Serbo-Croat, he gave to Edvard to review.

"It just may be," Ben said, "that I can buy, you can sell, Customs can process, and we can ship, all quite legally. In fact, that's the only way I myself can do it. If it takes something fancy, I'll try to find you someone else. I'm not about to pit myself against centuries of Byzantine scheming. I don't think I'd like the prison here. Understand me, please, Edvard. I'm not pretending righteousness, I'd just be an incompetent smuggler."

Edvard was shuffling through the papers. "Don't worry about it yet," he said. "Maybe your simple American cunning is the way. I'd never have thought of it."

"Thought of what?" asked Ben.

"Why, doing what you did as a private citizen and getting these papers authorizing private export."

"Authorizing?" Ben looked at the older man with surprise.

"That's what the papers say," Edvard replied. "You may have everything we need to do it right here." He smiled at Ben. "My friend, that was an absolutely brilliant maneuver. Only someone with your innocent face could have tricked them like that."

"Tricked them?" Ben was taken aback.

"Why of course. My hat's off to you. And you talk of us

as Byzantine. Child's play next to this. Let me tell you this, if ever there's another war, I want you working for our intelligence service."

"Edvard, what the hell are you talking about?" demanded Ben.

"Don't tell me you don't realize what you have here!" Edvard said.

"Not unless I've learned to read Serbo-Croat in three days."

Edvard smiled. "You're too modest. Imagine getting papers already signed, sealed, and giving Customs export authority approval. All we have to do is fill in the content form. 'Private handicrafts, arts and crafts, painting and sculpture.' There. Will that sound honest enough to you?"

"Of course it will. You mean that's all you have to do?" Ben was astonished.

"Look my friend, I've been exporting for years, fish of course, and never once in my life have I seen so-called blank forms given out by Customs, which are already signed and stamped. Yours here are approved for the shipping of whatever we fill in on them. I could ship you the Mestrovic statue out there in the park with these papers. Don't pretend you haven't managed it all."

"By accident," said Ben. "I have no idea what happened."

"No?" Edvard leaned over and patted him on the arm. "Then don't tell me, I don't want to know. If you forged them, fine. If you stole them, fine. If you bribed someone—and I imagine that's what you did, although how you found someone that fast I can't imagine—all the better. Bribery, you understand, is something our council couldn't consider even though we know it's sometimes done. In any event, it is a pleasure to do business with you."

Ben felt light dawning. He reflected on the scene at the

Customs office. Chaos, naturally. Someone must have prepared the illegal forms for someone else, no doubt on a bribe. The clerk Ben had been talking to, obviously not in on the deal, had simply seen the familiar package—the office must distribute hundreds of them—and had thrown it to Ben. The miscreant clerk who'd presigned the forms, whether he saw what happened or would find out later, would not be able to say a thing. Lordy. Edvard was right. They were home free.

"The art work will be shipped to you and Valeria this week with an honest bill of lading," Edvard was saying. "You sell the things as you see fit, take a forty percent commission after costs, send the rest of the money to our council treasury officer, and we'll all be happy. Is that a deal?"

"That's all? No contracts, nothing more for me to do? That's it?"

"If you approve." Edvard was very businesslike.

"I approve," said Ben. "How could I not?"

"Well Anya," Edvard turned to his wife, "don't you think Valeria's young man here is a clever friend for the family to have?"

Anna looked at Ben with so steady a gaze, appraising him, he felt, that he could not but return her look and was held by it. He felt himself shiver, without knowing why.

"I'm very tired, Ben," she said. "Come back this evening. We shall have a serious talk."

Ordinarily Ben would have politely demurred; one does not wear out one's welcome, especially with a hostess so deeply fatigued. Yet Ben sensed in Anna's words not an invitation but a conclusion. She compelled him to an accord. As he left the apartment, Edvard having walked him to the door, he felt that Edvard looked at his wife with the kind of alarmed curiosity with which a husband looks upon his own wife in her first labor.

Ben spent an indulgent afternoon swimming on a public beach some kilometers from the town. A local bus carried a crowd of pleasure seekers on the return. The bus stop was at the intersection where Diocletian's Palace commands a view of the wharves, of the spotless white express ferries and the incongruously putrid harbor waters. The stench of sewage from a landward wind hit him.

He was only a few feet along, walking toward his hotel, when he was stopped by a man. Yugoslavs dress well and cleanly, even though the proletarian uniform is usually washdress for women and sport shirt for men. This man was an exception. He wore a black suit, dirty with grease spots. His tie was stained and his soiled white shirt was open at the collar. His hair was black and straight, bright with oil. He smiled broadly at Ben, revealing several gold-capped biscuspids beneath his bushy moustache. He blocked Ben's path as he spoke. The man's grin was a Halloween lantern.

"You're an American, I can tell." The fellow beamed.

"Right on the button, Charlie."

Ben surprised himself with his own hostile response. He surveyed the other as one might before a fight. They were about the same height, but the other man was older, about forty-five, and stockier than was readily apparent beneath the drape of the black coat. For all his toothy smile, the fellow looked tough. Ben had been a boxer in college and was used to sizing up the opposition. He'd been glad from time to time that he knew how to use his fists. On one such occasion, set upon by a liquored-up tough in downtown Portland, Ben had been knocked into the open steel of a building under construction. He still carried the scimitar-shaped scar on the back of his neck. The incident had sent Ben not simply to hospital—along with the tough, who had fared worse—but to karate class as well. He'd had no black

belts in mind, just a sense of competence. Here on the
sunny avenue, surrounded by a throng of law-abiding
Yugoslavs, he was surprised to be thinking violence just
because this gold-toothed fellow was playing friendly. The
man went on.

"I bet you like Split, everybody does. You here alone?"

Ben didn't answer. The pitch would come soon enough.

The man looked downcast. "Listen, don't think I'm
going to make any trouble, you've got me wrong. I just
hoped to talk to an American, that's all. I went to Milwaukee once and really liked it. Everybody was so nice.
You been to Milwaukee?"

Ben made a bet that if he said "yes," old Gold-Tooth
would not pretend to know much of Milwaukee. Not that
Ben had ever been there himself. He tried it.

"Yeah, I lived there for a while."

"Oh, you did? Well, I just went for a visit, but a real nice
town. But listen, is there anything I can do for you here? I
was born here and I know my way around. Not that I look
like I'm doing too well, I know that, you must wonder what
a seedy-looking jerk like me is doing cluttering up this
workers' paradise. Well I'll admit I'm down on my luck and
wouldn't mind a little handout if you wouldn't take offense.
You know, just a few hundred dinars to keep body and
soul together." Gold-Tooth was hangdog now.

"Charlie, I'm told there's work for everybody in
Communism; why not go get some?"

"Don't you believe it, buddy." Gold-Tooth lowered his
voice conspiratorially. "Listen, I don't talk in public, but if
you want an earful on this goddamn country I can give it to
you. And I got friends, too, who can tell you lots of things,
just in case you want an eye-opener."

"No thanks, Charlie," Ben replied. "I'm just a happy
tourist."

"Well then, how about a girl? You want a really lovely piece of ass?"

"Charlie, you're a loser." Ben began to walk off, but Gold-Tooth grabbed his sleeve. The grin was servile.

"Look, Mister, I really only want to help. Isn't it true you're new here? Came in from Zagreb on that extra late plane just four days ago?"

Ben stopped. "So what? And how did you know?" He was bristling.

"No offense. I just know you're new and seeing you come off the beach bus by yourself, I figured you might be lonely. Honestly, I was just at the airport when you came in. That's all, believe me."

"You're right, Charlie, that's all. Now if you'll excuse me . . ." Ben stared at him aggressively, then turned and walked away.

The black-suited man walked behind Ben a moment and then turned slowly to wander away, finally to turn up a narrow street and disappear in a nondescript office building.

"Well?" The fat man seated behind the desk looked up as Gold-Tooth came in the frosted glass door of the small office.

"Don't bother me, Arso. Let me clean up." Gold-Tooth walked by the fat man to the rear, and disappeared. The fat man went back to reading the sports page.

Peko Bogdanovic looked at himself in the bathroom mirror of the small apartment situated behind the office. Slowly he pried the false gold caps off his sound biscuspids. He then pulled off the moustache, removed the two thin wax blocks from inside his mouth, which gave his cheeks their fullness, and carefully took off the oily-haired wig, revealing brown hair streaked with gray. He removed his clothes, threw them disdainfully through the door into the spartan bedroom, and took a shower. Some twenty minutes later a thinner-faced, clean-shaven, muscular and rather handsome man of about fifty came back into the office and went to his desk. Arso, the fat man, chewing a cigar, spoke out to him.

"Peko, goddamn it, how'd it go?"

Peko turned to the other from the typewriter into which he'd just inserted the paper for his report.

"He's the one Belgrade wants all right. Answers the description, speaks perfect American, went for the ploy about the Zagreb flight as though he were on stage waiting for the cue, and has the scar on the back of his neck."

"So," the fat man whistled. "Do you think there's something to it?"

"Arso, if Belgrade says that this comes from Director Savic, you better believe there's something to it. If the director says the world is round, the world *is* round, Arso."

The fat man looked puzzled. Bits of cheap tobacco plastered his lips as the cigar unfurled at the wet end. "But Peko, the world *is* round."

"Exactly, Arso, exactly. You do understand."

The fat man frowned and went back to the sports pages.

For thirty minutes Peko's typewriter drummed Arso's ears. Then it stopped and the paper came out.

The fat man put down the sports page and lit a fresh cigar.

"Peko, what do we do now?"

"Am I your boss, Arso?"

"For the last two weeks you are, Peko, and don't rub it in. You know I wanted that promotion as much as you."

"Right, so as the new chief of this office I tell you what we do and you don't ask me. Right?"

"Aw, Peko, what's got into you? We worked as partners

for years."

"Arso, what is Communism about?"

The fat man looked down, embarrassed. "Hell, Peko, I'm no theoretician. It's about equality, you know that, and workers owning the instruments of production, and the class war so that workers aren't exploited."

"Right. Now what are equality, ownership and class all about? I'll tell you . . . all those words are about power."

"Okay, okay."

"And that, my friend, is what my promotion was about, and that is what our own UDBA is about. Power. And don't you forget it."

Arso had forgotten for a moment just how mean his oldest and once dearest friend could be.

Peko went on. "Now, about the redhead. Belgrade's memo says that the scar is the only identification they have for the Soviet agent who was managing liaison in Montenegro for Djoko Stojanovic. You remember him?"

"Yeah. Friend of Dapcevic whom we took care of back in 1975."

"Right. We got nothing else from Stojanovic, so all Belgrade knows is that the KGB liaison man with the scar runs in and out of this country without any trouble. Until now it was assumed he posed as a Montenegrin and came and went from the Bloc countries. But what if the man Savic made in Zagreb, the guy who's here now, is the liaison? Makes sense doesn't it? It's a Western cover he uses. An American or English tourist today, a businessman tomorrow. Maybe he speaks German and comes in as an auto dealer out of Bavaria the next time. It's perfect. Why should he ever go to Montenegro? His network contact can meet him in Zagreb, Belgrade, here, and nobody is ever the wiser. No, it makes a whole lot of sense."

"What was your impression of the guy when you met

him?" Arso asked.

"Zero, which is just why I think Belgrade is right. No bluff, no nerves, no pretending, no denials. He's good, Arso. No wonder he could service a clandestine Soviet net for years right under our noses."

"Well, do we tail the redhead or run him in now?" asked Arso.

"We have a free hand until Belgrade gets my report. I say give him some rope. He won't see anyone publicly that we give a damn about, and he'll have some ironclad cover story backing up the whole trip. Give him a while to breathe, watch him at a distance. Wire his telephone in the hotel, and we'll see where he leads us. That's my plan. Even so, we check out everyone he does see publicly; one can never tell who'll be in the game with him and who he's using as patsies. I remember the last Soviet I worked in Belgrade was running fifty red herrings by us for every genuine agent we saw. We could have leaned on a lot of perfectly patriotic citizens if we hadn't been discriminating."

The fat man sighed. "Lots of trouble to check out fifty people. I hope this guy is a loner."

"No way," said Peko. "I'll bet you a month's pay-check on it. It's their method. Lots of contacts for you to see and none of them you care about and then, just time for a quick pass and he slips off and boom, by the time he's back in sight his business is over and you miss it all. I know. I've had it happen."

"Slippery bunch of bastards, aren't they?" Arso's pudgy face darkened.

"Dangerous, Arso, A knife at our throats every minute. It's not professional, but damn it, I hope this one gives me the excuse to kill him—after I do the interrogation, you understand."

"You think Belgrade will let us handle it by ourselves?"

"No chance. This is as big a case as Belgrade gets. There will be ten senior officers down here by tomorrow, you can bet on it. In the meantime, let's you and me put the bells on our Soviet friend's tail. And watch yourself, Arso. He'd kill us as happily as we'd kill him."

As Ben left the hotel to go to dinner at the Oposevics', he noticed neither the look of apprehension the hotel desk clerk gave him nor the fat man shuffling along on the other side of the street, the sports page crumpled in his left hand. His right hand remained free.

Peko stayed in the office to be certain his top secret cable to Belgrade went out "urgent." Internally, they used a secure telex network rather than radio. As the telex clattered with the Belgrade acknowledgment, Peko sat down at his desk, pleased with a good day's work. He would have been less pleased had he known that the UDBA headquarters telex terminal broke down just as the message was coming in. The message clerk hurriedly pulled the Split telex out of the machine, carrying it with him instead of putting it in the "urgent distribution" box, because the distribution box must be empty when the repairmen came in. The message clerk could not find the routing clerk and so gave the Split telex to the duty officer's secretary instead. It was nearly six o'clock, she had a date, and the duty officer was off having coffee. She put the message on his desk and left. The security officer, making his close-down check, spotted a top secret message lying on an already secured desk. He wrote a security violation notice for the erring secretary and, as his procedures required, locked the telex in his own safe.

Next morning, Savic would wonder why Split had not reported and Peko would wonder why Belgrade had not taken action.

SIX

Ben walked down one of the center arcades of the old Palace. One shop selling television sets had two demonstration models loudly blaring a night soccer game pitting Split against Slovenia. An excited crowd had gathered to watch.

Arso followed Ben cautiously, disciplining himself. He sucked up his stomach and held his breath against the fragrant distraction of a lamb cooking on an outdoor brazier. And then Split scored with a hard boot past the sprawling goalie. Arso had 500 dinars on the game. His eye moved to the TV screen for only a second, confirming the shouts of the crowd at everyone's good luck. Again self-discipline imposed itself as he returned his sporting eyes to follow the redhead with the scar.

Arso's heart thumped violently. His man had disappeared. Arso began to run, shouldering people out of the way. Down the stairs to the art shops, back again to the darkened doors of an old temple turned lecture hall, sideways into a dead-end corridor and from it to the quai, running, running, running, running. Nothing.

Arso's hand shook as he called Peko at the office. Peko had gone. Arso called him at home. No answer. Arso, wiping his face with a handkerchief, ran again. He now had a good deal more to lose than 500 dinars on a soccer match.

Thirty minutes later he found Peko at home.

"He gave me the slip," whined Arso. "I don't know how he did it, Peko; I had my eye on him every second but some damn tourists walked between us and poof! he was gone. Sure as hell he must have spotted me. Tonight must be his night for an agent meeting. I told you, Peko, we needed a two-man surveillance team for this one—two men anyway."

Peko was fuming. Arso was lying. The bastard probably had been reading the sports page again. But it was true, there should have been two, if not three, on the surveillance team.

"God damn you, you fat slob," Peko hissed into the phone.

Arso relaxed. Thank God he'd been clever enough to shift the blame to Peko for not assigning a bigger squad. Now Peko was in more trouble than Arso. Well, he grinned to himself, if Peko wants to be boss, let him explain to Belgrade. Arso played his card. "Gee, boss," he said—it was the first time Arso had addressed his old partner as "boss"—"if Belgrade finds out they'll have our ass."

"*Our* ass?" Peko screamed. "You lost the tail."

"Sure I did, boss, sure, but after all, Belgrade had told you what a big fish he was. They're not going to like learning I was the only one tailing him and you were in the office."

The quiet was palpably hostile. Finally Peko spoke.

"You bastard! All right, I'll meet you at the redhead's hotel in fifteen minutes. Maybe we can still find him."

"Sure boss, we're bound to."

Smiling broadly, Arso walked from the phone booth to an open-air cafe table. He ordered spaghetti and sat back, enjoying the sportscast. He had Peko by the balls. Leaning back, Arso let himself imagine the glorious moment when he himself would catch the KGB man as he serviced a drop or met an agent. Peko better look out, Arso thought to himself, old Arso was going to make out just fine.

Ben, as ignorant of Arso's less-than-fancy footwork as of the darker world into which he was falling, walked pensively, thinking about his return home the next day. Preoccupied with that, a few minutes later he knocked on the door of the Oposevics' apartment. Edvard opened it, his face grave. Ben sensed that something was seriously wrong. He held out his hand to shake Edvard's.

"What is it, Edvard?" he asked. "Aren't you feeling well?"

"It shows then, does it?" the other replied.

"Something's wrong. Is Anna all right?"

Anna's voice came to him from the kitchen, from which the fragrant vapor of paprika goulash drifted into the living room.

"Thank you, Ben. Yes, I'm all right. Edik, you give Ben a big slivovitz; take one yourself. Here, I'll bring you some good goat cheese. Dinner will be awhile. I think we'd better begin our talk now."

Anna, carrying a sturdy wooden tray, walked slowly into the room. She was, Ben could see, every bit as tired, as worried, as she had been at noon.

Ben suddenly felt himself tired, depressed and nervous; the contagion of their feelings was gripping him.

"Something wrong with our export scheme?"

Edvard waved his hand, dismissing the query. "No, Ben, no. You set that up beautifully. My men are already moving the things through Customs. It will all be cleared by tomorrow, and then out on the first ship."

"That's fast," said Ben.

"We can be fast now, thanks to you. A little grease helps the slide. We have a proverb, 'one hand washes another, money washes both.' That and a little *veza* is what keeps it going."

"*Veza?*"

"Influence, favors, connections. With *veza* everything is possible. I have *veza* on the docks and with the ships; after all, what else should I do with my authority?"

"Yes, of course," Ben nodded. Edvard was admitting to an aspect of life at which Ben only guessed.

"You are surprised, my friend, that I speak so directly to you, is that it?"

"Yes, a little," replied Ben. There was no point in pretending.

"It is important that we be very honest with one another." It was Anna who spoke.

"Of course," said Ben, asking himself, what the hell is this all about?

"Don't misunderstand, please." Anna reached out her hand and grasped Ben's own. She held it, like his mother would have in a moment of pleading. "Edvard and I must be honest with you. Frankly, we are afraid."

"Afraid?"

Edvard spoke. "Yes, Ben. Afraid."

"I'm sorry. Is there anything I can do to help?" As he said it he felt his stomach tighten. What was he getting into now?

"Ben?" Anna was looking directly into his eyes, her blue ones troubled.

Ben drew in his breath, as though ready for a plunge into cold water. "Yes?"

"We must trust you. May we?"

"Of course you can." How could it be otherwise, he wondered. Whatever else he was, Ben counted himself trustworthy.

"Take my hand, Ben."

Ben let her grip his hand. Edvard watched them solemnly.

"We have no one else we can turn to," Edvard said. In his face Ben no longer saw the soft fat of the plant director's easy life, but the hard lines, cruel lines even, of a fighter. That was the face of the war hero Valeria had praised. Edvard, Ben realized, was tough.

Anna was talking. "You've been good to Valeria, and she trusts you. You've been good to us here, helping with the ikons and statues, and very clever about it too. You have an innocent face, Ben—most Americans do—but here in this life in Yugoslavia, in the Russia I came from, there are no innocents."

"You came from Russia?" asked Ben.

"Oh yes. I was a nurse in the Soviet army when it came to Yugoslavia. That's when I met Edvard."

"Oh."

She went on. "So I must ask you about your innocence."

"I don't understand."

"Are you really the good-hearted, easygoing business-man that Valeria thinks you are, that you say you are?" It was not his mother asking if he had stolen cookies from the jar; Anna was more like, it seemed to Ben, a female Saint Peter, sadly omniscient, offering him the opportunity for confession.

"Well, Anna, I think Americans are not used to being so serious, certainly not about themselves, unless of course they are just conceited. It's poor form, at least in the little town I came from, to talk about oneself too seriously."

"You're evading my question, Ben, and you have the right to do so. Only it would help us so much if you trust us."

"I do," protested Ben.

"Then are you what you'd have us believe?"

For the first time since the moment he'd decided to

divorce, to leave advertising, to start a new life, Ben was reflecting upon himself, even though he realized that whatever Anna was driving at had nothing to do with what he knew himself to be.

"Well, I'm really not a businessman. I never was and don't intend to be. My parents died young, leaving me some money. I did advertising because a friend of my father's got me the job when I finished university. I think I liked the phony excitement of it for a while, and I did like the money. And I guess I liked conning people a little, at least being able to persuade them. That part I'm ashamed of. As for now, I started the art shop because I like art, not business, and frankly I don't care about the money much; I have enough anyway, and I'm sure the place will succeed on its own. With Valeria it can't fail. As for innocence, well I don't imagine you want to hear about my sex life. I like girls, and Valeria especially, although I haven't told her how much I think of her."

Ben paused while they waited.

"I don't really know what else there is to say." He spread his hands, looking from one of them to the other.

"But you are an American?" It was Edvard who asked it, deadly serious.

Ben grinned. "How could I be anything else? Ben Cornelius, born in Cornelius, Oregon. Father Rowland Cornelius, grandfather Ben Cornelius again, mother Missouri Adams, named after her grandmother."

"Do you have any experience in intelligence, Ben?"

Edvard's question stopped Ben dead in his thoughts. "Do you mean as in spying?" Ben's face carried his astonishment.

"As in spying," Edvard agreed.

"Hardly. How could you ask?"

"In the Balkans it is a common profession, and the way

you handled the Customs business made me think you had some special skills."

Ben smiled. "I'm flattered, but no, nothing so adventuresome as that."

"Do you know anybody in your American embassy in Belgrade, Ben? Do you know anyone anywhere in the CIA?"

Ben smiled no more. He looked Edvard in the eyes and spoke slowly, for he remembered he was in a Communist country. Something had happened.

"That is a serious question, Edvard. Do you suspect me of something? Have I done anything to offend you? Have I put you in jeopardy with some silly tourist's remark to a stranger?" For some reason Ben recalled the unpleasant fellow on the street with the gold-capped teeth. Had that meant something after all?

"To the contrary, Ben." It was Anna who spoke. "You arouse no suspicion, you do nothing wrong, we simply must know if you have any connections that might be put to use."

"Good Lord!" Ben stared at these two deadly serious, loving, frightened people. What was on their minds?

"And so I ask again," Edvard said, "about your connections."

"I don't know anyone in Belgrade. As for the other question . . ." Ben's voice trailed off.

"Yes?" Anna and Edvard waited tensely.

Ben considered the situation. He did have a cousin in the CIA, second cousin really, met him at family reunions from time to time and they traded Christmas cards, his cousin Jeff's coming from around the world. Jefferson Cornelius Grenn—and his being a spy was Jeff's business, that much about spying Ben did know, and Jeff was too good a man to be betrayed. Where, in fact, Jeff was these days Ben had no idea; certainly not in the Balkans.

"I don't betray confidences," Ben spoke slowly, "and, rather than lie to you, let's just say I can't answer your question."

Edvard smiled gently, Anna seemed relieved. Ben couldn't account for their reactions.

"We now discuss a matter of life and death," Edvard said. "We tell you everything, Ben, and these lives are in your own hands. Do you understand this?"

Ben found himself pulling his hand away from Anna's, withdrawing from them. Fun was fun, but enough was too much. The export caper had been enough, scary even, as he'd seen how his hosts were willing to involve him in risk. He'd managed, by sheer luck of course, to handle that and stay honest. And now suddenly this elderly couple—and they did both look older tonight than they had yesterday— were talking to him about life and death. That was hardly his metier. Here in this room, for the first time in his life, there was an odor foreign to him: fear and deadly business.

Ben heard himself say sensibly, "I'm sorry, but I just don't want to take on a responsibility like that. I've no experience, I have a business in Oregon to run, I'm not a hero."

Edvard looked at Ben for a time, and then said, "I'm glad you're not a hero."

"Why's that?" asked Ben, quite surprised.

"We have a saying here, 'Behind every hero is a traitor.'"

"Behind or inside?" Ben wasn't quite sure what was meant.

"It can be the same," was the reply.

Ben dismissing this Balkan conundrum, went on. "I'd like to help you but really, I don't want to get into something over my head. You must understand that, surely."

Ben found himself looking at Anna, that beautiful old woman, wanting her to forgive him, feeling inside himself a rising sense of shame.

"I understand, Ben, of course I do." There were tears in her eyes.

The old man nodded his head. This was, after all, the world as he knew it too well.

"Well, I guess I should get going. I want to get reservations for the trip home tomorrow." Ben could hardly wait to escape; he nearly bit himself speaking with his now dry tongue.

"But no, Ben, the goulash is ready. You can't leave without having your dinner. We know how you feel. You don't have to run away from us, we do understand." Anna's soft eyes forgave him.

"Christ," Ben muttered to himself, his mind a clutter of ugly feelings, a faded picture of himself as a boy throwing a snowball up at his old aunt's place, in the wild country beyond Cornelius town, and running away when it hit the visiting Methodist minister.

A vision of himself in one of those interminable scenes with Constance, clamming up rather than telling her what he really thought of her sharp-tongued selfishness. A recollection of himself with the boss at the advertising firm, level-headed while the old fart ranted and raved. Ah, that Anglo-Saxon control. Careful Ben who'd never yet kissed Valeria and who, virtuously again, was flushing her family right down the tubes. You are sweet, Ben, he told himself, really a dear.

"You will stay for dinner, Ben. It really is a good goulash and I'd hate to see you leave feeling so bad."

Ben felt himself blush redder than his hair. A string of invectives ran through his mind, all aimed inward. Anna took his arm and guided him to the tiny table in the old kitchen. She held her head high, her chin proud. No beggar in her, Ben saw, and as he'd told her, no hero in him.

"Christ." This time he said it out loud.

The old couple looked at him, puzzled.

"Christ." He said it again. Now Anna was perturbed; Ben could sense she didn't like swearing.

"All right, let's have it." The words rushed out in furious relief, leaving sensible, prudent old Ben somewhere far behind.

Edvard grinned and went out to get the slivovitz. Anna nodded silently and began to heap goulash on Ben's plate. Edvard poured a tumblerfull of the fiery plum liquor and pushed it to Ben, taking another for himself.

By mealtime's end, Ben was glad he was at least half drunk. How could a sober fellow, an American innocent at that, otherwise agree to do what he had just agreed to do: arrange a senior Soviet general's defection and, in the process, oppose CPS, the Forward God, that death-bent computer humming away behind the Tatra? What was the Waltz? Some kind of macabre dance to be sure. Anna seemed to know no more than that. Her brother Pyotr had been right, at least if he wasn't just selling some bag of tricks for reasons Ben couldn't imagine. But tricks couldn't be ruled out, the possibility that Pyotr had invented the whole thing for some purpose of his own. Hell, Ben thought as his brain cells swam in slivovitz, maybe it was all for some purpose of the Soviets. Stay a week or two in the Balkans and you begin to think like they do, dolls inside the wooden dolls inside the wooden dolls. But if the general spoke true, then Ben had agreed to do only one little thing.

"Save the world, that's it," he mumbled as he fell asleep on the front-room couch, nicely tucked in by Anna with a pillow under his head.

Three hangovers. Three blessed evening maidens turned next morning's hags. One belonged to Ben, a little harpie with whom he could live 'til coffee chased her away. The second belong to Peko, born of rage and nerves when the redhead failed to show at the hotel, who wrapped her arms around his skull and squeezed his headache tight all day. The third crone belonged to the UDBA security officer who'd picked up Peko's cable the night before to lock it so securely in his own righteous file. That fellow had made a night of it when he learned a grandson was born to bear his name. The security man called in sick, saying he had the flu. A small lie, but consequential, for Savic, called in by his boss—the university students were threatening once again to riot—had nothing on his desk to remind him of the suspected KGB agent, code-characterized now as L-IMOT. The business slipped Savic's mind under the Interior Ministry's higher priority worries.

The UDBA people are not incompetent. They perform, Savic saw to that, quite neat professional work, "simplifying cases," running quite a pleasant little dictatorship, not much fuss or bother and quite conscientious about shedding as little blood as possible. Not many trials, just enough to remind people to keep their mouths shut about democracy and such, and by no means generally obnoxious. Arso was, of course, an asshole, Peko knew that, but most of the time he'd done his work. As for Miko, the new man in the office, he'd looked promising. What the hell, then, had gone wrong? Peko asked himself. Peko was beyond anger, almost beyond self-reproach. He'd reached almost a purely intellectual level trying to figure it out, this business of the redhead, L-IMOT, disappearing. KGB he had to be, because no one else but a real professional would have left the UDBA branch in Split with only mud on its face.

When L-IMOT hadn't returned by morning to his hotel, Peko had put Miko on the stakeout. Miko was ordinarily a craftsman and Peko had not imagined that between Miko and the checkout desk so much could be lost. Miko had to go to the loo. He had told the desk clerk to watch for the redhead, to stall if he wanted to check out. Something had gone wrong, probably L-IMOT made it go wrong. Mother of God, Peko thought, how he'd like to get his hands on those Soviet infiltrators.

Someone had called the desk clerk away to a room upstairs, a bellboy had minded the desk, L-IMOT conveniently came in and checked out, nonchalant as could be according to the bellboy, and that was it. The clerk came back, Miko came back, and it wasn't until Miko, getting nervous himself by that time, had queried the clerk—and then it was 12 noon—that they'd come up blind. L-IMOT with an hour's grace, too many buses and three planes—one Zagreb, one Belgrade, one Zurich, all gone. It wasn't that the airport people hadn't seen the "American." Everyone had seen him. Or so they said.

No two stories were the same: he'd come in, he'd gone to Zagreb, Belgrade, Zurich. Ticket stubs? Oh yes, hundreds of them, but this was Yugoslavia and this morning's paperwork somehow went out with the garbage. L-IMOT's fine hand again? Peko didn't put it past him. If so, the slippery bastard had a network that included someone at the airport. Not impossible, and UDBA Split would start working on that full time. They'd damn well better, Peko knew, because if this thing fell through, Peko did not particularly want to go on trial for treasonable negligence. He'd put enough people up on the charge of "crimes against the State" that he knew it took only one signature by Savic and one well-prompted judge, in a quiet, "no admittance" courtroom, to stow him in Posaravac prison 'til his grandchildren were gray-haired.

Peko had sent the cable to Belgrade: L-IMOT had left Split for who-knew-where. Peko sat glumly at his desk scratching the stubble on his face.

The teletype in the tiny communications room clattered back. "Transmission acknowledged." That was all the cable said. They were, he concluded, as screwed up in Belgrade as in Split. It was time to go home to bed. Without a word to Arso, Peko left the office.

Ben Cornelius had looked at himself in the mirror during the few minutes it took him in his hotel room to pick up his bag, packed the day before in erroneous anticipation of a homeward journey. There were new lines on his face. Even his hair looked a darker auburn, perhaps verging on ruddy brown. When he was younger it had been, he was sure of it, bright red. Had he aged in one night? To wisdom? One might hope for that, but at the moment, age's components were sadness and fear. He was entering some world of deceit, already carrying knowledge to which no one else, save the Oposevics and the Soviet general staff, was privy. Knowledge? That word was insufficient for what Ben carried. His mouth tasted bitter. The slivovitz? Ben told himself not to bother with such lies; beginning soon he would have to lie too often to others to waste them on himself.

He picked up his bag, hurried down the one flight of stairs, threw money on the counter as the indifferent bellboy handed him the bill, walked briskly to the street and hailed a passing cab. At the airport, now alone—for he'd agreed with Anna and Edvard that the connection between them must not be renewed until some momentous next step was in the offing—he'd boarded the Belgrade plane, which Edvard had booked for him by phone, and settled in for the flight to the city on the Danube.

SEVEN

There is a tourist aid desk at the Belgrade airport, with a sign above advertising assistance in obtaining reservations. Ben made for the desk, pleased to note how beautiful was the girl behind it. She smiled as he approached.

"I'd appreciate your helping me find a hotel."

Her gray eyes danced for him. "Delighted to help. What price range?"

"I'm tired, so I'd like to indulge myself in something extravagant. What's your best?"

"The Moskva is supposed to be the best, but frankly I don't think you'd like it. Noisy and too expensive for what you get. Try the Metropole. It has a park on two sides, trees on the street, and music in the dining room. If you have a girl you can dance."

Ben couldn't help but grin. "Your English is perfect. If your advice is half as good, I can't lose."

She looked up at him, her five-feet-four to his relaxed, well-muscled five-eleven. "I learned my English here," she said. "Would you believe that?"

"Why not? You look a trustworthy type to me."

She lifted her head, pursing her lips in mock seriousness. "Ah, you must be an American, and new here. Too trusting. Fact is, I lived with some relatives in Detroit for a year."

Ben kept smiling, but took her words to heart. He *was* too trusting, and it wasn't everyone he'd meet who'd be so kindly an instructor as this charmer.

"I am an American, I am new here, but I'll do my best to follow your advice. On the hotel and the trust."

She nodded approvingly, spoke into the phone in Serbian, and scribbled a confirmation form.

"I assumed you wanted a single room?" There was interest in her voice.

"Regretfully, yes," Ben replied.

"No regrets now," she admonished. "A married man must behave himself away from home."

"I'm not married," said Ben.

"Ah," said the girl, "then how will you enjoy the dancing at the Metropole?"

"Beats me. Maybe I can advertise."

"Mister . . .? She glanced down at the paper, pencil poised. "What is your last name?"

"Cornelius. Benjamin Cornelius."

She wrote his name on the form and looked up again, smiling. "Mr. Cornelius, I think that charm of yours will be advertisement enough."

Ben felt embarrassedly pleased. "That's very kind of you, but I think you bring out the best in me. After all, how many strangers can expect this kind of welcome in a strange country?"

"It's not strange to me, it's my home. But you're right. The way of the world is not to welcome strangers." The girl shrugged, a wisp of sadness on her face now. Ben revised her age upward, guessing now at about twenty-eight.

"Well," he said, "I am grateful for your help."

"Have a good stay." She was not smiling as he turned and moved toward the outside door.

Ben was distinctly displeased as he left. That girl was

rather special and here he was, walking away from her. His eye fell on a candy stand near the street exit. Damn, he thought, why not? He bought a box of candy and returned to the counter. The girl cocked her head as he approached.

"Didn't like the hotel?"

"Worse yet. Didn't like leaving you with inadequate thanks. Bought you some candy. Share it with your husband."

She accepted the box. "No one has ever done this before, and I don't have a husband."

They looked at each other, directly, appraising. Ben spoke. "Would you have dinner with me tonight? I don't dance well but I can manage to keep time."

Her face was politely grave. "Mr. Cornelius, I would be delighted. I'll meet you in the hotel lobby at . . ." she glanced at the steel watch on her wrist, ". . . at about seven. Is that convenient?"

"It's perfect." Ben was beaming now. "Now may I know your name?"

As he asked, three bustling Germans stormed the counter demanding help. The girl, her brown-black hair brushing across her forehead, winked at him and said only, "See you tonight," and then, in German, attended to the portly storm.

Ben had checked in at the Metropole—the girl was right, it was excellent—and was now on his way to the U.S. embassy. There was, he felt, no use delaying the hard part. Lacking any knowledge of what to do, and recalling that cousin Jeff and most CIA people abroad worked under embassy cover, he had decided to ferret out the spooks in their nest.

The embassy is on Milosa Street, on a hill, the tree-lined street paralleling the Sava River on its way to the Danube.

A pleasing avenue, like many in Belgrade, reminding one, curiously, of places one has never seen. Nostalgia, Ben reflected, for the unknown place. Racial unconscious? Fragments from movies? He couldn't say. On the way here in the cab he'd noted the well but informally dressed people sauntering along. How disciplined were the pedestrians at corners, how careful the drivers. More streetcars than autos, and trees in abundance not overwhelmed by buildings, for most were no more than four stories. A comfortable city. He could understand why Miss Who at the airport had returned home from Detroit.

He walked up the steps to the embassy reception area. A thin woman sat at the desk, looking bored.

"Yes?" she said, glancing up.

"I understand my cousin, Jefferson Grenn, may be assigned here. The political section, I think." It was Ben's first lie in the service of God-knows-what.

She leafed through a thin booklet. Ben estimated the staff to number less than seventy-five. "I'm sorry, there's no Grenn listed."

"Oh. Well in that case, may I see one of the political section officers? Perhaps he can tell me about my cousin."

She spoke into the phone. "Mr. Saunders' secretary will be down in a moment to take you upstairs. Please take a seat."

A few minutes later Ben was past the guard, past the locked doors, down the hall and into the sparse office of Mr. Saunders. It did not have a lived-in look. Mr. Saunders either did little or did it elsewhere. Saunders himself was a young fellow, about twenty-nine, black-rimmed glasses, blond hair already balding, thin, watery blue eyes and large ears. He was impeccably dressed in Belgrade embassy summer casual: blue-striped seersucker trousers, blue short-sleeved shirt, and loafers. He smelled of lotion. He gestured to Ben to sit down, sat himself uneasily erect like a Sandhurst subaltern with piles, and spoke in a good Eastern-school accent.

"And what may I do for you, uh . . ." He glanced at Ben's card. The "uh" was disdainful. "Mr. uh, Cornelius."

"My cousin, Jeff Cornelius Grenn, is with one of the branches of our government. I was advised he might soon be posted here. Do you know him?"

"No." Saunders leaned back, tapping his fingers impatiently.

"It's important that I find either my cousin or one of his colleagues." Ben was putting it as delicately as he could. One does not, after all, ask for a CIA officer and expect him to be delivered up.

"Just what is your business, Mr. Cornelius?" His tone verged on impertinent disdain.

"I am, as my card indicates, a dealer in art and antiquities," replied Ben.

"Perhaps our commercial section can help you. I am not a commercial attaché, you know."

"It's a political matter of some sensitivity which brings me here." Ben stared directly into those smug eyes. Saunders flinched and fingered the calling card. Round Two to me, thought Ben.

"I am the junior political officer. You can speak freely to me. We receive all kinds of information here."

"I'm sorry Mr. Saunders, but I couldn't possibly entrust my information either to a junior officer, or, indeed, to someone who was only State Department."

Saunders' outsize ears began to quiver irritably. "I am afraid that there is no one in this embassy except State Department officers, Mr. Cornelius. As for the senior officer, I am delegated by him to deal with people like yourself."

It was infuriating. Yet Ben was, he realized, blocked. It would be so easy once one knew something about the embassy and how to make the right connections, but to an outsider, indeed a suspect outsider, it appeared, the embassy procedures were an enigma. But one more try, just one more push against this pipsqueak.

"Let me put it to you a little differently. This is a matter of extreme importance. It is and must remain highly confidential. It's a matter which must be in the hands of an agency which is in the right business, do you understand? Now, Mr. Saunders, the truth is that after your little performance here with me, I simply don't have any confidence in you, and, as you say, you are only State Department in any event. Now please, be a good fellow and go find me a man I can do business with, okay?" Ben got up from his chair and leaned forward aggressively.

"I told you . . ." Piles Saunders was choking with anger.

"And I'm telling you," Ben broke in, furious, "I've got a Soviet defector to get out from behind the Curtain and I'm not going to deal with you. Now, go call your daddy, you tinhorn asshole!" Ben had been known to lose his temper; it was a family trait, and this—well, it was too much even for a reasonable man.

Saunders barely managed to whisper it. "A defector? You fool! Don't you know our offices here aren't secure for conversation?"

Ben closed his eyes in humiliation. It had just burst out of his lips. He had to do something to get Saunders to listen. How was he to know that the goddamn embassy offices might be bugged? Idiot, he told himself, you've blown it. If you're going to play with the big boys you damn well better learn what the world is like. He sighed and sat down again.

"My apologies," Ben said. "I didn't think about that."

Saunders glared at him, but his faint smile testified to his satisfaction at Ben's greenhorn mistake. After briefly savoring his triumph, he picked up the phone on his desk, dialed, and spoke.

"I've got someone here whom you should see. I'm bringing him to room 34. Can you come down immediately?" Saunders then turned to Ben, his voice flat with the wear of their encounter. "Come along. I'll take you to the man you want to see."

Room 34, on the third floor, was undecorated, but, as the man who called himself Arthur Robinson was saying, it was a secure conversation area. Robinson was not what Ben had expected; he was an even younger man, no more than twenty-five, with an uncertain manner. Not one's idea of a spy. Not another Saunders, thought Ben, but by no means impressive. He was at least courteous, after the fashion of Easterners of good family and good school, but with little apparent spark.

"Now first," Robinson said, "if you could tell us who you are and in as much detail as possible what it is you want."

"I'm . . ." Ben paused. At this stage he wondered if he could trust anyone. "My name is Smith. Alfred Smith. I'm from Berkeley, California. I'm in the media game, and I represent a very senior Soviet who would like to come across."

Robinson was matter-of-fact. "Do you have a passport by way of identification, Mr. Smith?" The tone was cold, disinterested. They were alone now. Saunders had left.

"When the time comes." Ben wasn't sure why these people, at least these two, worked so hard at being supercilious.

"I see. And what can you show me then?"

"Mr. Robinson, I'm an amateur at this game, but I do know we can't get anywhere without a modicum of trust. Now obviously I have to trust you, I have nowhere else to turn. So let me begin, if you don't mind. Can you show me some identification?"

Robinson stared hard at his visitor.

"Me? I told you who I am. Obviously I work here in the embassy."

"I gather that, but still, it would be reassuring to me to see who you are. Some kind of identification you understand."

Robinson began to reach for his wallet and hesitated, drawing his hand back. "Well, I don't happen to have anything on me at the moment, but I can get you something later." The young man was embarrassed.

Ben was firm, teacher to child. "You see, you give me a phony name, are suspicious when I give you one, and then you can't even back it up. Look, there's no room in this for more than one amateur, that's me. But so far I've met that irrevocable amentia Saunders, and now you come along without even a decent alias."

Derek Rylander was by no means happy. This was his first posting overseas, his first meeting with a walk-in, and in spite of being trained for such occasions, he felt much the new boy in town. It was routine to give false names to strangers, especially when they might be provocateurs, but in this situation, in the embassy itself, it had been Derek's own idea to put the spook forward. Now he was hoist on his own petard. His refined fingers drummed on the table nervously as he wondered how to handle this situation without botching it utterly.

It seemed that Mr. Smith had read his mind.

"Come now, there's no need for any further nonsense. We've got serious business on our hands. Now who the hell are you?"

Derek sighed. "I'm Derek Rylander, assistant cultural attaché. Here." He proffered a card from his wallet. "That ought to satisfy you."

Ben took it and handed Rylander his own card. He held out his hand. "Here, let's shake hands a second time now and get off on the right foot."

Derek was humiliated. He had lost command of the situation entirely. Cornelius, or whoever he was—at this stage who could tell about that?—had moved in and deftly taken over. What could he do? Derek shook hands like a defeated college debater.

He summoned the strength to begin again. "Well now, you say there's a Soviet defector? Who is he and how did you come to be here on his behalf?"

"Mr. Rylander, I'm not being coy, just cautious. I have to feel my way along. This is all new to me and I don't want to screw it up. There are not just lives at stake, Mr. Rylander. If my information is correct, world peace could be at stake."

Derek relaxed as he picked up Ben's own uncertainty. "So you're not sure of your information. Well at least we can share some doubts." Derek smiled wanly. "Do you have anything you can give us that would help us assess this situation, some sign this chap of yours is real?"

The words were sharp, but Ben acknowledged the truth of the implication. What the hell did Ben know of his general except what Anna had said?

"You've got a point. I can't guarantee truth. I simply think that it's highly probable that what I have is the genuine article."

"You have it then, I mean in your physical possession? Some documents to prove this man's value some way, so we can evaluate him?"

"I do have some documents. I don't read Russian, so I can't tell you what they say. But my client, frankly I can't think of anything else to call him, says these papers will demonstrate he's genuine. Here.''

Ben handed over a sheaf of paper that Anna had given to him, papers that her brother, she said, had given her explaining that no intelligence agency buys just promises. Pyotr, who knew the world of espionage, knew there would be persuading to be done. Anna had carried them out under her clothing. She'd given them to Ben. Now he placed the packet of thinly folded Russian pages stamped with red security ink on the table. Derek picked them up. He did read some Russian.

"Military documents I see." His eyebrows raised. "General Staff . . . what's this?" He puzzled over some words, "Central Sector Strategic Planning and Intelligence Staff—well that's arcane enough. Yes, Mr. Cornelius, these do look interesting. You understand the people back home will have to evaluate this material. They'll be fast, I assure you, but in the meantime there's nothing I can say or do. You understand that, I hope."

"Sure. I'll wait. How shall we get in touch?"

"Do you want to tell me where you're staying?" Rylander asked the question doubtfully.

"Why not? I'm at the Metropole. Room 42."

Rylander smiled. "Well Mr. Cornelius, you surprise me."

"Why? I told you we had to proceed on the basis of trust. I mean it and you'd better mean it too or else this whole thing will go sour. Now, about our getting in touch . . ."

"I think it's safer if you call here. Now you have to realize that any phone line in this country may be tapped, certainly every one into any embassy is. Some of the rooms in the Metropole are too. It's funny, for example, how guests of the embassy always get put in the same rooms. But if you call in from a public place, the post office or railroad station, and ask for Mr. Arthur at this number"—he scribbled a number on a slip of paper—"they'll put you through. If our office tells you Mr. Arthur is gone for the day, you'll know there's no message yet. If we tell you that Mr. Arthur will be back in fifteen minutes, it means we should meet. Now, if you call every four hours or so from 8:00 a.m. to 10:00 p.m., that will do.

"If there's an emergency I'll find a way to get in touch with you. Most likely I'll just be in the hotel lobby when you come down. If I am, you walk on outside without any hint of recognition. Take a cab to the Moskva Hotel. Wait in the lobby there, where someone will pick you up. Now we'll use that same routine if when you phone you're given the 'back in fifteen minutes' message. Just go to the Moskva, wait in the lobby, and when someone comes over to you with the Wall Street Journal in his hand and asks if you follow the stock market, if you like Benguet B, that will be our man and your man. It might even be me. Do you have that?"

"Simple enough."

"Good. Now be sure not to say anything on any phone that could give any hints. Don't write. Don't talk. Belgrade is a listening kind of town. Now, are you safe?"

Ben was surprised at the question. "Well, I don't see why not. I haven't breathed a word of this to anyone but Saunders. My front here is good, for I really will look around for art and antiquities. What can go wrong?"

"Murphy's law, Mr. Cornelius: if anything can go wrong, it will. Now, if you do have an emergency, if, for example, you're followed or even sense something amiss, don't ignore it. Assume the worst. If that happens, call immediately and ask for Miss Riley. That will alert us and we'll act accordingly."

"In what way?" For Ben it was a new world unfolding. Derek rather liked this amiable Oregonian, or whatever he was. Why not be franker with him . . . after all, if the man was a Soviet, there'd be no revelations in it.

"Damned if I know, Mr. Cornelius. I've only been overseas six months. You don't have to read spy novels to guess that we'd try to find out who else was surveilling you, and of course we'll do our darndest to find out if you—and your friends here—" Rylander shook the papers in his hand, "are genuine. But how all the wheels within the wheels grind, that is beyond my knowing. I am, as I think you may have suspected, but a callow youth." Derek grinned disarmingly.

Ben welcomed the humor. "Well, you're smarter than I thought and I'm dumber than I thought, and I am glad to have met you Mr. Rylander—or may I call you Derek? You'll be getting my phone calls, Mr. Arthur, be sure of that."

"Derek it is, Ben. And when you call don't use the same public place too often, and do keep looking over your shoulder, will you? If you are the genuine article, we don't want to lose either you or your friend."

Derek couldn't have been more serious, nor could Ben have ever felt more somber than when he walked out that embassy door.

Steffie Hebrang—actually her first name was longer and harder to pronounce but he'd settled on that—appeared punctually at seven, sitting primly in the lobby. His intuition had told him she was all very cheery and worldly-wise, but not the sophisticate who'd be at ease calling a man's room from a hotel lobby. Belgrade seemed quite an old-fashioned place, for all the progressive proletarian noise in the local English-language paper. The dining room was an example: mustachioed waiters in black tie and tails, ornate high ceilings, panels of French doors opening to the

park-view veranda, and an orchestra straight out of the
Vienna woods.

She was soft, feminine in his arms, with a buoyant
perfume like fresh apples, and she was very pretty; straight
nose, high cheekbones and forehead, thin bones, freckles,
soft dark hair, fine warm lips, and a figure quite perfect
indeed. She was talking while they danced.

"Ben, do Americans ever dance waltzes like these?"

"Steffie," he replied, "to Americans, Strauss is only the
partner in the firm that makes blue jeans."

"But you waltz quite nicely." She smiled as he swung her
wide to the music of "Wine and Roses."

"I dance badly, Steffie, but better than it might have
been if my parents hadn't insisted I take lessons. And my
older sister practiced on me. Naturally I hated it."

"Naturally. I have brothers too. You know, this is the
first time I've ever been here at the Metropole. For us
ordinary proletarians this is high society."

"You sent me here without having ever been here?"

"Certainly. We tourist aides keep up-to-date on the
fancy places, but we can't afford them."

"I thought this was successful Communism. Jobs for all
and a commissar in every pot."

"Ben, you mustn't joke about it. We are pretty lucky.
We can talk about the shortcomings. But be careful, or
rather I have to be careful, about speaking out too freely.
This isn't America."

"Why'd you come back then, if you don't particularly
like having to keep a lock on your tongue?"

"I told you Ben, it's home. My whole family, except my
older brothers who work in north Europe, live here. I can't
help loving where I grew up. Besides, I'm not political. I
like my job—look what fun I'm having today because of
it—and really what I want to do is work, get married, have

kids, enjoy the sun in the park, be with my family. This is a good country for that as long as you don't get political." She paused. "Are you political, Ben?"

"Do you mean, do I vote? Sure I do, usually for my cousins because in our little county it seems half the people there are relatives."

"That's very nice, but what I mean is, are you here for anything that's political, I mean like journalism or meddling, or anything of that sort? After all, you haven't told me what you do." She was looking at him carefully.

"You haven't asked. But if you want to know, I'm a dealer in art and antiquities and I have my own store in Portland, Oregon. I came here to buy ikons, statues—that sort of thing."

"Well, I'm glad of that. If there's anything that's okay in this country it's business. We're the world's most capitalist Communists."

"I've noticed that already."

She picked up on his tone. "Don't you approve?"

"Sure I do. Why not? After all, the last stronghold of liberty is free enterprise. If you folks don't look out, you'll all be laissez-faire democrats in another few years."

He was careful not to talk about politics during dinner. She focused on exchanging family statistics and gossip as though that were really all that interested her, that and friendly interest in his own plans.

"How long will you be here in Belgrade, Ben?"

"Darned if I know. Long enough to talk to your export people, the art dealers, and see what bargains there are in my line. Maybe a week."

"Do you know anyone here, Ben? Does anyone know you?"

"No. Well, in Split, yes, some relatives of a friend, but not in Belgrade. Except, of course, for you. Frankly I feel so lucky in meeting you I don't much care if I meet anyone else."

Steffie lowered her eyes, almost blushing. "That's good of you to say, Ben, but if you're going to do business here you are going to need to know people a lot more important than I. Our bureaucracy is pretty messed up and indifferent most of the time. To get ahead you're better off if you have some *veza*. Do you know what that means?"

Ben nodded. "Back home we call it 'juice' but here I'm plumb out of it. Don't worry, I'll just make my way and hope for the best."

"That's a pretty casual way to do business, Ben. Are you sure you're serious?"

"Sure I'm sure. Why else would I be here?" As soon as he said it, he realized he'd been too offhand. Steffie was giving him a hard second look.

"Ben, are you lying to me?" she asked.

To be accused of lying hurt. Then his incongruous situation hit him. Of course he'd been lying to her all evening, about why he was in Belgrade, about his plans, even when he had said he was not "political." What in heaven's name could be more political than this business —no, this mission; that was what it was, a mission. He hadn't realized how easily lying had come to him, how natural it was under the compelling need he now shared with a Soviet general he had never met.

Steffie was right; the new Ben had been conning this sweet, innocent girl. Innocent? The alarm bell rang softly. What had Anna said about the Balkans? What had Steffie herself teased him about at the airport? "Too trusting," she'd said. Ben tried to clear his brain. Maybe it wasn't an accusation, just a test, or maybe just a matter-of-fact inquiry. He realized he didn't know how to answer.

"Well?" she asked again, without smiling.

He gritted his teeth, the new Ben, liar to pretty girls and personal agent for General Pyotr Myagkov who wanted to save the world. He looked her in the eye.

"No, Steffie, I'm not lying. What could there be for me to lie about? Here, look at my card." He reached in his wallet and gave her one. "Look at that. Name, address, business, it's all there. Keep it, check it out with anyone you want. It's all me. You can have my fingerprints if you want." As he said it he felt uncomfortable. Actually he didn't want to give his fingerprints away. I wonder why not, he thought. I wonder just where all this is leading.

She read the card, nodded and placed it in her handbag. "Ben, what you do is your business," she said. "It's just that, well, Belgrade is a funny place and all of us get used to living a life that isn't quite what we say it is in public. It's Serbia's history; we've never been free for long. Serbs have developed an instinct for preservation against the odds. Do you know that in Zagreb there's a stone where in the sixteenth century the Austro-Hungarians executed the leader of a peasant revolt, Matija Gubec, seating him on a red hot iron throne and crowning him with a red hot iron crown? 'Be king,' they said as they fried him on that skillet. And do you know that in Nis, that's a town south of here, the Turks built a tower from the heads of peasants who rebelled against them in 1804? Did you know, Ben, that just a few years ago the government uncovered a Soviet underground spy network near here in Montenegro? Those are the same Soviets whose troops raped and killed as they came in to liberate us in World War II; the same Soviets who want to take over our country now. I'm not political Ben, I told you, but no Serb is apolitical—not after all those Austrians, Turks, Nazis, and the rest. I'd just hate to have to worry about you Americans, Ben. You know your country has taken a rather anti-Yugoslav line."

"Not anti-Yugoslav, Steffie, but maybe anti-tyrant, and maybe a bit dubious about the glories of Communism. But I don't want to talk politics at dinner."

"You are political, Ben, even if you say you're not." She was clearly ill at ease.

"And you are political, Steffie, because you have to be to survive." He reached his hand across the table, intending to squeeze hers by way of reassurance. She moved her hand away.

"It's late. I have to be at the airport at seven tomorrow morning." She was rising, leaving the table.

"I'll take you home in a cab, Steffie." He was walking beside her, unhappy at the tension between them.

"That's extravagant. I'll take the streetcar."

"I'll take the streetcar along with you."

She stopped as they reached the front door of the hotel. It was about 10:30. In the lobby, the music of Strauss waltzes from the dining room could be heard, lilting and romantic.

She looked at him, her gray eyes serious. She held out her hand, formally, to shake his. "I'm going home by myself, Ben. I think it's better that way."

"But why, Steffie, why? I hope I haven't said anything that offended you. I feel like an oaf with your walking out on me like this."

She smiled softly, sadly. "Please don't think you need to apologize. There's nothing you've said that's out of line."

"What is it then?" Ben was really upset. He liked this lovely girl and here she was, running away.

"I like you, Ben. I like you very much, even if we have just met. That's the problem."

"Good Lord, Steffie, what's wrong with that? People ought to enjoy liking each other, not having to run away from one another."

"That's true, ordinarily, but I think this is different."

"Why?" Women were, Ben realized, a puzzlement to a man, no matter how old and wise he thought he had become.

"Because," she held his hand in hers now, the grip warmer and sweeter than her earlier formal handshake, "my intuition tells me so."

He was annoyed. "And what," he asked, "does your intuition tell you about me?"

Her eyes were sad, cool, and as wise as Athena. "That it is not right for me to see you," she said. And with that she leaned forward and, kissing him on the lips, fled through the front door of the hotel. A bellboy standing at the counter nearby watched her go, eyeing her legs approvingly and, turning to the puzzled Ben, grinned.

When Ben tried to call the airport the next day, asking for the tourist aid desk, the telephones were not working. He considered taking a cab out to see her, but upon reflection, felt it better not to push. Maybe he would have, he thought, if her judgment hadn't shaken him so. Perhaps it was as she said, he was a danger to her and to any other local people he'd meet. This was, after all, a police state in its own quiet way, and who could say where this mission of his would lead him? Steffie might very well be right. He was still thinking about the implications as he walked toward the post office to make his regular, but so far unfruitful, call to Mr. Arthur.

EIGHT

The Embassy of the Union of Soviet Socialist Republics is at Delegradska 32; with its grounds it occupies almost an entire block. The main building, thirteen stories high, is among the largest in Belgrade. Inside the compound, behind the high wire fence, are a number of small structures, including the reception building that functions as moat and portcullis to defend the looming Soviet keep behind. One floor removed from the ambassador's eyrie on the thirteenth floor is the *Residentura* of the KGB. Its smaller sibling and sometimes rival, the military GRU, is quartered below on the fourth floor next to the military mission and attaché's quarters. The KGB Resident, like the ambassador—the latter not always his superior—has a grand view of Belgrade and the Danube plain. What they cannot see visually they observe readily enough, thanks to modern electronics, a subscription service to every Yugoslav newspaper, periodical and journal, and a network of agents and in-place officers, believers true or wise enough to feign it. There are also opportunists and partisan ethnic factionalists who, unaware of history, are deluded by the promise that the USSR will assist their petty nationalist causes.

Yugoslavia is a country that the USSR, voracious Eurasian shark, one day intends to swallow. The KGB

Resident in Belgràde, General Valentin Petrovich
Pavlichenko, is the tooth of the shark.

Every morning at 8:05 the senior staff gather in General
Pavlichenko's conference room. The carpet is green, the
chairs red leather, the table polished oak. Wire rods
outside the window are deflectors against alien micro-
waves; wire mesh inside the walls and a permanent sweep
apparatus provide audio security. Photographs of the Party
Chairman, bushy-browed and growling, and the KGB
Director, thin-faced with expressionless eyes, hang on the
wood-panelled walls bidding those seated beneath them to
mind their manners. It is an honor to sit in this room. It is
satisfying. Each one seated here is absorbed in one sensa-
tion, sweet Power.

Pavlichenko's deputy each morning commands the
agenda and, like a symphony conductor, bids each section
chief report. The minor business comes first: political
developments, agent handling, routine surveillance reports,
personnel matters, equipment problems, new identifications of opposition officers, blue cables from Moscow; the
normal business of intelligence. It is no more thrilling than
an Iowa factory manager's meeting to review the widget
business. But there is a difference; here one risks one's
head.

Pavlichenko waited, wondering where the dirt would be
this morning.

Forty-five minutes later, all was still well. No complaints,
no problems. The Resident might be able to take a long
lunch; the secretary of the First Counselor was ready and
waiting for him in her flat—well, her husband's and hers—
in the apartment house adjoining the compound. He loved
rolling down that sweet valley of her bosom, plunging into
the warm wet bush of tightly wrapping thighs. Happily
preoccupied, he felt the beginning of an erection. At his

age, with his worries, that was welcome indeed.

The general didn't want to notice the glum look on Major Komiakov's face. Vadim Vladimirovich Komiakov was in charge of the First Department, First Chief Directorate, which in Belgrade was inconsequential. Elsewhere the First Department was central, for it was targeted against the United States and the United Kingdom. Pavlichenko knew Komiakov well enough; morose, ill-tempered, he always held back the bad news 'til last. For Komiakov anything new was bad news, for the fellow was an incompetent. Except in marriage; his wife was niece to Army Chief of Staff Kulikov. That was why Komiakov was a major, why he was in Belgrade, why he was in this conference room, and why the Resident couldn't do a thing about it. The happy lump behind the general's fly subsided. It would be another typical day after all.

"All right, Major Komiakov, what's bothering you?" The Resident's tone was resigned.

"A difficult problem, Comrade General."

"Of course, Major, I could tell from your face. What's happened?"

"We have a tape from the American Embassy office surveillance. My department doesn't know what to make of it."

"No?" There was, the Resident knew, no use trying to hurry the fellow.

"Shall I play it?" The major started to put a tape recorder on the table.

"No, Major, please don't. We have a lot to do today and we can't play everything you hear from the Americans and British. I'm sure you can give us a brief report."

"Yes, Comrade General. Well, it seems that someone is brokering a defection."

"A defection?" His voice sharp, General Pavlichenko

leaned forward. "By whom, to whom, when, and where, Major?"

The major looked as if he were about to cry. "I knew you'd ask me that, Comrade General."

By the holy heroes of the October Revolution. Pavlichenko thought, how much am I to stand? Quietly he said to the deficient one, "Yes, Comrade Komiakov, I must ask you that."

"But I don't know, Comrade General. The tape doesn't say. May I read the summary my staff have prepared?"

"By all means, Major, by all means." He had seen to it that the enfeebled one had a very sound deputy.

"Someone, a fluent English speaker, told a man representing himself as Saunders that he had a defector. That's all we have, Comrade General."

The general smelled a rat. "There's nothing more on the tape Major? Nothing?"

"No, Comrade General."

"And why not? Surely a conversation beginning like that one leads somewhere, to questions, to verification, to arrangements, surely something."

"Yes, Comrade General."

"But not this conversation? Can you tell me why not?"

The major's eyes were red, his hands shaking. "Our surveillance apparatus became defective, Comrade General, the tape is garbled. We only have the words 'I' and 'defector to get.' The rest is gone. As you know they use . . ." The general noted it was "they" not "we," now that there was trouble. ". . . They use microwave sensors as well as the newly developed diffused reciprocating . . ." the major paused, hoping that was the way to pronounce the word he was reading from notes, ". . . reciprocating acoustical holographs. Anyway, our machinery failed. Someone," the major licked dry lips, "someone accidentally tampered with the power switch to the acoustical monitoring apparatus."

"Oh," said the Resident, his voice controlled. "And just who did that, Major? It is not your responsibility, working through the communications personnel assigned to you, to prevent such accidents?"

"Yes, Comrade General," Komiakov spilled words like a little boy explaining the broken cookie jar, "but it was the cleaning woman. She did it. She thought it was the light switch or something."

General Pavlichenko nodded slowly. He felt not just sixty-two years, but a century old. He sighed, conjuring a vision of quiet retirement in the countryside near his childhood home. There would be no lunch today, not even if he had time for it. The general dismissed the staff, retaining only his deputy. Lieutenant Colonel Yakov Fedorovich Lenev.

Back now in the Resident's private office—sumptuous as any ambassador's, with velvet rust draperies, rugs from Asian Russia, a teak bar set with silver cups for vodka, richly upholstered chairs—the general loosened his tie.

"What do you think, Lenev?" he asked.

"I think, Comrade General"—when alone together they were informal—"that we have no choice. We must assume the worst."

"Which is?"

"That a defection is intended, that the defector is a Soviet, and that the Americans will follow through."

The Resident nodded. "And so?"

"You know what it means, cables to Moscow, deleting of course the cleaning lady and the equipment failure, and our plan, subject to Center's guidance of course, to put everything we have here onto it. We have to assume, I think, that the defector, since he is being brought to the Americans here in Belgrade, is either one of our own people here in Yugoslavia or someone directly neighbouring who can come here easily. Bulgaria, for example, or Hungary, or Roumania. It can't be a Yugoslav. They are free to travel and don't need help."

"And our first step?" the Resident asked.

"Increased physical surveillance of the people in the American Embassy we suspect to be CIA. What else? I don't know."

The Resident nodded. "We could try to run in a stalking horse before the Americans get their hands on the genuine article. That would foul them up, inserting our own defector into their system. We'll also want to raise some strong doubts in their minds about any defector. Let them worry about it being a provocation. The CIA group here is small. They don't have the facilities to assess a provocateur and handle a genuine escape simultaneously. If we stir up enough dust, get privy to their actual defector evacuation procedures, we can buy time for our Department V to take executive action. Propose that to Moscow in a cable, Lenev."

Lieutenant Colonel Lenev hurried from the room. The Resident, burdened by a real defection in his own territory, sat back in his chair and stared at the wall. He sat quietly for some time before he fixed his course of action. The first priority was to get the intermediary, the man on the tape.

The Resident buzzed for Lenev.

Blagoje Savic stared out the window of his Interior Ministry office, into the blue sky of mid-September Belgrade. The chief of the communications surveillance section, bustling like a bird, was setting up the portable movie projector on the table. There were four others in Savic's office, senior deputies, all respectful.

Savic turned to a tall, cadaverous man standing by. "All right, Potiorek," he said, "tell me again, what have we got here that's so important that I have to see it rather than being home in bed."

Potiorek, number one deputy to Savic, answered. "It's a segment from the monitoring film of the U.S. Embassy," he said. "As you know, we keep the embassy under photo surveillance twenty-four hours a day. I think we've picked up someone of interest."

"Oh?"

"Yes, sir. Do you recall Draza Stavonic, who we believe is the head of the Croatian revolutionary group in Sweden? We think this is him in the film, coming out of the embassy with one of their political officers. Watch carefully. You'll see the two exchange something and shake hands. I wanted you to see it, sir, because you know Stavonic by sight better than anyone else. We have the still shots blown up, of course, and our lab thinks it's him; but he's changed enough, or disguised enough that we can't be sure. As I recall, sir, you worked on his case before you became director."

Savic nodded. He had, indeed, worked on the case, and had tried to eliminate Stavonic several times, but the man had been too slippery. Well, if he'd come back to Yugoslavia, this time they'd get him. Why would he be at the American Embassy though? Savic disliked Americans on principle. He suspected they might be keeping in touch with Croatians in case they could put them to use if Yugoslavia's stability were threatened. But would they be so stupid as to see Draza at the embassy in broad daylight?

Savic rested his head in his hands as the film began to run. Figures walked up and down the embassy steps, and pedestrians went by. Finally, there appeared a dark-haired man in the company of a younger man with balding light hair and glasses.

"That's the man, sir."

It was not Stavonic. As the film rattled on, showing the pass of a book and a handshake, Savic looked at it intently. Another figure was walking up the embassy steps.

"Hold it!" Savic cried.

"Stavonic, sir?"

"Hell no, but the one going up the steps . . . do you know who that is?"

"No, sir. Looks like an American by his dress. We've nothing on him that the photo clerks recognized."

"You wouldn't. Tell me, what have you heard from Split about L-IMOT?"

"I don't know the case, sir. I'll check it out."

"You check it out this minute." Savic spoke angrily. "And get me a blowup still of this fellow right now!"

"Yes, sir."

Within twenty minutes Potiorek had returned, glossy photo and Split cable traffic in hand.

"It seems, sir, that Split lost L-IMOT. He gave them the slip. Very professionally done, they say. There was a small filing difficulty in the cable room, that's why you didn't hear about it sooner."

"I'll say they lost him. And I've found him. What the hell is going on in that cable room? Get that mess straightened out!"

"Yes, sir. And what about the photo, sir?"

"It's L-IMOT, all right. You say Split lost the tail, eh? 'Very professional' they say. What's their opinion then?"

"That he is KGB, sir, as you suspected."

"As I suspected." Savic preened himself. "Damn it, Potiorek, I have to manage this agency and run the cases too. Isn't that a fact?"

"It seems to be, sir. You were the one to pick this fellow

up in the first place, and now again. Why would you think a senior KGB officer running liaison for the Montenegrin Soviet networks would show up at the U.S. Embassy? A bit risky, isn't it?"

"Potiorek, if our file on this fellow is even half right, risk means nothing to him. And we want him more than any other Soviet running internal operations against us. Look at him. He must be using an American cover.

"All right, Potiorek," Savic was pleased with himself, "we'll get him this time. Put out this photo to all UDBA, top priority. Report when and where L-IMOT is spotted."

"Alert the police, sir? Begin a search?"

"Potiorek, you're a halfwit. No, we don't want to scare him off. Put it out to the police and there'll be some idiot hauling him in. And no going around the hotels showing pictures, either. Who knows who's working for him to warn him off. I don't want him *in*, Potiorek, I want him found and I want twenty-four-hour surveillance, all of his faces, because I want to know how he handles his network, who are his agents, how the Russians are getting money and arms to his people. Let L-IMOT run on a long leash. Long, but strong."

"Yes, sir." Potiorek left the office. One thing Potiorek was sure of. Savic was lucky.

Miles Saunders telephoned Derek Rylander at 4:00 p.m. The two of them were recently arrived in Belgrade, were both young, and were starting families. They often saw each other socially since ties with the local people were difficult. It wasn't good for a Yugoslav with ambition to be seen spending too much time with Western diplomats. Resident foreigners were thrown in with each other, or with the local radicals; writers, for instance, or dissidents, who were avoided by the more conservative foreign

officials. Their job, as they saw it, was to build a bridge to
the legitimate authorities, not to antagonize them.

Miles Saunders was building bridges to power. Here the
regime was power, and however much they might be aloof
officially, the Yugoslavs approved and rewarded his cir-
cumspection. His reports were full of little goodies—he
was proud of that—dropped by unofficial officials cultiva-
ting a careful young man like himself.

Miles was aware of some inconsistency. He was, after all,
a liberal, but then so were most of the State and CIA
personnel. But the liberalism of home didn't apply here.
Communism was really just the logical extension of liberalism, first to democratic and thence state socialism. It had
passed beyond the awkwardness of democracy which was
controlled by big money. by capitalism which favored
lenders over debtors, stockholders over workers, conservative economists over welfare programs. Inconsistent
perhaps, but not illogical, that Miles, while here as an
accredited representative of his country, favored the
successful dictatorship of the proletariat. After all, he told
himself, if Yugoslavia became a parliamentary democracy,
wouldn't the capitalists return to begin the cycle again?

It followed that the powerful forces at home that favored
American democratic imperialism were wrong. Miles had
welcomed the gutting of the CIA; nevertheless, the
Agency, in his view, was still a danger because it worked
darkly and might return to being the ugly monster that had
run "pacification" in Vietnam and tried to kill Castro.

Meanwhile, Miles traded what he gleaned from his
friendly unofficial official Yugoslavs. Derek traded Miles
what Derek learned of Agency policy. There seemed no
more to it than that, just gossipy camaraderie, which made
each other's reports to their superiors look better.

"Dinner tonight then, at my house?" Miles was confirming it.

Derek agreed. They were having drinks in his fine house in Grocka, elegant by Yugoslav standards, with its swimming pool and veranda. Miles lived only a few doors away. Their wives sat chatting: shopping, babies, and servants.

"Well, how'd that bastard I sent you turn out?" Miles asked.

"Bastard? You mean the so-called Oregonian? I don't know how he'll turn out. He's got some fancy documents we have to go over. If he's real, I'll be up to my ears in work."

Miles' mouth was warped in anger. "I've never met anyone I've detested so much. A real manipulator. You look out for him. My instincts tell me he's trouble."

"Really?" Derek was too new to be sure of his own judgments. Miles, a cum laude from Princeton, was someone Derek respected.

"You bet. Aggressive. Vulgar. A dangerous man. If he's what he says he is, I'll eat your cables without ketchup."

Derek felt uneasy. "Do you have anything special to go on?" he asked.

"Just my assessment, that and the fact he knew too much and purposely blew himself. From the start he knew I wasn't Agency. And he told me he wanted to bring a Soviet defector in from behind the Curtain, when he knew damn well I wasn't the one to be told and that the office might be bugged, as though it was all nicely rehearsed." Miles was furious.

"That's interesting." Derek sipped his martini. "So you think he's putting on his own show, eh?"

"I do."

"Why would he bother? I mean, why blow it to you?"

"Well, let's say he's working for the Soviets and they blow you running a prohibited operation here in Yugoslavia—the kind of thing that would get your whole station thrown out persona non grata. That would put a dent in you all for a while and make you all public wherever you go."

"Yeah, I guess it could happen."

"It does happen, Derek. You know that."

"Not often." Derek was on the defensive.

"Only because you don't take every walk-in who offers to sell you the Kremlin."

"We'll be careful, Miles. Besides, it's not my job to evaluate him."

"Even if he were real, Derek, it has a bad smell to it."

"How's that?"

"The Agency has enough mud on its face. How will the Soviets feel if you pluck out some bigshot and embarrass them? Another Svetlana, for instance. That will raise hell with detente just when everyone is trying to make it work. In my opinion the Soviets really want to keep things stabilized, keep their military budget down, and have money for consumer goods. If they don't want a war with us, then what do we care about how many planes they have in their hangars? Satellite technology was good enough for our SALT negotiators, why create troubles with this cloak-and-dagger stuff? You know as well as I do it never leads to anything but hard feelings and high taxes at home to support a clandestine service."

"It's my job, a good living, overseas assignments and nice promotions. Don't cut me out of my slice of the pie." Derek was smiling.

"Eat your pie, I don't care. But nobody's forcing you to take in another Soviet stray. Let him stay where he belongs and contribute something to his own society if he's all that idealistic. Those defectors are a pain in the neck."

"I never met one, Miles. Neither did you."

Miles replied heatedly. "We both know how to read,

don't we? Thank heaven for a free press. If it weren't for the press no one would ever know about all the dirty business from the Bay of Pigs and since. Defectors are the same; just traitors to their own. We buy treason. It's shameful."

"Spying is a dirty business, Miles."

"Exactly, Derek, and you're too nice a guy to accept that without a struggle. I tell you that you can do your job, file your reports, serve your country and the world, and not take in every Benedict Arnold who's gotten in trouble back home and wants to hightail it to America for safe haven. Don't be part of that, Derek, please."

Derek finished his drink. "I need another martini, Miles. I agree with you, at least generally, but it's my job. Granted when I joined the Agency I didn't expect to be doing exactly this—that is, not shepherding in some defector."

"Traitor," Miles injected harshly.

"Okay then, traitor. But it's my job."

"Not necessarily, Derek." Miles had filled both the oversize martini glasses. The two men were on their third.

"Just hold back on this phony Oregonian. Tell your boss that you suspect he's a Soviet. That'll stop it for a while. Or if they insist, go through the motions and let it fall of its own weight. I know the Western journalists here in town. The right word from me to any of them will blow this defection sky high. Why not?"

"I couldn't do it, Miles. Somebody might get hurt."

"That's their problem, Derek. If the American and his Soviet buddies want to play spy, let them. It's not your problem. You're all violating Yugoslav law too. Think of the hell I'll get from my government friends here if this thing comes to their attention. We've got a stable government in Belgrade, Derek, we ought to keep relations going as well as we can. And with the Soviets. Really, isn't it the main aim just to keep things peaceful?"

"Aw hell, Miles, you know I'm stuck. Let's forget it. You got some more martinis?"

NINE

In one of the communication rooms of the *Residentura*, the four walls are banks of tapes, the reels starting and stopping, rotating silently on their spindles. Beneath are consoles with headsets. Switches allow the operators to select the tapes, marked by locale, for example, "UDBA incoming lines" or "French Embassy" or "Soviet Embassy, Ambassador's secure line." There are speed controls, for a clerk trained in signal detection can run a tape at higher than normal speed and, scanning, identify whether or not it is of interest. But routine tape audit is a bore and clerks in the KGB, as elsewhere, play games to alleviate the tedium.

Today's task was, however, unusual. Before each set of consoles were oscilloscopes. In front of each clerk was a printed oscillogram; each also had beside him the special tape containing those few important words uttered the day before in an office in the U.S. Embassy, first clear and then quickly garbled conversation about a defector. Today's job was to match the recollection of the spoken word to any incoming ones on today's audio surveillance traffic, and then to match the voice print of the man uttering the word "defector", the sound-wave printout of which was now before them, with the oscilloscope on the counter presenting current transcriptions. A difficult job, perhaps impossible, but it was an order. The operators' focus was on English language lines: embassies, foreign press offices, a few selected residences.

An elderly clerk was addressing the supervisor. "On the U.S. Embassy tape, Comrade, about every four hours a voice close to the one on the graph, and repetitive, like a code, keeps asking for the same thing and keeps getting the same response. Do you want to hear it, Comrade?"

Comrade supervisor did. His ears, too, found the voices similar. The voice-print match could only prove they were not dissimilar, but the recurrent question about Mr. Arthur did seem a code.

Lenev presented the findings to the Resident.

"We can't be sure, Comrade General, but it should be pursued."

"Assume the man is genuine," the Resident said. "Assume he keeps calling the U.S. Embassy because he is waiting for their signal to act. When they give him a different answer on the phone, or he asks a different question, something important may be happening. Assume all that. Our job is to find this man and find the defector. Department V can then kill them both."

"Yes, Comrade General." Talk of killing made Lenev circumspect. With his name, Jacob, the sting—and sometimes the knife—of anti-Semitism could not be avoided. For Jacob, protection lay in being cruel first. The Jew might always be an animal to the Russian, but Jacob would be a cobra and not a dog.

"This man," the Resident went on, "is playing the part of an American. Given the history of these things, it is not likely he is one; Americans do not move so easily in and out of the Bloc doing errands for our senior people who take it into their heads to cross to greener pastures. But since this man is playing the American, let us look for one. How many Americans would you say there are in Belgrade, ones staying more than a few days in September?"

"No more than a thousand, including tourists and business people."

"Good. We begin to look not for the needle but for the weasel in the haystack. Put men on the U.S. Embassy. Check the hotels. Circulate men through the foreign residential areas, post some at that import bookstore downtown, in the basement where the English section is. This man could be a translator from one of our allies; tell our people inside the Pact embassies and trade missions —Polish, Roumanian, the rest—to keep their eyes open."

Ben knew he had three kinds of trouble. The first was impatience. Two full days had passed and all he heard was that Mr. Arthur was still not in. Second, he was getting bored. There were just so many books, museums, and movies. Third, he could not stick around without making a show of work. His first visit to the State Foreign Trade Office had told him that the run of art and antiquities in Belgrade wasn't much. His treasure trove from Split had spoiled him; what antiquities were available on the open market were few and costly. As he walked away from a gallery of government culture, much of it but one step removed from the Soviet painting of "girl enraptured by tractor," Ben was disgusted. He needed someone to talk to, and a break in the tension.

The break came. His call told him that Mr. Arthur would be in in fifteen minutes. Things were moving at last. He walked from the railroad station to the Moskva Hotel; he had to force a leisurely pace.

In the Moskva lobby, at exactly 6:15, Derek appeared carrying the newspaper, asking about Benguet B shares on the market. It seemed silly to Ben, but even imbecile ritual was welcome. They chatted idly, amiably, as Americans first meeting might, with Derek inviting him to a drink.

"I know a good place, lots of local feeling, over by the river. Come on, let's take a cab."

"Fine," said Ben, playing the role of new acquaintance. "You show the way."

Derek did. One cab and then another, one block on a streetcar, a zigzag walk, a dodge through a bus station, thence to a corner where, at exactly 7:41, a car sped to the curb, a door opened, they hurried inside, and the car sped away.

Six seconds had elapsed at the stop.

"Okay?" asked the older man driving.

"Okay," said Rylander, watching the traffic behind them.

"I'm Cowan," said the driver, not turning around.

They had been driving for an hour as dusk fell, as if Cowan were waiting for night, checking to be sure nothing followed, turning, turning. By now they were driving through a fine residential area. A street sign said Octoberski Revolution.

The houses were large, with large lawns surrounding them. The car turned up a driveway and stopped at a gate. Cowan punched a button on the dash, the gate swung open, and they drove up a tree-lined drive. The big house was dark but for a dim light over the front porch. The three men walked up the steps and into a hall where only a blue night light glowed. A cellar door was opened and they descended. Another door at the bottom and finally lights; a pleasant room, decorated like a tavern with a bar, stags' heads, colorful steins for beer, oak panelling. A party room, but no party there. And no windows.

Cowan was about fifty, lean, sharp, blue-eyed, graying, with a long nose and long neck.

"Sit down," he said to Ben. The chairs were leather. Soft. He gestured Ben to a red one with a high back. "What'll you have to drink, sir?"

Ah, thought Ben, so it's sir. I am moving upward, even if it is in a basement world. "Scotch, if you have it," he said. "I'll take it neat."

Cowan walked to the bar and poured the drinks. Each sipped quietly, waiting. Above, the house was silent.

"Well," began Cowan, "your documents interest us, Mr. Cornelius, and so does the man behind them. How did you come by them?"

Ben let the Scotch warm his tongue. "I'll tell you when I'm ready, Mr. Cowan, and that will be when I'm sure you're ready. As an amateur I've learned it's easy to misstep. I want to be sure that if I fall I take only myself down with me."

"Admirable," said Cowan. "Cornelius is obviously a noble breed. Trace it back to Caesar, don't you?"

Ben was surprised. "So my Aunt Mabel tells me. She read it in a book."

"And your Aunt Mabel is a MacIntosh, is she not?"

"No, a McKinney."

"The McKinneys own the Portland Globe, do they not?"

"No, just a small town paper."

"That would be your cousin Frances's husband, would it not?"

"No. There is no cousin Frances. There is a Virginia."

"So there is, and who then would Jefferson Grenn's line be?"

"Old grandfather Ben's daughter's line."

"So it is," agreed Cowan, "and that's the house of Tillie Maude, is it not?"

"It is, but she was cousin."

Ben had read somewhere that when an Australian

aborigine was crossing the desert and met the local tribes-
men there, the stranger and the locals would sit and
exchange genealogies. Two days or three they'd sit by
the fire telling of cousins extended by fifty and generations
back a dozen. If they found kin, the stranger was
embraced, fed, and given safe conduct. If no kin, the
stranger was killed. Ben looked at Cowan-not-Cowan, for
the name was a lie.

"Just like the aborigines. If I miss do you kill me?"

"Like the aborigines, Mr. Cornelius, but no, we just
don't give you a second drink."

"Is that the worst?"

Cowan was a serious man. He hadn't smiled yet, nor held
out his hand. He kept appraising Ben.

"There may be worse. You want to try for bingo?"

"Don't threaten me, Mr. Whoever."

Cowan raised his eyes. "No threat, Tovarish. You asked,
that's all. Another drink?" The question was in Russian but
passed so easily that it didn't ripple.

"Tovarish yourself, and if you asked me if I want another
drink, sure. But now it's your turn."

"Shoot," said Cowan.

"Derek here is embassy, but you could be anybody,
worse than anybody if Derek gets confused about which
side he's on. Whose house is this?"

"First Secretary of the U.S. Embassy."

"Is he upstairs? Will he vouch for you?"

"He will but he's not home. If you like to read documents
you can see mine."

"All say Cowan?"

"Yup."

"Does your printer do five-dollar bills too?"

"Touché. He could, of course, but it's illegal."

"So how," asked Ben, "do I know you're CIA?"

"Because I have a letter for you from your cousin Jeff, hand delivered by air courier today, and he says I'm one fine fellow you can trust. His letter to me says the same about you."

"Show me," said Ben.

Cowan handed Ben his letter. It was from Jeff, and it described the man "Cowan" in detail. Jeff gave him no name.

"Wouldn't it have been easier," asked Ben, "to let me meet you in the embassy? Cut out all this nonsense that way."

"Never cut out the nonsense in this business. It saves lives. After your slip in Saunders's office, you better bet the Russians have a permanent doorman at our embassy. The Yugoslavs may have taped you too. You don't need all that company."

"No, I'd say not."

There was a pause. Derek was fidgeting with an ice tray from a refrigerator under the bar.

Ben felt at ease. If Cowan was to help him, help his Soviet general, they'd do it their way. Ben stretched his legs, put his arms behind his head, and said nothing.

"You're pretty cool, Mr. Cornelius. Do you broker defections very often?"

A serious face, was it a serious question? Ben couldn't be sure.

"No."

"Have you been in the business?"

"What business?"

"This business. The spook business."

"No."

"You're not doing too badly for a beginner."

"Time will tell," said Ben, meaning it.

"Time will tell," said Cowan. He meant it too. He then

said, "A Soviet general. Is he real?"

"As far as I know," Ben replied.

"Who does know?"

"His family. I'm their intermediary."

"And they are . . .?"

"Yugoslav."

"A Soviet general of Yugoslav blood? Come now, Mr. Cornelius."

"Try a Russian girl married outside, with a brother who's a Soviet general. That okay?"

Cowan nodded. "That's okay. And this general wants to come over."

"So I'm told."

"But your contacts could be putting you on. The family could be working you for the Soviets to work us."

"It's possible," said Ben.

"Yes," said Cowan, his face stone. "The woman wants us to contact her?"

"No. She wants me to be the intermediary."

"Okay, so you're the cut out?"

Ben nodded. "That's her rule and I respect it."

"She pays you?"

"Not a penny."

"You do it for love, then?"

"People sometimes do kindly things for others, you know."

"Oh yes," said Cowan, "I know."

"I like her, I like her niece, I like her husband, and thanks to them, I'm about to make a pile of money in the antiquities trade back home."

"In the meantime, do you have enough money to tide you over for a week or a month or whatever it will take here?"

"No, I'll have to arrange for some credit." Ben had been

thinking about that problem. He'd brought a few thousand dollars along in traveler's checks, but a month here would finish that off.

Cowan reached into his coat, brought out a fat wallet and began to peel off bills.

"Here's a thousand in local currency. There'll be more when you need it. Don't flash it or splash it. Now, sign this receipt." He pushed the money, a paper and pen over to Ben.

Ben frowned. "What are you buying?"

"We hope a Soviet general and your courier service. I won't insult an idealist with the idea of profit, but you can have more if you want. I need the receipt signed."

"If I were Soviet, I'd damn well not want my name on that. You could blackmail me."

"If you were Soviet you wouldn't give a damn, believe me."

Ben believed that tone of tired, worldly conviction. "Okay, I'll sign. But I've got a thing about names. You know my name, I get to know yours. Otherwise I sign this receipt 'Cowan' and you explain to the bookkeeper how you lost the money at the races."

Cowan leaned back, studying Ben. "You're a nervy son of a bitch. But all right, the name is Franklin. I'm a counselor at the embassy."

"Good job?" Ben inquired impishly.

"Cornelius, you are a son of a bitch. How do I know whether it's a good job or not? It's my cover."

Ben held out his hand. "Good to meet you Mr. Franklin. Now let me sign your receipt."

Franklin turned to Derek, still behind the bar. "Well, Rylander, how do you read it?"

"Looks okay, sir. Only big hump on the chart was when you asked him whether he was working for love."

Franklin turned to Ben. "Congratulations. You just passed."

"Passed what? What are you talking about?"

"Lie detection, Mr. Cornelius. That big, soft chair you're sitting in measures your respiration rate, pulse, blood pressure, body temperature and muscle activity in the gluteus maximus muscle. That's what you sit on."

"I'll be damned. It feels like an ordinary chair."

"That's what we pay it to do. Now with that bit of technological legerdemain over, let's get down to business. Where's your Soviet?"

"Sure the house isn't wired?"

"Hell yes, I'm sure. It's swept daily, there's a monitoring panel under the bar there that's keeping Rylander busy, and I've a technician upstairs making doubly sure."

Derek spoke up from behind the bar. "If I'd known about all these gadgets, sir, I'd have studied electrical engineering instead of political science before joining the Agency."

Franklin was not interested in the young man's humor. He turned again to Ben.

"Now, where is your Russian?"

"Southwest Poland, near Skawina. There's an underground forward base there: computers for intelligence, a forward computer battle command post for the whole central western sector."

"What's your general do?"

"Commands CPS." Ben explained as best he could what the CPS was. Anna herself had not been very clear.

"Yes, the documents referenced that," nodded Franklin. "And why does he want to come over?"

"Several things, as his sister sees it. One is a revulsion with the system; bit by bit it's gotten to him. He came from an educated background. He reads English and French. He thinks. Made his way by dint of sheer technical genius and a low political profile. He's sick of Gulag, sick of corruption, sick of the same things that have bothered every Russian intellectual from Tolstoy to Solzhenitsyn. That's just the background though. The second thing is, his alienation from his family. His wife's an opportunist, his kids are high-living Party tramps. There's nothing there for him and no one he's close to. The real clincher is that he's been made privy to a top secret plan by the General Staff. They call it WALTZ. Anna says it's some kind of assault on Western Europe."

Franklin's eyes opened wide. Behind the bar, Derek took his eyes from the monitor.

"You mean the bastards intend an invasion? SALT, detente and nuclear war notwithstanding?" Derek was shaken.

"I don't know," said Ben, "just that her brother told Anna there was a plan, now official, for an overt move. She got the idea that it was not open warfare, but something sneaky."

"And your general has the plan?" Derek asked.

"Has it and is on top of it. That CPS of his is no small potatoes," replied Ben.

"Whew!" Franklin whistled. "All that crap coming out about satellite surveillance superiority, but when the big one comes it comes the old-fashioned way, cloak and dagger style. How long is your general willing to stay back there if we can set up communications with him—via Krakow for example? We can place a handler in Krakow."

"He wants to get out now. WALTZ operational planning is under way. Who knows when it will come off? He's got to get it out to us as soon as he can."

"WALTZ comes out, but the general doesn't have to. We don't want him coming out. He's more valuable to us sitting right where he is in CPS, cozy with the Soviet General Staff."

"What do you mean, you don't want him coming out?" asked Ben in irritation. "That's what I'm here to arrange, a defection."

"There are two kinds of defection, Mr. Cornelius, the kind we want, which is in-place, and the kind we want less, which is coming over. Just think how much this man is worth to us staying on the inside and keeping us up to date. Once he comes here, all he has to tell is history."

"WALTZ isn't history yet. When it is we may all be dead."

It was Derek who spoke. "Sir, it strikes me that we can't let the general cross over physically. If he does, it will raise all kinds of hell with detente. The Western press will turn against the Russians, public opinion follows, there'll be that old-fashioned anti-Communist mania again. I think this kind of thing ought to be kept close to the chest. Besides, if he comes out, the Soviets will know we know about WALTZ and just think up something else if they're intent on probing us."

Ben turned to Derek. "I didn't say 'probe,' I said 'assault.' There's one hell of a difference. And as for anti-Communism, you tell me if John Q. Citizen ought not to be told the USSR is planning to bury him right soon. A man has a right to defend himself." Ben spoke angrily. Derek ignored him and spoke to Franklin.

"My own advice, sir, is that we insist the general stay in place. Put a handler in Krakow to service his communications. Let him sing for his supper." Derek was snide.

Ben was beginning not to like the downwind smell of young Derek.

"Well?" Franklin's lined face was kinder now, sternness gone. "What do you say, Mr. Cornelius? Will you help us persuade your general to stay in place?"

"I'm sorry. No. His sister promised him, I promised her. It's that simple. I think what he has to bring us is enough. Sing for his supper? It's insulting. You can help get him out or not, that's your decision. Mine is that if you won't get him out now, I won't go one step further as intermediary."

"You'll cut the link, is that it?" asked Franklin, "let WALTZ go on just to spite us?"

"No. There are other intelligence services besides CIA —British, French, Israeli, German. I'll try them. Maybe they'll be more grateful than you and settle for having the world saved now."

Derek interrupted, his voice angry. "We've got to make him see it our way," he said.

"How would you do that?" asked Franklin.

"There are ways, sir."

"Oh? Are there?" Franklin's tone was sarcastic.

"Yes, sir."

"I've heard your opinions, Rylander. You're the new breed, anti-dirty tricks, against covert action, maybe even against the Clandestine Service itself, for all I know. Your kind is for nine-to-five hours, satellite technology, lots of paperwork filed. You surprise me, wanting to come down hard on somebody who's on our side. You offend me, Mister Rylander." Franklin emphasized the "Mister." "Mr. Cornelius here is taking a lot of chances on behalf of our country and that general of his. Furthermore, we need him. One doesn't usually go around threatening friends. I must confess I find you inconsistent."

Ben's eyes had narrowed as he'd heard Derek's threat. He got up and slowly walked over to the bar. He was bigger than Rylander and, he now knew, tougher.

"I was just beginning to admire you, Derek," Ben said. "Now I'm thinking about breaking you in two. Don't you ever threaten me again, do you understand that?"

Derek backed away from Ben. He was badly shaken by his boss and by Ben's menacing posture.

"I'm sorry, sir," he said to Franklin, "but I just thought we should pursue our country's greatest advantage."

Franklin assessed the junior case officer. "And I'm sure you're going to file a separate dissenting report which says just that, aren't you?"

Derek flushed, stammering, "Well, I think it's my duty to, sir. I think you don't have the right to go along with this fellow on his terms."

"Headquarters does have some role in this decision, you know, Mr. Rylander." Franklin's tone was cold.

Ben knew he wouldn't want this courteous, steel-eyed man for an enemy.

"I have a duty to file separate reports, sir, if it's a matter of conscience."

"And your conscience, aside from wanting to squeeze Cornelius here, tells you that Headquarters is wrong and I'm wrong?"

"Headquarters?" Rylander looked surprised.

"Yes," said the older man. "You see, they've already agreed to the general's defection on any reasonable terms Cornelius here sets." Saying that, Franklin turned to Ben. "So you see, Mr. Cornelius, your general will have it his way. We'll get him out as best we can and as fast as we can. How that works depends a great deal on you."

Ben nodded, saying grimly. "And on Lady Luck."

"To say the least," replied the senior officer, and raising his as-yet-untouched glass of bourbon, he offered a toast. "To luck, Mr. Cornelius, and to your general, who might yet do us all a very good turn."

Ben raised his glass. "To luck and to the general, sir." Ben was glad to call a man "sir" when he'd earned respect.

For the first time, Mr. Franklin's face softened.

"And to you, Mr. Cornelius, who's had the guts to get this thing moving."

TEN

Ben, in his room at the Metropole, was looking in the mirror at a man he didn't know. There stared back at him a fellow with brown hair and eyebrows, gold-rimmed glasses, puffy cheeks, a clipped moustache. Norman Borg, a Hoosier with a wallet full of papers to prove it. His clothes, electric-blue sport shirt and tourist-red trousers, were an affront to everything a decent tailor held dear, but they had advantages. One was that the flat shoulder holster cradling the short-barreled .38 Smith and Wesson was invisible beneath the loose bulk of the shirt. As Mr. Franklin had said, it was usually only in the movies that spies carried guns, but in this case circumstances were unusual.

When Ben, carrying a small suitcase containing Norman Borg, had stopped at the front desk for his key, there had been a message. It was from Steffie.

"Please call me in the morning." It gave a number.

After breakfast, Norman once again in the suitcase, Ben dialed the number. Steffie answered.

"I'm glad you called, Ben. I was feeling bad about the other evening. Can I see you again?"

"Of course, Steffie, but I'm going to be out in the countryside looking for art to buy for the next few days. I'll call you as soon as I get back."

Ben was delighted to hear the cheery voice again.

"Ben?"

"Yes?"

"It's really important that I see you before you go." Her voice was serious. Ben asked himself if, from now on, everything was going to be serious. He knew the answer.

"Okay, I'll come to the airport now." Ben was not going to tell her he would be at the airport anyway in the afternoon to travel to Split as Norman Borg.

It was a very good-looking Steffie, eyes shining, a becoming lavender blouse tight against her breasts, who greeted Ben gravely at the tourist aid counter. She suggested coffee. In the coffee shop, they took a corner table.

"Ben, I'm taking a big chance telling you this. It's just exactly what my intuition told me might happen."

"What?" Ben had respect for intuition. The human brain knew things it didn't know how it knew, of that Ben was sure.

She took a deep breath. "There's a UDBA man, our secret police, who's a friend of my brother's. He's assigned to the airport here. He stops by and chats with me when he has time, actually he flirts, but he's married and besides— well, I don't like him. I don't agree with his work, Ben, but that's private, between you and me, right?"

Ben nodded. He couldn't have been in greater agreement.

"He asked me to help him, Ben. He showed me a picture, and said it was one of the most wanted men in the country. If I saw that man in the airport, I was to call him immediately."

"And?" Ben pretended nonchalance. His heart was beating.

"It was you, Ben. Your picture."

"Oh."

Ben would have preferred a more imaginative response,

a fine theatrical lie, but he had none on tap.

"Oh," he said again.

"You're in trouble, Ben."

Ben nodded. "Sure looks like it."

"Do you know why?"

What fine excuse could he invent? He could have used a little training, some time to practice being a spy. Norman from Terre Haute he was sure he could manage, even the .38—at least he'd shot one a few times in Oregon—but Steffie confronting him with this . . . Besides, she could tell he was lying, testing him. He dare not fall for that kind of feminine trap.

"Didn't pay a parking ticket maybe?" Ben smiled at her ruefully.

"Ben, don't joke with me. This could be life and death."

Her words caught his stomach.

She reached her hand out for his, and held it tightly for a moment. "The UDBA man says you're a Soviet spy, Ben. The biggest one in Yugoslavia."

"Me?" Ben didn't have to invent the squeak of surprise in his voice. It came naturally. "You're kidding. Somebody's nuts!"

An old response from a different time, a different place, before Anna and Pyotr. No, no one was kidding, no one was nuts. UDBA was in this thing already, and they were— Mr. Franklin had told him about UDBA—not the kind of people who made jokes.

"No, Ben. Not kidding." She was clearly afraid.

"Steffie, I'm not a Soviet spy."

She sat looking at him.

"Don't you believe me?" Good Lord, she might not! This was the Balkans. Why should she believe him?

"I don't know, Ben. That's why I had to see you, to decide."

"Why?"

"I'm a Yugoslav, Ben. I hate the Soviets. They want to take over my country. If you were a Soviet spy, I'd be the first one to want you dead. I'd kill you myself if I had the chance. That's what I have to decide right now."

"You mean you're not sure?" The old Ben's voice squeaked.

"I have to be sure," she said.

"And if you decide I'm a Soviet spy?"

"I'll tell UDBA and be glad when they shoot you."

"Great! And you think I'd just sit here and let you do that?"

"No, I imagine you wouldn't just let me do that. I imagine you'd kill me first."

"Jesus!" This was one gutsy woman. "So?"

"I did take a gamble, didn't I?" Her face was so lovely, she so uncertain and yet fiercely proud. Ben was moved by this brave, decent girl.

"Relax, Steffie, you're still alive and I want you to stay that way a long, long time. Turn me in, don't turn me in, but I'm no Soviet spy."

"I believe you, Ben. I've made up my mind." Once again her hand reached across the table to his.

"Steffie, you are crazy. If I'd been a Soviet spy I probably would have killed you. For Christ's sake, don't ever take a chance like that again! Not ever."

"I didn't know what else to do," she said.

"So now what?" he asked her.

She smiled at him. "Now go off wherever it is you're going, and promise to buy me dinner when you come back."

"I promise." Ben meant it. She'd earned more than a dinner.

"But Ben," she had obviously just thought of it, "you

can't go far without UDBA spotting you. You don't hide easily you know, not with that ruddy American look of yours and UDBA with your picture. Although the one thing lucky is that their photo is black and white, and only your profile. They'll have to see you just right to be sure."

"Profile? Any idea where it was taken?"

"No." She looked thoughtful. "There were some steps in the background and a tree in the foreground, like one of our quieter downtown streets."

"Could it have been the American Embassy?"

"Yes, of course! I'll bet that's it," she agreed.

"Yeah." Ben nodded his head. Probably UDBA routinely filmed the entrances to major foreign embassies. He was beginning to plot the standard moves of the spy game. An amateur had very little time in this business to become an expert. Ben felt a cold chill down his back.

"I'll get by, Steffie. I'll wear a cap maybe, dark glasses, grow a beard. I'll look like a typical north European."

"Yes, I'd say that would do it. The photo was only profile. Please Ben, do be careful. And for God's sake, don't tell anyone what I've told you. You know, I face a life sentence for what I've just done."

"Good Lord!" Ben hadn't thought of that, but she was aiding and abetting a Soviet spy—or so UDBA would say.

"I owe you a lot," said Ben with feeling. "You're a wonderful person."

"I'm a fool. But please, Ben, don't misunderstand me. I didn't do this because I'm some silly girl infatuated with you. I don't want you getting the wrong idea. I just felt UDBA was wrong. Oh, I knew you were political, but I knew in my heart you weren't Soviet. I don't want you to be the victim of an injustice in my country, Ben. Someday I want this to be a country of law, like England or America. Doing what I've just done is the only way I can show where

I stand on that. Do you realize, Ben, that since the war no one politically accused in our country has ever been found innocent in court? Not once."

"No, Steffie, I didn't know that."

"It's true."

She squeezed his hand. "Kiss me goodbye, Ben, and go. Get those dark glasses and the cap. And come back safely. We won't have dinner in public any more; it will be at my sister's apartment. You can stay there when you come back to Belgrade; she's away and I have the key. But don't stay longer than you have to, Ben. Get out of Yugoslavia as fast as you can."

"I will, Steffie. I promise."

"And good luck, Ben, whatever it is that you're doing." She looked at him.

"Just buying antiquities, Steffie. I told you that."

"Ben, I've just risked my life in prison. Please don't spoil it by lying to me. Not again."

Ben was shaken. In the midst of deceit, this girl was standing up for what she knew to be right. It was to protect people like her, principles like hers, for which Ben's general was defecting. That was why Ben was here. Yet as Ben was learning to lie, Steffie was teaching him the real value of truth. He smiled at her.

"Your're right, Steffie. I won't be buying things. Maybe some day I can tell you what it's about. Be sure of one thing, we're on the same side. You'll be pleased with me if it works."

"I know I will, Ben. I know that."

They kissed lightly on the lips. It tingled nicely. Ben went off with a warm feeling. He bought dark glasses and a fashionable Dutchboy cap at a notions shop in the lobby. It was a pre-Norman Borg precaution and Steffie would be pleased.

Norman himself would emerge from the Metropole an hour later to return to the airport.

When Ben as Norman passed in front of Steffie's tourist aid counter, she looked at him without recognition. Norman had passed the test.

That evening the Rylanders and Saunderses were having dinner together at Miles's fine house. They sat on the veranda overlooking the swimming pool. A young man with a B.A. degree and a few years' experience at pushing papers would not, in the U.S., be enjoying such luxury. But such amenities are soon taken for granted as proof of one's worth. Miles had reached that self-satisfied state early on; his opinions bore the stamp of his overpayment. Derek, on the other hand, while enjoying the perquisites, was untidy with self-doubt. He was aware that things here were rather better than they might be at home, but he was worried.

Derek had gone too far with Mr. Franklin the night before. He'd become used to cowing the older generation during this last decade when, in America, impertinence had passed for wisdom. The Chief of Station, Luke Franklin, proved no such patsy. Derek was shaken. He'd finally come up against a man who reflected back to him the truth he knew about himself.

The threat of a dissenting cable was sheer bluff. Franklin might well have let him send it off, but it would have been, Derek realized, digging his own grave. Headquarters had either consented to or commanded Franklin's position to approve the general's defection. Derek had pushed too hard. Now he found himself the victim of his own impertinence.

Derek couldn't tell his wife; she would hardly be sympathetic with the idea of recall to America. He couldn't talk to the other Agency staff; indeed, he was not allowed to discuss the case with any but Agency people in the need-to-know category. But Derek had to do something to cover his ass.

Miles was his best friend, the veranda was hardly likely to be bugged, the evening was warm, and Derek had already had two martinis. He was upset enough to badly want a third martini, which Miles was now pouring. The tinkle of ice against crystal was reassuring.

"Well," asked Miles, "how's our Mr. Cornelius coming along?"

Derek grunted. "Can't talk about it. You know that."

Miles's eyebrows went up. "U.S.-Soviet relations at stake, U.S.-Yugoslav relations at stake, and you can't talk about it. There is, you know, a Freedom of Information Act predicated on the grounds that Americans have the right to know who is pulling which rug out from under them."

"Secret business, you know that." Derek glowered.

"I have a top secret security clearance, as you know," said Miles, miffed. So many people used security clearance as a device to be exclusive; the snobbery of "in" bureaucrats. Miles knew that well, having done it himself often. "Don't pull that clearance crap on me."

"Lay off me, will you? I've got enough troubles." Derek looked as miserable as he felt.

"Ah," said Miles, smiling. "You need a friend. Come on, what's gone off track?" Miles was solicitous.

"It's a mess. Cornelius is the real thing, or so Headquarters says. He could be Andropov and the CIA wouldn't know."

"Andropov?"

"KGB Director in Moscow."

"Oh. So you think Cornelius is a fake?"

"Maybe."

"Oh come now, you're not going to decide war or peace on the basis of 'maybe.' If there's any doubt, you can't go ahead. I told you the other night, Derek, if this blows up we're all going to be hated here."

"So what?" Derek was looking bitterly at his martini.

"Don't be foolish. You can't let this go on. It's just one more CIA disaster; perhaps history will call it the 'Danube Disaster.'"

"Don't rub it in, Miles. I'm sorry I joined up. I should have gone Foreign Service like you."

"My dear fellow, I couldn't agree more. And you can still transfer, but not later if this thing goes sour. We wouldn't have you." It was his turn to be exclusive.

"What the hell do you expect me to do? Tell Cornelius that I won't let his general come out even if Headquarters says he's got bed and board waiting?"

"It's gone that far, has it?" Miles shook his head knowingly, clicking his tongue like a gossip at a back fence.

"Yes."

"Well, aren't you going to stop it?"

"How can I? Franklin hates my guts."

"Ah, that's the cat who got your tongue, is it? I sympathize with you."

Derek sipped at the drink. "I tried to buck him on the defection and he called my bluff. Now I'm in trouble and he's handling Cornelius. You know who's handling the general?"

"No, who?"

"Cornelius himself."

"You're kidding!" Miles was amazed. "Civilians are never allowed to handle any kind of case, that much I *do* know. And something this big! Ridiculous! Who is he really?"

"He's just there, the faucet on the pipeline. If he doesn't

move it, nothing flows. Set it up himself. Tough son of a bitch. Mean. He damn near hit me the other night."

"You too?"

"Yes. You were right about him. Vicious. Has things his own way. Moved Franklin, moved Headquarters. Damndest thing I ever saw. Imagine it, a civilian, an amateur, handling the biggest defector since Penkovsky. Maybe bigger."

Miles poured his own third martini. "How's big Ben going to do it?"

"Damned if I know. How do you run a submarine out of Poland?"

"Ah, Poland, is it? Very good. Hard place indeed for submarines."

"Yeah. Shouldn't have told you. Expunge it from the record, will you? Poland, I mean?"

"Certainly," said Miles amiably. "What do I care where he is, I just asked how he's coming out."

"Like I said. Submarine. Or hot air balloon, they're all the rage these days. Coffin? Disguised as a nun? How do I know. Let Cornelius and Hardface worry about it."

"Hardface?"

"Old Luke Franklin."

"That he is," agreed Miles, "but now, what are we to do about it? The whole thing is a mess."

"And how," said Derek glumly.

"Well, if you won't do anything about it, I will."

"Yeah, you do that, Miles. Tell Hardface to go fuck a duck."

Miles snickered. "No, no, Derek. Nothing so direct. Just leave it to me. I'll handle this thing as it should be handled in a democracy."

"Yugoslavia isn't a democracy."

"Who cares about that? Certainly not the Yugoslavs.

Come on, Derek, how about one more martini."

"Right on." Derek was slurring his words, Miles not far behind, as the two toasted the democratic solution, whatever it might be.

The Writers' Club occupies a lovely old villa not far from the Parliament buildings in Belgrade. In good weather, dining is outdoors under a canopy of linden trees. Service is excellent, the food superb, the diners an exciting group of successful artists, government propagandists, journalists. Those in government who like to think of themselves as artistic dine there. It is a good place at which to be seen. Conversation is lively: who is sleeping with whom, who has just parleyed a sycophantic article into a promotion, who is slated to be ambassador. Here one would not want to spoil the atmosphere with tedious talk of injustice or tyranny. Besides, UDBA dines at the Writers' Club too, where even the Interior Minister fancies himself on the *rive gauche*.

It is a broad-minded club; foreigners are allowed membership if they are high society. Miles Saunders was having dinner with Joshua Seymour, a syndicated New York political columnist. Miles's wife was there; so, too, was a pretty French blonde who worked for *Le Monde*, and after hours for herself, in bed.

"I have something very, very hot for you, Josh, but it is absolutely not for attribution." Everybody was a little drunk. Miles had been working up to this moment all evening.

"Have I ever revealed a source, Miles?" Joshua spoke with hurt reproach in his voice, as to an old friend. The old friend, Miles, was someone he'd met at a reception the week before. In Josh's business, intimacy varied as a function of the copy provided. Miles, a talkative young diplomat, looked like an especially good source. Josh, here to do *the* definitive piece on Yugoslavia, in ten days, needed all the inside stuff he could get. Doder of the *Washington Post* had spent four years here writing a book on Yugoslavia. Josh thought that if it couldn't be done in ten days it wasn't politics, it was political science, and that was for professors.

"But I mean this is hot, Josh. Detente versus cold war, maybe even cold war versus hot war."

Joshua closed his fat eyelids, opening them slowly, the gesture of a man fatigued from a surfeit of knowledge. "Trust me, Miles, my paper and I are a force for peace. We'll treat your stuff with reverence."

"Reverence?" The little French girl gave her customer the fish eye.

"Reverence for the truth, dolly, reverence for peace."

Miles gave the French girl a dirty look. "Please, Francine, talk to my wife. This is private."

Francine sniffed and turned away.

"Well, Miles?" Josh turned his head sideways, offering his confessional ear.

"I have very good reason to believe," began Miles conspiratorially, "that the CIA is about to create the greatest threat to peace since the Berlin blockade. They are setting the stage to present to the world a Soviet defector, one from the very highest circles, who will warn that the Russians are about to attack Europe, the U.S., China. If he is believed, the West will have every reason to argue for a preventive nuclear first strike. World War III may begin and we will begin it, just as the Soviets have always feared. Naturally, only the NATO leadership, plus perhaps the Chinese, will be privy to this material. There is no way the people of the world can judge for themselves if this man is what he claims to be, or if what he says is true. Certainly no one, not even the president, will know that this defector

may, in fact, be a creation of the CIA, a man whose script
was written by the hawks to destroy detente."

Joshua Seymour stared at Miles. "Miles, this has got to
be hogwash."

"I wish it were."

"Holy Toledo!" Joshua Seymour was rarely impressed
by anything he heard; he'd played with words enough to
know that almost everything that passed for news was
gossip. "You got proof?"

"I can get you an interview with a CIA man who's been
involved. Naturally, you'll have to protect him."

"You got any documentary evidence? This one is too big
to go on without some back-up."

"Maybe the CIA man has some documents. I know he's
seen them. I don't know whether he copied them. If he did,
what he has is in Russian, with nothing to prove CIA
involvement in setting this up, if that's what happened.
Now you understand, Josh, that I can't guarantee this is
what the Agency is doing. I just say it is highly likely, based
on my own access to certain events. I can only guarantee
there is a defector in the wings with the story I've told you
tonight."

Josh's mind was racing. "You've got the story angle, all
right. Nobody has to prove it is a CIA theater, but as you
said, the question must be raised. The public has a right to
know, Miles. A right to know."

"Exactly, Josh. They have a right to know." Miles thrust
his glass down hard on the table.

"Miles, baby?" Joshua said, "can you get me next to this
defector?"

"No. He belongs to the Agency. He's as deep a secret as
Ultra as far as they're concerned."

"Not now, he isn't," said Joshua.

"No, but we won't find him until they're ready."

"Can't we get next to anybody in the pipeline?"

"I could tell you, Josh, but I can't. I am sworn to secrecy, after all I don't break confidences. Still and all, there's a little I can give you by way of background."

"Let's have it, baby."

"The Soviet defector is being handled, that is, his case is being personally supervised, by an American. His cover is that of a businessman, but of course no one in his right mind would believe that. He has to be somebody big that the Agency has sent in. The important thing is that the entire operation is being run out of Belgrade. That way the Yugoslavs will be implicated, making it look like this country, a Third World leader, is cooperating with NATO and the Chinese to oppose the Russians. It's not true, of course, but those guys in the Agency are more Byzantine than anyone can imagine."

"Miles, that doesn't do much for me. The Belgrade angle, that's great, really great. But an American businessman, what the hell! There are millions of them."

"I know, Josh, and I'm sorry, but I've got to live up to my secrecy obligations. You know that."

"Oh sure, sure." Seymour was annoyed. He'd give this State Department fathead one more prod.

"Come on, Miles baby. I promise not to print it, not one word. But give me a hint so I can get next to the operation myself. You know, maybe just so I can stumble on this fellow."

Miles gave Josh a severe glance. "For your sake, Josh, I wouldn't want to do that. These boys play rough. They'd kill you as soon as look at you."

Seymour paled. "They wouldn't. I'm a journalist."

Miles enjoyed the drama as it edged toward sadism. "Oh yes, Josh, they will kill you if they can, because you already know too much. One of the risks of life over here."

Calm, Miles reached out his hand to grip Seymour's shoulder. He smiled reassuringly.

Joshua looked at him hard. "You actually mean that you've put my ass in a sling, you bloody bastard?" Seymour was shaking with fury.

"You've got a duty, Josh, bigger than yourself. The public. They have a right to know."

"You make me sick!" Seymour grabbed Francine's arm. "Come on, dolly. Let's get out of here."

Francine hissed at Miles, *"Espèce de salaud."*

ELEVEN

"What is it, Lenev?"

Lieutenant Colonel Lenev stood in front of General Pavlichenko's desk grinning, a sheaf of papers in his hand. It was the grin of a shark.

"Comrade General, a bit of luck. We have a nice tape from the Writers' Club last night. On your orders it was wired yesterday."

"Well, let's have it."

Lenev summarized, with an effort to stay cool, the conversation between Saunders and the New York journalist.

"Well, well. There is progress!" Pavlichenko exclaimed. "An American posing as a businessman, that's something, and the State Department thinks the CIA is setting the stage for an international defamation. The war hawks want the excuse to strike first. What is one to think of that?"

"Anything is possible, Comrade General. If it's true, Russia will make the first strike."

"That option is always ours. I remind you that Comrade Lenin advised, 'Revolutionary activity consists in using the enemy's policies, especially when these policies are preparing his own destruction.' The West is not the only power capable of either cunning or a first strike. We may be able to put this wile of theirs to work."

"Yes, Comrade General." Lenev nodded vigorously.

The Resident drummed his fingers on the desk top. "If it is a CIA operation, if the defector is to be their own man, it is every bit as imperative that we nip this in the bud as it is if the defection is genuine. So now we must suspect this curious American businessman of putting on a show that day in the Embassy as the first act in the CIA's conspiracy against the doves in their own government."

"Yes, Comrade General."

"Does such a truly treacherous scheme remind you of anyone, Lenev?"

The aide-de-camp knew he had to give it a try. "Trotsky?" He offered the name weakly.

"I was thinking more of Beria. It is a plot worthy of Beria himself."

"Yes, Comrade General." One did not, the aide knew, speak lightly the name of that arch conspirator, dead on his way to the master stroke against Khrushchev.

"Yes," the Resident was musing, "worthy of Beria himself. If so, our 'businessman' is no small opponent."

"Exactly, Comrade General."

"Unless, of course," Pavlichenko continued thoughtfully, "there is a further wheel within the wheel."

"Which would be, Comrade General?"

"Yasha," it was rare the Resident called him by his first name. It signalled intimacy in conversation, a conspiracy between friends. "What if elements in our own Politburo wished to generate an irresistible argument for a surprise attack on the West?"

"What, Valentin Petrovich?" Yasha used the first name and patronymic, acknowledging the change in the level of intimacy, but still respectful.

"What more clever an artifice than insinuating their own

people into the American government and thence the CIA
to create such a ruse as this? They situate their imposter as
one of our defectors. They give him just this story to tell.
They arrange for this terrible warning to come to the
NATO leaders. At the same time, they assure, as has now
happened twice, that the whole plot comes to our official
attention. My cable to Moscow Center will faithfully
describe it all. Moscow Center will, in turn, alert the
Politburo immediately. By tonight, the highest leadership
will be aware that it is possible that elements in the
American government are creating a provocation that
would justify a Western first strike. That, in turn, necessi-
tates that our General Staff place us in a first-strike stance.
Presto, Yasha! Our defector posing as their defector posing
as our defector provides the irrefutable argument for war,
all according to plan."

"Yes, Valentin Petrovich. I see." Yasha considered
what had been said. "Our defector posing as their defector
posing as our defector, according to plan." It was so
insidious that it compelled belief. Anything that a paranoid
conceives becomes possible. If it is possible, there will be
those who consider doing it. If there is an interest to be
served by doing it, it will be done. This is not only the
mentality of madmen; it is one way for the mind to work.
Among our Soviet elite, there is a Darwinian selection for
such thinking. Those who fail to sense that others' imagin-
ings can power anticipation, and anticipation action, refuse
to admit the reality of the Soviet world in which they
live.

Lenev asked the Resident, "What will you cable Moscow
Center?"

"All the facts at hand."

"And this possibility you raise?"

"It is not wise to involve oneself in disputes among the

leadership, Yasha. I only speculated privately on what could occur."

"But you may be correct."

"Of course, but if I saw it, then anyone who reads the cable will see the possibility. Others are less likely to consider it if I convey it as a speculation, for my motives in raising it will be suspect, as if, for example, I opposed the first-strike faction in the Politburo. No, the possibility is so evident that a child will see it. Let them discover it. We here will stick to the words on our tapes for the time being. As for the American, since we now know his cover is to be open, check all the hotels and the Yugoslav trade groups. Get me the names and descriptions of every American businessman who's been in Belgrade these last few days."

Norman Borg arrived in Split, took the public bus to town, went through stores, walked byways, and was sure he was not followed. Luke Franklin had instructed him in the elements of surveillance detection and evasion. Ben was glad; it was past time to get help in this business.

Anna and Edvard were cold and suspicious to Norman, but suddenly overjoyed to see Ben. As they had dinner together, Ben told them what had happened.

Perhaps it was to be expected that Anna's first question was about Steffie, tentative, worried. "Can you trust her, Ben?"

"I daresay. She went all out for me. Tell me where I could find someone else to do that for a stranger."

"Valeria would do the same, Ben."

Ah, Ben understood. Aunt Anna was in there pitching for Valeria. Ben almost chuckled. It was true he hadn't thought of Valeria much these last few days.

Edvard voiced the real concern. "If UDBA has been alerted, Ben, if for reasons beyond us they think you are a

Soviet spy, we all have to be very careful."

It was an understatement. For Anna and Edvard it could mean life in prison, even the firing squad, Ben realized, if UDBA acted on the same kind of hearsay evidence that had revved them up about himself.

"No more hotels for me, Edvard, and only disguises when I visit here. Is there some storeroom in this labyrinthine old palace where you can hide me for the night?"

"Yes, lots of hidden nooks, some not slept in for fifteen hundred years except for bats, rats, and a ghost or two."

"Just what I need," said Ben, hoping it was.

"But what are we to do about Pyotr, Ben, now that you've made contact? How will he get here?" Anna asked the question nervously.

"A lot depends on him, Anna, and a lot on luck. Somehow, he'll have to find an excuse to get closer to Belgrade. Skawina is, from all the CIA people tell me, way out of their reach. If he can get to Roumania we can set up some kind of exit."

"He told me that he can get to any of the Warsaw Pact countries," Anna said. "As commander of CPS he regularly visits the forward Soviet and Pact armies, inspects the communications, reviews their status, that sort of thing."

"But Anna, that's very good indeed!" Ben was immensely cheered by that news.

"What shall I tell him, Ben? You'll have to be very exact. It will take me some time to put all of it into recipes. Thank goodness he gave me that little dictionary he made up. He always loved puzzles as a child. He has such an elaborate mind, Ben."

"I'm sure he does, Anna, or he wouldn't be where he is today."

She shook her head. "It's so hard for me to imagine, Pyotr having to leave."

"Do you trust him, Anna? Are you sure he's doing this on his own and not out of duplicity?" Ben had to ask the question.

"I know Russians, Ben. I know why you ask. Things like that do happen. But I also know Pyotr. He's my brother. I swear by the Holy Virgin, by the blood of Christ the Savior, that I believe him and have full trust in him. I have my reasons. Good reasons. That's all I can tell you, Ben."

"I think you can trust Anya's judgment, Ben," said Edvard. "She really does know her family. Pyotr has been closer to her than anyone."

"That's enough for me."

"What do I tell him?" asked Anna.

Ben consulted his memory. The Chief of Station had reviewed with him a hundred contingencies, the best of which was what Anna had just reported: that Pyotr was free to go to Roumania on military business.

"Can he commandeer a small military plane, Anna? Fly it out himself or hijack it?"

"Oh no, he was very clear about that when we talked. He's not a pilot. The Pact countries are very careful about where planes fly. They'd shoot it down if it deviated from the flight plan, Pyotr was sure about that."

"Does he have motor transport? Can he get a car or truck to get out into the country?"

"He seemed to think he could. He's a commanding general after all, and has every reason to visit any military area for which his unit has responsibility. I don't suppose he could go to some remote place without a good reason, unless, of course, it was to go fishing . . ."

Ben interrupted. "Does he fish or hunt, Anna?"

"Why certainly. He adores sports, fishing particularly. He goes as often as he can. That's one of the advantages of the military; the officers all use the restricted areas and have the soldiers tend to them as servants. Why, it's no different from the days of the czars."

"So Pyotr could get to Bucharest, for example, and from there to a district military headquarters with time off for fishing?"

"I think so. I know he's done it before. All the general staff use their privileges like that. Pyotr even went to the Transylvanian Alps a couple of years ago."

"But Anna," Ben was beaming, "this is wonderful." Ben had been briefed on the geography. He had the map in his briefcase, as well as in his mind's eye.

"I'm glad you think so. But Mount Hategului, where he was fishing, must be seventy-five miles inside Roumania."

"That's not as far as Skawina, believe me," Ben said. For the first time, he began to think that this whole crazy scheme he and the Chief of Station had concocted might work.

For the next few hours the three of them worked on the details of the message that was to be sent as a family recipe to Pyotr.

Ben spent the night in an old storeroom in Diocletian's Palace, under the eaves, accessible only by a wooden ladder. Apparently designed as a pigeon cote in the fourth century, it still functioned as one. It was the pigeon guano capital of the world, thought Ben, with the only advantage being that everyone else who might know about it—and that could be only the most adventuresome of the small boys who lived in the building—would want to be there even less than he did. Edvard gave him a tent-like covering, a thin mattress, and a loud ticking clock. The clock, Edvard had said, would keep the pigeons away. Perhaps it did, Ben was too tired to notice. Here in this stinking eyrie he felt he could sleep 'til Diocletian's second coming.

The next day, Norman Borg, camera swinging over his

shoulder, took the express bus to Belgrade. It was a long journey but Norman, Hoosier tourist, was surprised at how much he enjoyed it. A few of the Yugoslavs on the bus spoke a little English but only one, a young girl about seventeen, was friendly. She shared her oranges with him; he bought her dinner in Sarajevo. World War I had started here. The Balkans, mother to war. Ben felt a chill at the thought.

In Belgrade, Norman took the streetcar, using the marked map Franklin had given him, to a stop four blocks from the safe house—an apartment in a busy residential district. The key to the door worked and the safe house itself was pleasantly furnished, the bar stocked, the refrigerator full. Norman liked the way the Chief of Station ran his shop.

Ben spent one boring day reading. The next day, wearing the change of clothes provided in the safe house, he met Franklin at noon in a busy downtown restaurant remarkable for its noise, ugliness, and bad food. Fortunately the beer was good. Ben began the conversation in low tones, telling Franklin the good news of Pyotr's mobility. He reported the instructions he had given Anna to encrypt in her batch of family recipes.

"That's good news," said Franklin, his face nonetheless grave. "And now for the bad. Look at this." He shoved a telex facsimile copy of the prior evening's New York newspaper across the table. It was a short article by Josh Seymour, dateline Belgrade. Most of it dealt with what Seymour considered the unique and successful worker-run Communism of Yugoslavia. The last lines of the article alluded to a breaking story. They read:

"Rumor among the diplomatic corps here is that a major international incident is in the making. A top level source revealed, in an exclusive interview, that the Yugoslav Government—which is fastidiously neutral in the conflict between the U.S. and the USSR—fears that both governments are planning to use Belgrade as a scene for provocations. While no one is certain what is in the wind, one reliable official stated that the U.S. is using Belgrade as a transit point in an underground railroad for top Soviet defectors. American CIA agents are operating clandestinely here with bravado not seen in that Agency for some years. The diplomatic community is asking, why? Some suggest that at least one major Soviet defector planning to pass through here is not genuine, but a made-in-America plant who will be surfaced in order to exacerbate U.S.-Soviet tensions. Thus, the defection of a senior Soviet official shortly to be announced by the CIA may be a victory for the American hawks. In a later column, I shall be reporting further on these critical, peace-endangering developments."

Ben looked at the Chief of Station. "Somebody's got his monkeywrench out, looks like. Or do you think it's a coincidence?"

"In this business coincidences are like babies; if you don't know how they're made, you're in trouble. I don't think this is anything but intentional," Franklin said. "There's a leak, a security violation. The Russians and the Yugoslavs are now on notice that a big defection is brewing. It's also evident that someone wants to discredit our defector in advance."

"The Soviets?"

"They would if they could, of course, but if they knew about this, your general would be dead by now. No, it looks more like somebody who is—I use the phrase euphemistically—on our side."

Ben was outraged. "It's a betrayal."

Franklin had a melancholy smile. "Betrayal is the business we're in. You'd better be prepared for trouble. For one thing, it drastically reduces the resources available to me in running this operation. I'd hoped we could run it using just our station staff; I don't like to bring in agents and staffers from outside if I can help it. But now I'm trapped."

"Surely you've got ample staff in the station here?"

"Start with me, then take Rylander, Sam Munson, whom you'll be working with, and finally Jim Potter—if he gets well in time—and you'll have the picture."

"Four people, with one out sick?"

"Mumps, can you imagine? No fun at his age, but in the meantime the three of us constitute the Belgrade tentacles of the worldwide octopus that everybody is always moaning about."

"I had no idea. I really did think of it as omnipotent, somehow."

"About as omnipotent as a punch-drunk prizefighter. Anyway, with this piece by Seymour facing us, we don't even have three men, we have two."

"How's that?"

"Since Sam has been out of town since you've been here, he can't be the leak. And mumps is mumps. That leaves one suspect, our good friend Derek Rylander. Counterintelligence, CI we call it, is already in on this because of the Seymour article. I've no choice. I've got to suspend Derek pending CI's investigation. They can have a team out here in two days, not that it will help; Seymour's not about to reveal his sources.

"Which means that I wait for outside help to come in to get your general out of Roumania. If the general waits too long to get to Roumania, the Soviets may find him first. If he gets there too soon, I don't have anybody to send in to get him, excepting Munson. And it's a three-man job, at least."

"Doesn't Bucharest have people at the station there, or agents in the field who can bring the general out?"

"You don't appreciate the ramifications of what I told you about this post. There are just enough staffers in Bucharest to make a bridge game. Headquarters has already reviewed Bucharest's capabilities; that cable traffic has been going over my desk since you came back from Split. We'll have to bring people in from Europe or Stateside."

"Why can't I go in to get the general? I've come this far, I may as well go the full route. Besides, I've never seen Roumania."

"I can't let you do it," Franklin said. "You don't have the tradecraft, the skills, should you need commo, explosives, what-have-you. Your .38 won't fend off the Roumanians. Besides, if our people go in and are caught, if they're not shot—accidentally, so to speak—then they enjoy diplomatic immunity. They simply get sent back home with egg on their faces. If you go in, you are really a spy. If you're caught you can be very dead indeed."

"How can there be immunity for a diplomat conducting espionage in a country to which he's not accredited?"

"Technically you're right, there can't, but for the regulars, the old boys, spying is quite comfortable. There is a kind of informal agreement between us all. No KGB officer would ever be hurt knowingly by a Western case officer or vice versa. The worst that ever happens is you get caught and serve time until somebody whips up a prisoner exchange. These days that can happen in a matter of months. It's a no-risk game for the regulars. By definition, anybody with diplomatic cover, anybody who is a case officer operating in a country where the informal rules apply, is comfy. There are some countries which haven't joined the club yet: Albania, Iraq, Libya, China, Cuba . . . the nuts and the radicals, of which the Soviet Union is by no means one. And there are, of course, the irregulars who don't enjoy the club's protection; that's most people who get caught up in the business: agents, informants, guerrilla forces working for a clubman, bystanders. You're one of those without protection."

"If it makes the difference in getting the general out, I'll take that chance." Ben's tone was firm.

"I can't turn you down flat, but it shouldn't be necessary unless the general rushes off to Roumania right away. I'll be straight with you. I've run agents into the USSR from submarines off Murmansk and Yalta, I've run them into Peking from Hong Kong, and of course into the East from right here. I've lost most of them. It's true you'd go in on a short-run mission, but I can't tell you you'll have any better luck than most of the people who've worked for me, or others like me. Most are dead. That's how this business really works. The employers go to diplomatic receptions, the work force ends up in shallow graves. Do you know what the younger men in the Agency call me?"

"No."

"Hardface. They're right. This is not the kind of game that makes a man prone to smile. Oh, Rylander can smile. He files reports and seems to talk to reporters, but he's never sent an agent into Roumania knowing what the agent didn't know, that five who went in before him were already dead. Derek Rylander smiles too easily. No matter what the CI boys find, I'm going to make a Christian out of him."

"Meaning?"

"Folklore has it that Christians are sober, trustworthy,

hard-working, loyal, God-fearing. Rylander could use some of that."

"So could Miles Saunders!" said Ben.

"Ah yes, Rylander's best friend. Princeton's contribution to the next Soviet-American friendship society. You may be right. Miles and Derek may be in this mischief together." Franklin looked at Ben appraisingly. "You know, you've got pretty good horse sense, Mr. Cornelius."

"Thank you, Mr. Franklin."

Ben mused about the use of last names. People could be too quick with pretended intimacy. Real respect was better conveyed with a last name.

"Assuming now that the general does get to Roumania, have you figured out what happens then?"

"I'm working on it. I won't tell you unless you need to know. I'm sure you can appreciate the rule."

"I can. In the meantime, I'll be waiting to hear from Anna. What do you think, shall I stay Norman or shift to someone else? I see there's an Irishman waiting for me in the apartment. I saw the clothes, documents, and makeup. But I've never been an actor. Can you tell me how to put on a beard?"

"Sure, when the time comes. Meantime, stay Norman and stay out of sight."

"I'd like to call Steffie to let her know I'm okay."

"Sure, but don't use the safe-house phone, and don't see her. Ben Cornelius is sure to get picked up by UDBA, and Norman is best off not socializing, even with pretty girls. Boring I know, but just sit tight and read all those safe-house books until you get word from Anna. She's writing you care of American Express?"

"She's writing to me there as John Duncan. You gave me his Express card and wallet papers before I left for

Split."

"Good. Call me when you hear from her."

Ben called Steffie at the airport that afternoon. She was obviously relieved that he was safe. She wanted to see him immediately. It was painful turning her down.

"Believe me, Steffie, I do want to see you and I promise you that dinner, but under the circumstances I'd better delay it."

"But Ben, remember I'm cooking."

"I appreciate that but even so, let's wait until a more auspicious time. Do you understand what I'm trying to say?"

She did. Both were circumspect over the phone, even though its chances of being bugged were low.

"Things will straighten out soon enough. I promise to call you soon and I will see you."

They were both disappointed.

Lieutenant Colonel Lenev sat with the Resident as they reviewed Komiakov's report of that morning. There had been two hundred and forty-two transient Americans in Belgrade the day of the conversation between Saunders and his visitor about a defector. Komiakov and his crew had debriefed their paid agents in hotels, bribed their way to the State Trade Mission visitor files, and burgled the current visitors' visa files in the Foreign Ministry. Of the two hundred and forty-two Americans, two hundred and forty-one were accounted for.

The missing man was identified as Benjamin Cornelius of Oregon. A full physical description with a copy of the visa photo accompanied the papers given to General Pavlichenko. Cornelius was registered at the Metropole, but had not picked up his key for several days.

"Our man," said the Resident.

"Yes. Komiakov has done a passable job for once."

"And no doubt alerted UDBA while doing it."

"No doubt. UDBA will want to know what we're after."

"With that article in the New York papers,"—the Resident had received it via Moscow—"they'll have a good idea. We shall all be looking for the same fellow."

"No doubt a different fellow now, Comrade General."

"No doubt. Still, a beginning. How many men do we have working on this, Lenev?"

"One hundred and thirty-eight, Comrade General."

"And how many are in the CIA station here?"

"Komiakov's First Directorate estimates six. That would be about normal."

"Good odds. The six are under surveillance?"

"On and off, Comrade General. They are not so easy to follow, they break loose from time to time. The Chief of Station, for example, is an old-line professional. He has slipped surveillance a number of times."

"What's Komiakov been using? Old women and cripples?"

"No, Comrade General, but this is hostile territory for us, and until today most of the staff were simply trying to identify this man Cornelius. We don't have that many trained surveillance teams here. Old Hardface is very, very good. And Komiakov you know, well . . ." Yasha raised his hands in a gesture of despair.

"Tell Komiakov not to lose him again, Lenev."

"Yes, Comrade General."

"And Lenev, when Komiakov does find Cornelius, he'd better not lose him, no matter if his brother-in-law is General Kulikov himself. Even the Chief of the General Staff can suffer embarrassment."

It was, the Resident realized, time to set up a goat, in case this operation went wrong. Komiakov had been trouble enough, but had been untouchable because of his connections. Now things were different. The sacrificial goat would be readied.

TWELVE

Seventeen books, much good liquor, and six days later, "Norman Borg" took his daily walk to the tiny American Express office. Ben had expected a spy's life to be exciting, but these last days had been interminably dull. It must be tedium, not danger, that drove spooks out of the game.

Today the letter from Anna to John Duncan had arrived. In the code he'd worked out with her, her letter told him that Pyotr would be in Roumania on the seventeenth. He would, as the station's plan had specified, go fishing on the eighteenth. Ben recalled the map. It was about a hundred and sixty miles from Bucharest to Targa Ju, from where a dirt road led to Baia de Arama. From there, Pyotr was to hike upstream toward Mount Gogul, a 2300-meter peak closer to the Yugoslav border. The plan called for him to hike west, staying south of the peak, toward the headwaters of the Cerna River. He was to fish the Cerna, heading downstream toward the town of Baile Herculane, about twenty miles from the high headwaters. There were trails and small villages, and nothing suspicious in an elite sportsman enjoying the early autumn season. The Cerna joined the Timis River near Baile Herculane and soon after met the great Danube. The Yugoslav-Roumanian border follows the Danube, as does the main highway. Baile Herculane is only twelve miles from that border.

The general had been told to camp on the Cerna, ten miles down from its source, to await the contact agent. The signal was prearranged.

Ben called the station with the formula message, "We'll be able to repair the Xerox copier this week," the signal for the letter's arrival.

Mr. Franklin was to meet Norman Borg at a popular international tavern near the embassy at 7:00 the evening after that message came in. It was imperative to avoid surveillance. If either sensed his own or the other's surveillance, they were to make no contact. Neither was to acknowledge the other until ten minutes had elapsed after arrival.

Ben was prompt, but it was nearly 8:00 before Luke Franklin appeared. The place was, by now, crowded. One took a place as best one could, joining large tables already ringed with customers. There was no free table, not even two chairs together. Franklin finished one beer and walked to the newspaper rack by the rear wall, for here, as in much of Europe, the daily papers are kept in eating places for leisurely reading. Ben joined him there. They talked while standing.

"Sorry I'm late, but there was a very able surveillance squad on my tail. By the cut of their clothes, I'd say KGB. Took me this long to shake them, and I started at 6:00, too, just to be on the safe side."

"Sure we're clear now?" Ben was bothered by the news.

"I'm never sure of anything, but I think we're okay. Now, what's your news?"

Ben told him of Anna's letter.

"The seventeenth is the day after tomorrow." Franklin was distressed. "Which means contact and pickup will be on the fourth or fifth day from now, or maybe never."

"What's the matter?" asked Ben.

"Damn near everything."

Ben had a sinking feeling. Didn't anything ever go right in the intelligence business?

"In a nutshell," Franklin went on, "the counterintelligence people visited Josh Seymour, and he threatened to write them up in the papers. They fled New York screaming. Those CI boys can't stand daylight. Here they only had Rylander and me to work over. No surprise to anyone that Saunders's office, and all the other embassy offices, all the telex and phone lines, damn near everything but our unit—which we do keep secure—were hooked up, through the phones of course. Soviet equipment mostly, but a UDBA tap on the main switchboard as well. Rylander claims he's clean and so does Saunders. Saunders insists you're a Soviet and that the Russians gave the defector story to Josh Seymour as disinformation. He and Rylander both have charged me with doing an inadequate assessment of you and leading Headquarters down the garden path. The new chief of SB—Soviet Block—at Headquarters is a smart but nasty man named Barbour. CI has relayed the Rylander accusations to him, and he's called me home to give my side of it, to defend myself is putting it more plainly. In the meantime, Barbour has cancelled the team that was coming down here from Paris to help us get our general out of Roumania."

Ben was stunned. "You mean they're bringing you home right in the middle of this just because Rylander and Saunders are lying to save their ass?"

"This is a nasty trade, and it's nastiest right inside the family, as you can see. Don't worry, I can handle myself. No junior case officer is going to put the monkey on my back—unless, of course," Franklin gave Ben a long look, "unless you are Soviet. But in that case I'd have it coming."

"Do you want me to talk to the counterintelligence people?"

"Absolutely not. You are our most cherished property at the moment. There's no way we could keep UDBA and the Soviets from following CI to you. You'd be burned right away."

"Where do we stand, then?"

"I stand knee-deep in unpleasant cables, the general looks to be going back home to Poland after fishing, and NATO better start worrying twenty-four hours a day about when the WALTZ we never found out about is to begin."

"We can't let that happen, Luke." In this moment of crisis, Ben found himself using the first name. "Are you under orders not to go in to get the general?"

"No, Headquarters authorized the action. We even managed to get the Roumanian support we need. Some rather old-fashioned resources have been dredged up, but they ought to work. The trouble is, Ben, we don't have the team to do it. Potter is still sick, and that leaves Munson and the technician. Period."

"Still time to get Headquarters to reverse themselves and send down the Paris backup," said Ben.

"You don't understand Headquarters. They're so damn busy trying to protect themselves that they've lost sight of what it is we're trying to do. Seymour's article and Rylander's charges are more important to them than WALTZ or NATO because the flak at home is political. Congress will pick it up, the President will be on the Agency's back, and the State Department will say just what Saunders says because he's got the ambassador here worried about bad publicity and local relations. So what if we don't get the general out? The Agency, the Executive, can't be blamed for what we didn't do, or didn't know. But bad publicity? Why, the very thought of it sends those pansies running to hide in their flower beds."

Ben was quiet for a few moments before he said, "Luke, I told you that I'll go in after the general. It makes sense anyway, since I'm the best one to identify him and make sure they've not put a ringer in. As you know, I've seen the family albums. And he's more likely to trust me, because I know his sister and the family. We'll just have to rig an operation that an amateur can handle."

Franklin sighed. "All right," he said. "I am ready to let you do it, Ben, if you remember what I told you about the risks. It will be you, Sam Munson, and the technician. Munson and the technician both have diplomatic passports. I'm not even sure I could get authorization for a government-paid funeral for you."

"I'll go in." It was a cold determination that Ben felt, flowing from what, he now saw, had all along been inevitable. He was facing possible death, on a mission that might be pointless, were Pyotr lying—or mad. But if Pyotr was sincere, nothing could be more important. He was surprised at how calm he was.

"All right," Luke was saying, "you're on. You and Sam will go to Orsova on the main road. You can't go off the highway by car, because the whole area is a restricted border zone. Bucharest station will get you from Orsova to the general. They will get you back from the pickup point to the main highway. From there back it will be your show."

"I'll have the general's help," Ben said. "If we move fast enough, he won't yet be suspected by them."

Luke remained grimly in the present. "We've been lucky that UDBA and the KGB are still beating the bushes. I want you out of sight until tomorrow. Stay Norman Borg today. Stay in the safe house. Before you leave the safe house, change into the clothes that are there. For the beard, all it takes is a thin layer of cream on your skin, then the spirit gum to stick it on. You'll be surprised how easy it is. At noon tomorrow you're to meet Munson here."

He wrote out an address. "If there's a tail on you and you can't shake them, show up anyway. Munson will be equipped to get you out of there. You'll stay with him from then on. I won't be able to see you again; too many KGB on my tail, and I can't do you any more good now anyway. Munson will know what to do. It's damn tricky as you'll soon find out. That's it. Good luck."

"Thanks." Ben was about to shake hands but realized that any gesture might attract attention to the two of them so casually lounging against the back wall of the tavern. He did say, "Good luck to you, too, Luke."

"Save it. You'll need it all." Franklin left quickly, disappearing through the door into the night. Ben waited briefly, then followed.

Major Komiakov stood at attention as he presented himself to General Pavlichenko. He had begun his report at the 8:00 a.m. staff meeting, but the Resident had shut him up and told him to report after staff.

"All right, Comrade Major, let's have it." The Resident's face was angry, angrier than Lenev, sitting nearby, had ever seen it.

"The good news, Comrade General, is that we have found someone to tie us to Cornelius."

"Yes?" The Resident was surprised. What he'd been hearing from this clown at the staff conference was only bad news.

"Yes, Comrade General. We traced all the telephone calls from Cornelius's room when he was at the Metropole. There was only one of interest. It was to the tourist desk at the airport, their private line. It's not listed, so we assumed he would have to know someone there. One of my men posing as UDBA checked it out. A clerk at the ticket counter nearby thought she remembered the tourist girl talking to someone answering Cornelius's description. We waited and photographed the girl. Then—again posing as UDBA—our man asked her about Cornelius. She denied knowing him. But at the hotel when we showed the picture to the staff, a bellboy remembered seeing them together. They'd kissed goodbye at the door as she'd left him one evening. We presume they're intimate. I've ordered a twenty-four-hour surveillance on her. We've tapped the tourist office line and her house; she lives with her parents. So far nothing, but if Cornelius is around, it stands to reason he'll get in touch with her."

The Resident's face relaxed. This was better news than he'd expected.

"Well, Komiakov, that's not too bad. Still, I think you may be overdoing it, having our men use UDBA papers so much. That's risky business."

"I realize that, Comrade General." The major's face became very depressed. His tone made the Resident suspicious.

"Oh?"

"Yes, Comrade General. Our man who interviewed the girl at the airport was arrested there, fortunately just after he'd given the camera to his partner."

"Arrested?" The Resident glared at the major.

"Apparently by UDBA, Comrade General, and within just a few minutes of talking to the girl."

"So she knew that he was not UDBA, even though his documents were perfect?"

"It would appear to be the case, Comrade General."

"And how do you imagine, Comrade Major, that this little girl could detect such an excellent forgery?"

"Our staff discussed that, Comrade General. It is the

opinion that she must herself be UDBA. Naturally she would know who at the airport is and isn't UDBA. I fear that is the only explanation. It may also explain her interest in Cornelius."

"How very cleverly managed, Comrade Komiakov. And our man, can he be identified as KGB? If so, Soviet-Yugoslav relations are in for a very bad period."

Komiakov hesitated, pushing his toe against the carpet.

"Well?" the Resident roared.

"It is possible, Comrade General. He is a regular staffer here. No doubt the Yugoslavs will have his photograph on file."

"I see." The Resident turned to his aide. "Lenev, you know UDBA fairly well. What will they do?"

"They have several options, Comrade General. They can hold him incommunicado and put on a show trial. With UDBA documents on him, that will not improve our image here. If they want to avoid such a major incident, they can release him quietly with a non-public protest from their Foreign Ministry to our ambassador. Or they may just keep him in prison. They might shoot him, but I doubt it since he's a pawn they might use in an exchange with us some day. I think they will opt for the quiet prison cell."

"I agree, Colonel Lenev. It will be up to Moscow to decide whether our ambassador asks for him back. That is unlikely. It embarrasses us and puts us in a position of being blackmailed."

"So, perhaps," Komiakov ventured quietly, "there's really no harm done. One man shot or in prison in return for this information: doesn't the Comrade General agree it's a good trade?"

"Ask me that, Major, after I know the Yugoslavs have decided against a show trial. If there is a trial, I shall be recalled to Moscow." Pavlichenko, the old fox, knew this time he might lose his bushy tail to the hounds. As Resident he was responsible. He shrugged. There was nothing to be done.

He looked sternly at Komiakov, this idiot. "Now Comrade Major, as you were about to report in the staff conference, what about the surveillance of the CIA staffers?"

"Yes, Comrade General. We have had considerable success in that all those we believe to be CIA staffers have been continuously watched. There was one brief failure."

"Yes?" The Resident was suddenly oppressed with fatigue. He knew what Komiakov would say.

"The team did lose Chief of Station Franklin, General Franklin I believe is his rank, Comrade General. He evaded surveillance at 7:08 p.m. yesterday, and we didn't pick him up until he returned to his house by taxi at 11:32 p.m. The watch on the embassy says he did return there at 9:04, leaving again by cab at 11:15.".

"Plenty of time for a meeting with Cornelius or anyone else, even with our defector, should he already be out. You recognize that, don't you Komiakov?"

"Yes, Comrade General."

"Dismissed!" The Resident shouted the order.

The major left the room. The Resident leaned back in his leather swivel chair to stare at the ceiling. Lenev quietly departed. He knew the Resident's moods. This one could go on for days.

Patrick Brown, the wallet papers showing him from Shannon, carried a lightweight Irish wool plaid jacket over his arm as he walked briskly to the trolley stop. With bushy eyebrows and a well-trimmed, curly beard, he was every bit the well-off bachelor tourist. Of Norman Borg, he had kept only the camera. Patrick paused here and there as he walked, looking at the shop windows. He strolled across the park, bought roasted chestnuts from a vendor, watched the doting young fathers with youngsters in their arms. From shop-window reflections, glances as corners were turned, it appeared that Patrick had no followers.

Patrick arrived at the address, a narrow side street off Proleterski Street, between the embassy and the Metropole Hotel. It was a tiny flower shop hugged by a tobacconist on one side and a ladies' dress shop on the other. As he entered, a tall, blonde woman of about thirty, busty under a thin blouse, greeted him in English.

"You're Mr. Munson's visitor?"

"That I am," affirmed Patrick Brown.

"Please come with me." She led him behind the counter, through a small room where flowers were prepared, into a back room, which was a kitchen. In these old buildings, tradesmen evidently lived behind their shops.

"He'll be along in a moment," said the girl. "Do you want some coffee?"

"I'd like that," said Patrick.

As she moved to the ancient stove, a side door opened and a gray-haired, powerfully muscular man entered. Gray-eyed and pale-skinned, there was a faint resemblance to the Nordic blonde. The man held out his hand to Patrick.

"Glad to meet you, Mr. Brown. This is my niece, Kirsten."

The three shook hands all around, Munson explaining that his niece had married a Yugoslav who taught in the university here. She ran this little shop. She and her husband lived here during the week. They had a grander house in the country.

"My uncle tells me that his Consul General asked Sam to show you Yugoslavian birds. Sam's an avid birdlover, of course, but I've never met a wildlife society executive before."

So that's what he was. Sam would have to get him out of this before the conversation went much further. Sam did.

"Oh, we'll have a splendid time in the country these next few days. Markus from the Swedish Embassy is coming along too, I think. Come on, Patrick, finish your coffee. Let's be on our way." Munson looked at his niece. "I'll check the shop before we go."

"The bell hasn't rung. No one's come in," she protested.

"Just to be sure, that's all." Munson went quickly toward the shop and returned smiling.

"No customers in sight." He glanced at Ben, who understood.

"We're on our way," he said to his niece. "See you in a few days. Don't worry if we're longer; there are some splendid migratory pathways to be seen this time of year."

He led Ben down a back corridor which, several doors later, opened into a garage in which was an old Peugeot. Sam opened the garage doors; a narrow alley stood revealed. He surveyed it carefully before beckoning Patrick into the car. They drove out.

"I suppose I should do something to prove who I am," Ben said. He felt there must be some ritual at this point, otherwise how did either know the other was not a ringer?

"Not necessary for me," Munson said. "I checked out the clothes you're wearing before they went to the safe house. I also maintain the beard supplies. Your fuzz there is called a tile beard because it's squarish. Did you know that?"

Ben laughed. "But how do I know you're CIA Munson instead of KGB or UDBA Munson?" asked Ben.

"The Chief of Station anticipates all," said his companion, handing Ben a tiny tape recorder. "Go ahead. Play it."

Ben pressed the "on" button. He heard Luke Franklin's voice.

"Ben, if the man who gives you this drives a dumpy Peugeot, has gray eyes, gray hair, a lovely blonde niece, he can tell you exactly what I drank the first night you and I met in a basement. Ask him questions about who else was in the basement and what happened there. If you like his answers stay with him. If you don't, use your .38 to persuade him to let you off at the next corner. Now, erase this tape."

Ben did, and relaxed.

"The adventure begins," he said. "What now?"

"Like the famous Hungarian recipe for goulash, 'first you steal a chicken' . . . well, we steal a car."

"Just like that. Any car?"

"Oh no, we borrow a special car. Remember Markus, whom I mentioned to my niece? She is, by the way, unwitting. She believes I'm assistant commercial attaché, which, by the way, I am. The station doesn't have much by way of resources here so I exploit my family. If I weren't so slippery, I'd get them in trouble. Today, for example. Took me two hours to shake the KGB team on my tail. I must be getting old. Finally had to resort to measures I abhor. Two of the bastards were really breathing on me so I turned into an apartment house hallway, turned my gun on them, and pushed them both down a flight of stairs?"

"Really?" Till now, there had been no hint of violence so far in this game Ben was playing. His .38 smelled of it but it had seemed a gentleman's game of wits. Big-muscle Munson had violated the rules.

"I sense your disapproval," Munson said, "but they probably didn't hurt at all for they were, be assured, unconscious by the time they reached the bottom of the stairs." He paused. "If there was a bottom. It seemed to me like at least a double basement, maybe a pit. Oh well, I'm sure the KGB pensions wives."

"And you really did do that?"

"I really did do that," affirmed Munson. "If I hadn't, our little tour could not have left at all. Your general would be stranded in a trout pool in Lower Slobovia."

The Peugeot turned into a driveway before a small, neat building. Next door, a larger stone building flew the flag of Sweden on a pole jutting out above the entrance.

"Our Swedish allies," said Munson, "although they deny it. Today, thanks to Markus, they are allies indeed."

Munson stopped the car in front of the garage, unlocked and raised the door, drove in, and closed the door. The garage was immaculate. Two other cars stood there: one a black Mercedes with a fender flagstaff, the other a black Volvo.

"Your transportation, Excellency." Munson gestured to the immense Mercedes.

"You're kidding," said Ben.

"No. If one is to steal, steal big. Markus is my accomplice. He's the chargé d'affaires here. The ambassador, you see, is on vacation. The Mercedes is his car, but when he's away the chargé can drive it, or rather, have it driven. They have a Yugoslav handyman who doubles as chauffeur. Anyway, Markus is lending it to me."

"I should think he could get his ass in a sling doing that." To Ben the thing sounded crazy.

"Oh indeed he can," agreed Munson, "which is why he won't fuss to anybody about it. I've got Markus trained."

"How?"

"Easy. In the first place, we both speak Swedish. In the second, he's screwing Kirsten, whom you met, but neither Kirsten's husband nor Markus's wife is exactly in on that. Add that I play poker with a bunch which includes Markus and that I hold a marker for about $5500 with Markus's name on it. I traded Markus the $5500 for this car and his quiet tongue."

"You forgave a personal debt for CIA business? That's noble, but bad business," said Ben.

"To the contrary. Ignoble and good business," contradicted Munson. "Franklin knows all. The Agency reimburses me the five-and-a-half K and I get nice things written in my personal file."

"Unprincipled," said Ben, "but why do we want the ambassador's car? It's not likely to go unnoticed."

"No traffic in and out of Roumania goes unnoticed. If one is to be remarked anyway, it might as well be respectfully. Besides, haven't you always wanted to be a diplomat?"

It was the last thing Ben had ever wanted. He said so.

"Too bad, because you are becoming Markus Adolphson, the chargé d'affaires. I'm your chauffeur. When we go into Roumania, we do it in style."

"And getting out? Do we bring the general along as an adopted child?" asked Ben.

"You do pose a little problem there, I've got to admit," said Munson, "but each day's troubles are sufficient thereto. Your suitcase, by the way, is packed. And your papers. Markus would have hated that part, giving me his documents to forge, so I spared him. Plucked them from his coat at poker one night. He was so grateful to me the next day when I found them—under the table, I told him—you can't imagine it."

Ben could imagine it.

THIRTEEN

A file of cars waited at the border for Yugoslavian exit customs and passport checks and incoming Roumanian customs and visas. Uniforms in gray, gray-green, khaki, blue. Guns in many sizes, official talk in many languages, with pleasant greetings in none.

The black ambassadorial Mercedes, the fender flagstaff hooded but there for all to see, elicited courtesy and attention on both sides. Munson, wearing a chauffeur's uniform, began in Swedish and, that failing as he knew it would, spoke in English. Markus the charge had gray hair, wore dark glasses, dark gray pants, a high-sheen white turtleneck shirt, and had next to him, casually folded, an elegant black, lightweight-wool sport coat. Casual decadence was the mode. Ben as Markus was seated in the recessed cushions of the back seat, which was unusually high. He said nothing as the chauffeur handed his papers back and forth. The visas were for tourism only, nothing official. The guards on both sides saluted as the papers were returned. There would be a call to Bucharest alerting the Foreign Ministry. Should the Ministry in turn call the Swedish Embassy there, nothing would be amiss. The real Markus had been persuaded to cable Sophia saying he was making a short vacation trip that way.

Immediately behind them as they passed the border was

a young man on a motorcycle. No typical European scooter, this was a big, Japanese Kawasaki, all polished chrome and black. Markus saw Munson's eye flicker backwards to the bike. Was there something wrong? Munson didn't say.

The drive down the Danube is through pleasant country, with spurs of hills, small valleys, the great river itself. The highway is good, there are places to eat, and both country motor campsites and hotels in the small towns offer accommodations. Any vacation traveler can enjoy Bloc countries as long as he is willing to forego speaking frankly with citizens, being served graciously, or enjoying a standard of amenities much above that of a Great Plains wagon train of the 1840s.

After a lunch of sausage and beer, Ben's stomach hurt. Here he was, traveling behind the Curtain falsely documented as a Swedish diplomat, on a mission to spirit out a Soviet general, and he was griping about the food.

"We have to stop here." Munson pointed to the map as they sat in the big car after lunch. "The main thing is to be able to leave the car for twenty-four hours or so without being missed. This evening we make contact with Zanko, the Bucharest agent, exactly two miles out of Orsova, just off the highway."

"Have you ever been here before?" Ben asked.

"I drove through with my family once just to see the place. Diplomatic passport, of course."

"But the Belgrade station has pulled defectors out?" Ben hoped for reassurance.

"I can't tell tales out of school, but you can assume they have. Speaking generally, and don't tell the CI I told you, it's usually not such a rush. You know, a Minister decides he's had it, lets us know, and then waits in his office until the station has it all worked out. Maybe he stays in place for years. When he does come out, it's easiest if he just drives his own car over the border on business or drops in to stay on a routine trip abroad. The spookier you do it the harder it is. You save that stuff for the big ones. We used our own light plane trying a coup near here, but it got shot down. We also used a car trunk once, but the border police were on a big anti-narcotics kick and poked behind the trunk's false backside. Big surprise. Everybody got shot. That was last year. As you see, our record isn't spotless."

Ben said he hoped Sam was kidding. Sam said he wasn't. They drove in silence for a while, then Ben asked,

"I suppose you know where we store this buggy when we make our rendezvous point?"

"I don't," said Sam, "but our pickup better have a plan. This thing attracts notice."

"So does the motorcyclist on our tail," said Ben. "He's been behind us, off and on, since the border."

"I know," said Sam.

"Anybody you know?"

"Yep. That's Joe, our technician and commo man. He fixes cars that break down and, if we need a radio, he's got one on the frequency that gets us through to our stations in Bucharest and Belgrade. He'll stay near the car when we lay over."

"Well, that's a nice surprise. Does he cook?"

"Probably. He's also a mechanical genius and a damn good shot."

Ben was pleased. Here among aliens and enemies it was comforting to know that there was one lone man on a motorcycle who was a friend.

On schedule, in pitch darkness, the car reached the point on the map beyond Orsova. They turned off a dirt side road after driving north for one mile. They saw the lights of the motorcycle follow them as far as the turn, then disappear.

Maybe Joe was covering the rendezvous in case something went wrong.

Lights and motor off, they sat in the darkness and waited.

The knock on the car door made them jump. Sam opened the door slowly, a lighted flashlight in his hand. For the first time since he had carried it, Ben had his hand on his .38, the safety off, the weapon hidden beneath the folds of a sweater on his lap.

At first the man seemed an apparition in the flashlight's beam—dark brown eyes, brown skin, long black unwashed hair, even white teeth, bearded, an open leather shirt, a remarkable conical fur hat on his head. He was about thirty, handsome and quick-gestured. He must be a gypsy. And he smelled like one.

"Munson, Adolphson?" The gypsy's English was passable.

"Yes," said Munson, "and you are . . .?"

"Zanko." That was the right name.

"You came here . . .?" Zanko let the sentence dangle.

"To fish the Cerna," Sam replied. That, too, was the right answer, prearranged between the two stations.

"Okay," said Zanko, "let's get this car out of sight. Follow me." He ran alongside the front bumper, almost invisible in the night. A few hundred yards ahead he signalled the car down a narrow track, through a wood and to the edge of a field. A large haystack loomed. Zanko guided them slowly to its base. "Out of the car," the gypsy commanded. As they got out, a dozen men appeared from the night, all swarthy, all gypsies, all with pitchforks and most with the conical hats. Within a few minutes the haystack had moved. Like a broody hen, it enveloped the car.

"Okay." Zanko led them into the wood, along the

track. They soon came upon a campfire and a gypsy encampment, something Ben had never seen. They were, as in the old pictures, barrel-vaulted caravans, with horses still in harness. There was no one in sight except an old woman who, as the men approached, smothered the fire.

"Here, in my caravan," said Zanko. He showed them the sharply angled wooden steps that led up to a door in the back. The door opened and a lighted interior greeted them. No sooner were they inside than the wagon began to move. the lamp swayed, the sound of horses' hooves muffled on forest leaves and sandy soil.

"Good," said Zanko. "Now give me your clothes and change into these." He handed them filthy pants, faded shirts, well-worn leather boots, and ancient wool hats.

"Okay, now this. Rub it in hard before you put your shirts on—arms, neck, face, any place to be seen." It was a can of greasy stain, like shoe polish. "Rub it in, I said." Their gypsy was an impatient authority. They rubbed and inspected one another. Zanko made the final inspection, adding the stain to an earlobe here, a finger there.

"Okay, now put on the shirts."

Zanko looked them over. "Now the hair." He gave both men wigs of black hair, bowl cut and long. They were grimy to the touch. Ben took off Markus's gray hair and handed it to Zanko, who added it to the pile of clothes they'd discarded.

"All right, you're gypsies now. But don't talk if anybody other than my people are around, and keep out of sight as much as you can. Here." He handed them a tired deck of playing cards. "If someone inspects the camp, be sure they see you playing."

Zanko opened a carved wood chest and pulled out a full bottle of white liquid. It smelled of licorice, like ouzo, or arak.

"Drink," he commanded. Ben took a swig from the bottle and handed it to Sam. Sam licked his lips as the sweet, hot liquor went down. Zanko took the bottle and raised it to his own lips. A gurgling half-pint sped down. Zanko grinned at them. He walked forward carrying their folded clothes towards the front of the room, pulled up a floorboard, brought out a box, placed the items neatly in it, covered the hole again, and hammered the boards in place.

"Now, try to sleep."

He left them and went forward to join the man up front driving the horses through the night.

Ben heard the uphill creaking of wagons in front and behind. A forced march this, and a good thing too.

To his surprise, he slept through the bone-jarring ride; it was motionlessness that awakened him. The caravan had stopped. Bright morning sun peeped through the curtained windows of the wagon. There was a hum of voices outside. Ben got up—no need to dress, he'd slept in his clothes but for the boots—to look outside. Sam was still asleep. Ben went down the rickety wooden stairs to the campsite, to find other gypsies already gathered. Zanko was near a campfire tended by two women, both in long dresses, their heads covered by shawls.

Zanko got up as Ben approached and offered a tin cup of near-boiling tea.

"Breakfast?" he asked.

"Great," said Ben, sipping the tea cautiously. Zanko brought him a loaf of peasant bread and, tearing off an end, handed it to him along with some freshly picked berries. Zanko poured his own tea from cup to saucer and noisily lapped it up.

"Drink it our way," he commanded. "Otherwise everyone knows you're a *gadji*."

"*Gadji?*"

"No gypsy," grunted Zanko.

Obediently Ben drank his first saucerful of tea.

"We'll camp here until after lunch," Zanko said, "to rest the horses and do the chores. Then we move out. We should get to Baile Herculane by dusk and upstream on the Cerna by midnight. We should find your party shortly after sunrise. We'll come downstream a different path, bypassing Baile Herculane so they don't get to wondering about why we go up and down so fast. Back to your auto, with *bakht*, sometime the day after."

"*Bakht?*"

"Romani for luck. We need it," said Zanko, unsmiling.

"Who's the woman over there?" Ben had noticed a grand old woman seated in a chair, wearing a purple silk blouse embroidered with yellow fern leaves, a black skirt, a white scarf, and a gold chain. She was being attended by several other women.

"She's the *phari dai*, our wise woman. She has the magic. She knows you and your friend are with us. When she's ready, she'll send for you."

"She looks very queenly," observed Ben.

"Have the power, be a queen," replied Zanko.

"No king here then?"

"No king. Only a *voivode*, a chief."

"Will I meet him?" Ben asked.

"You have," replied Zanko. "I'm the *voivode*."

"Oh. Well I am honored, *Voivode*, to be your guest."

"We are honored to have you as our guest," replied the gypsy in a courtly way. "You call me Zanko. But as I warned you last night, you are to speak to no others. It is not good that English be heard in our camp: trees listen, horses hear, flowers talk."

"Do you expect us to have trouble?"

"A gypsy's life is always trouble in these countries. They

despise us, they try to make us settle in towns, they force us
into factories, they force our children into schools,
sometimes send us to camps. My father was killed in a camp
by the Germans, my uncle was killed by the Russians, my
brother is in a Roumanian jail. Communists do not like
independent people. Now I pretend to be a Communist so
that I do not have to be a slave."

"I'm sorry," said Ben, "sorry that you all suffer so."

"It has its advantages to you, my friend. Without a dead
uncle and imprisoned brother, I wouldn't be working for
your people in Bucharest. It is the wounded animal that is
most dangerous. Eat your bread. You will need strength."

Ben ate the coarse, dark bread. It was good.

Ben and Sam did nothing that morning except to observe
the camp life and keep out of the way. The *phari dai* looked
their way once as they sat sunning themselves, backs
against the spoked wooden wheel of the *vurdon*, the
caravan, but she was the only one even to glance their way.
Ben and Sam were careful to blend with that casual theater,
the game of not noticing, life saving should strangers be
about. But they did notice one girl especially, strikingly
beautiful. Bangles, beads, black hair, a winsome
smile—for Zanko only—and a low-cut blouse. In that
setting of the forest clearing, she was a kind of perfection.
Good guests, neither man even spoke of her to the other.

Lunch was served from a boiling kettle on wooden
plates, the utensils each man's knife, his fingers, and a large
wooden community spoon for a dipper. With the dark
bread and cabbage, the meat was delicious.

"You like it?" Zanko asked.

"Sure do," said Sam, his lips greasy. "What is it?"

"Our specialty. *Niglo*."

"Which is?"

"Hedgehog," said Zanko. "*Gadji* don't eat it, but then

many people are misled by appearances."

Ben sensed the larger meaning. "I think *gadji* underestimate the gypsies."

For the first time, Zanko smiled.

Dusk fell soon after the wagons rolled by Baile Herculane, traveling a dirt trail that left the village a mile to the east. Zanko was doing his best to keep local contact to a minimum. The gypsy aloofness served them all well on this journey. Men make their own *bakht*, thought Ben.

And other men ruin it. He saw the headlights of the jeep as the vehicle, swirling dust behind it, honked its way past the horses and wagons until it reached the head of the column. There it swung around, blocking the road. Five men, all wearing the gray-blue uniform of the border patrol, jumped out. Their automatic rifles were menacing, Ben saw, for he was sitting with Zanko on the driver's seat of the lead wagon.

"Ignore them if they speak to you," Zanko whispered. "Let me talk. This is routine. They will ask for papers, poke through the wagons, insult the women, threaten. The woman in back will speak for your friend. Do not worry," he paused before he said slowly, "yet."

The corporal spoke curtly to Zanko in Roumanian. Zanko replied in wheedling, deferential tones. The corporal, cradling his weapon in his arm, reached up for the papers. He snarled at Ben. Obviously his papers, too, were required. Ben pulled out the dog-eared, dirty identification papers that Zanko had given him the night before. The photo was so covered with grease that no matching of paper to carrier could be possible. Only the conical fur hat and long hair could be seen in the photo. It satisfied the corporal. He handed the papers back as his squad began to move down the line of halted wagons, their boots heavy on the wooden stairs, their arrogant voices loud in the forest night. No one attended the jeep.

Zanko nervously rubbed his thumbs over the reins. Down the line a horse whinnied, in the woods a screech owl hooted, in the distance an animal howled. A dog, wondered Ben, or a wolf? This was wolf country. A bat flitted by the parking light of the jeep. The owl screeched again.

Four of the five soldiers had returned to the jeep. The corporal asked something of one of them, pointing to a wagon behind them. The corporal kicked the dirt with his boot. It was then the scream of the woman pierced the night. The three soldiers looked at the corporal. The corporal waited. There was a second scream, again a young woman. Zanko's horse pawed the ground nervously, tail twitching, ears up. Zanko began to get down from the high seat, slowly. Ben could see he was taut, a coiled spring. The corporal levelled his weapon at Zanko, snarling him into immobility, and then, commanding a gun to be trained on Zanko, strode slowly toward the third wagon back.

Ben did not actually see the whip flick into the face of the young soldier, bringing a gush of blood around the eyes. He could only infer the lash. The whip had been in Zanko's hand all along. The soldier yelled in pain, dropping his weapon as his hands sought his bloodied face, his blinded eyes. The other soldiers, startled, raised their weapons to fire, but Zanko was already down, running to the wagon where the woman had screamed. The soldiers raced after Zanko. Ben jumped to the ground to grab the automatic rifle lying there. Its owner was rocking and moaning with pain, blood-blinded. Ben took up the weapon and ran behind the soldiers to the third wagon. He was aware of the screech of the owl close at hand. It seemed to be in his ear.

The wagon was swaying to the cacophony of a struggle within. The body of the corporal lay on the ground beneath the high steps, a great red rip along his side. The two soldiers were on their way up the steps when Ben shouted.

"Halt! One more step and I'll kill you." His gun barrel pointed between the shoulder blades of the man higher on the steps. Both swung around on him, readying their weapons. They could only turn awkwardly, balanced as they were on the steep wooden steps. Ben hoped to hell the safety catch was off as he dropped to a kneeling position and pressed the trigger. Kneeling was a forethought, making him a smaller target and making the angle of his fire high so as not to enter the wagon lower than the roofline to endanger Zanko and the women.

The gun jumped about in his hand as the bullets barked. Ben was conscious of the brass cartridges spilling out like cold sparks from a welder. Both soldiers levitated briefly as the bullets' force elevated them, then, gurgling and wheezing, they toppled from the steps to the ground.

Ben jumped over the bodies and clambered up the steps, kicking the door open. Inside was chaos. The beautiful gypsy girl, naked except for a torn blouse around her neck and her stockings, lay on the bed, her legs apart, her torso bruised with welts. She was gasping, her eyes staring vacantly. A man, naked from the waist down, was crumpling to the floor. In slow motion, he was sliding from on top of the woman as blood gushed from his neck. A strong man wielding a knife, pulling a man's head backwards by the chin when gripping from behind, would kill with such a sheep's throat slicing as that. Zanko was kneeling, his twice-bloodied knife in his hand. His face was in agony. He cried as he moved toward the girl, reaching almost blindly for something with which to shut out her violation. Ben, seeing a blanket on the other cot, handed it to Zanko.

"Zorka," murmured Zanko to the girl. He buried his

face against hers and wept. Slowly, a gasp at first but then welling up, the girl began to moan and then, her chest heaving, to cry.

Ben grabbed the naked feet of the soldier and pulled him across the floor. The man's buttocks were pimply, and he seemed smaller than he had in life. It was an easy pull, for the floor was greased with blood. Furiously, Ben dragged the body out of the door, letting the face crash down the steps, the nose bone crunching as it smashed against the first tread, until that body joined its two fellows on the ground. Only when that was done did Ben become conscious of the ring of gypsy men around him, and Sam.

"Jesus," said Sam.

Two of the gypsies crossed themselves. The others stood silently, staring at the heap of corpses. None stirred. They were pushed from behind by the *phari dai* as that fat old woman made her determined way up the steps of the caravan. As she passed, she stared bitterly at Ben. He heard her mutter *"Melalo."* She entered the wagon and, a few minutes later, a red-eyed Zanko came uncertainly down the steps, pale, uncoordinated, in shock. The men began talking in frightened whispers. An old man among them, his beard white, tried to calm them but, Ben sensed, they were near to panic. The old man turned to Ben and Sam and, in broken German, asked a question.

"He wants to know what they're to do," said Sam. "It's a good question, wouldn't you say?" Sam managed a thin smile. "You're not very slow on your feet, are you, partner?"

Ben, relaxing for the first time, felt his entire body shaking. Uncontrollable, as though he would vibrate loose. And yet, to his astonishment, as he looked at the gun in his hand, it was moving but slightly. Thank God I don't feel sick, he thought. He was surprised that all he felt was shock and cold anger.

"The bastards," he muttered.

"Former bastards," Sam corrected. "And now that you've got that off your chest, what in fact are we going to do?" Ben realized that Sam, like the white-haired old uncle there, expected him to decide.

Ben's voice was firm. "Tell the old man," he said to Sam, "to take the bodies and bury them in the woods. Keep the uniforms. Check on the fellow up front who got whipped, tie him up and tend to his eyes, if he has any left. Clean up the slaughterhouse. They'll have some lanterns. And Sam, ask if any of them knows a good place to conceal that jeep."

Sam spoke in German to the older man, obviously a respected elder. There followed a short conversation.

"They'll bury the bodies, have the women clean up, and find a place to hide the jeep," Sam reported. "You want to drive it in or shall I?"

"I'll do it, Sam. You supervise the cleanup. Be damned sure there aren't any spent cartridges on the ground. And have them repaint, stuff, whatever they can do to hide the holes I shot in this wagon. I want these caravans to be able to pass a hostile inspection. What time is it, by the way?"

Sam looked at his watch. "Nine-thirty. Why?"

"If Zanko was right on his reckoning, that will put us, counting the delay, about three hours from where our general is camped. Three hours by horse and wagon that is, but what do you think by jeep? About thirty minutes?"

"Depends on the road, but probably," said Sam.

"So if we take a chance and use the jeep, if—and it's a big if—there aren't any villages between here and the general, we can pick him up and get back, and, if we're lucky, still get rid of the jeep just after sunup. That way we can get this bunch here heading downhill again to camp a mile or two back. That may help save their ass."

"And if someone spots us in the jeep and wants a nice conversation in Roumanian?"

"We don't stop, Sam, not for anybody. Tell the old man I've changed my mind. He's to clean up, turn around, and camp in the woods off this trail two miles back down. We'll put on the soldier suits and go looking for our general."

The two busied themselves stripping the bodies. Gypsy women, kerosene lanterns in hand, were scouring the ground. Ben handed the bloody jackets to them, making signs for scrubbing and sewing.

"Those will be damn cold to wear wet at night," said Sam.

"We haven't much choice. The uniforms are only helpful at a distance, anyway. If anyone does spot us, at least it gives the *Tchurari* here an alibi. There'll be space between us and them."

"*Tchurari?*" asked Sam.

"Name of this tribe. Zanko told me."

"Ah," said Sam, "and does your wisdom also encompass what to do with that soldier boy they're bringing to us now? Christ, he is a mess."

A trussed-up soldier was being hustled toward them. One of the women was preparing a bandage, another had sprinkled herbs on the wound, stopping the flow of blood. Zanko's whip had been kinder than Ben had feared. The forehead skin was split to the bone, but the eyes were untouched. The soldier, recovered from the terror of what he must have thought to be sightlessness, was in an ugly mood, snarling and cursing. He had bitten one of the women caring for his flayed head.

"He's a problem, all right. We can't take him with us. If we let him go he becomes the death warrant of the *Tchurari*. If the gypsies keep him and get searched, the same thing, a death warrant."

"There is a solution, Ben." Sam's voice was penetrating.

"Murder him? Listen Sam, that was my first killing, but it was a fair fight. I'm no murderer."

"I suppose you expect me to do it?" asked Sam.

"No, I don't *want* you to do it."

"Well maybe the uncle here has an idea." Sam spoke to the elder in German. The gypsies huddled among themselves speaking Romani. The elder finally replied to Sam.

"They'll keep him," he told Ben. "Hanged if I know what they'll do with him, though. Hide him in one of their base fiddles?"

"Don't look a gift horse in the mouth, Sam. We've got to get cracking."

The jeep traveled slowly over the forest trail, bouncing and rattling. Sam was driving. Ben sat beside him, an automatic rifle across his lap. Zanko had assured them before they left that there were no habitations on the way up the Cerna to the fishing camp. Zanko had been exact, in his own way, about distances: past the first turn, over the old bridge, beyond the big rock, note the barren hill, stop at the pickup point where the two streams meet the Cerna, one from either side, "where the tallest pine tree grows."

"Rather hard for a stranger to spot in the night," Ben had said. "How about kilometers?"

Zanko had no idea.

A new moon came out as they crawled along. Ben used a flashlight from the jeep to find the bridge. He missed the big rock and bare hill nevertheless, but did find the two streams by stopping every hundred feet. It took them two hours to go fourteen miles. At least the *Tchurari* were safe, and if and when they found the general, the return would be quicker. At the two streams, by a big tree—how would he ever know in the dark if it were the tallest—they pulled the jeep into the woods. Spelling each other in two-hour watches, they tried to sleep.

Dawn came. The sun climbed behind the mountains and shot cheery hot rays into this wild, high country.

"Now, how do we find the general?" asked Sam.

"He's to show here each of the three days, fishing rod in hand, just after dawn. For breakfast trout, I assume."

"And you think he'll see this little army of ours and come over to introduce himself as a defector?" Sam asked the same question that had been bothering Ben.

"We told him to show at the map coordinate and wait for the high-sign. This is the map coordinate, or at least the nearest point on the road. Franklin was sure of that. Myagkov will be wary, but he's got a good cover and he should figure that anything that's here must be for him. He's making a double-or-nothing play."

"Exactly."

"So what the hell. All we can do is hope." Ben sat down on a log. It was a lovely morning in the mountains.

Sam was the first one to hear the whistling, a merry tune from *Petrushka*, perhaps. A fisherman came wading downstream, moving slowly toward them. He was a big man of about sixty with high rubber boots, a wicker basket on his waist, a fly rod, a straw hat, a yellow sweater, bushy eyebrows—and a surprise. For behind him trailed a younger fellow, lurching under his awkward load: a spare rod, a giant picnic hamper—it looked to weigh twenty-five pounds—blankets, and a transistor radio. He wore the uniform of a Russian lieutenant, a ludicrous dress in his present situation as angler's valet.

Ben and Sam had not counted on General Myagkov defecting with an orderly.

The angler scowled at the Roumanian soldiers, their ill-fitting uniforms, the laundered jackets still damp. The bullet and knife holes hastily sewn by the gypsy women gave the uniforms a seedy look. The general's aide, Lieutenant Zemskov, stared contemptuously at this derelict and rumpled pair.

Ben nodded politely to the angler, smiling, saying nothing. The Russian lieutenant spoke harshly in Russian. Sam and Ben gave the palms-up sign of noncomprehension. The lieutenant, to Ben's relief obviously out of languages, sniffed haughtily. The angler spoke, but not in Roumanian, of that Ben was sure. He tried another tongue, Polish, perhaps. Then German.

"Bingo," said Sam under his breath, returning a German greeting. "I'll ask him if his butler knows any German. If he doesn't, I'll find out just what kind of an entourage our general has in mind."

A German conversation ensued in which, as Sam told Ben, the proper identifications were exchanged. To specific queries about the general's sister Anna, there were satisfactory replies. As for the lieutenant, General Myagkov explained that to avoid suspicion his aide must initially come along until they went covert. The general was sure that they would think of some place to park the aide.

The general was genuinely at ease, as though encountering the CIA wearing Roumanian uniforms along the reaches of Mount Gogul was quite an everyday matter. Hands behind his head, whistling cheerily in the jeep's back seat, he seemed carefree. He had placed himself in the hands of the United States, that great power? What, his demeanor seemed to say, could possibly go wrong? There was something childish about this defector, Ben concluded.

Ben didn't know what the general told Lieutenant Zemskov, who was also quite at home in the bouncing jeep. He too had faith, hardly in the Agency, but certainly in Myagkov.

They had driven quickly for the first few kilometers. It

was not yet 6:30 when they encountered the foot soldiers, wearing the same gray-blue uniforms of the night before, but today with looks of concentrated boredom. The sergeant leading the sloppily arrayed platoon—obviously it was only a routine march—held up his hand as the jeep approached. Ben felt his neck grow cold, hairs bristling. Was calamity to come so soon? The sergeant began a Roumanian address to Roumanian corporal Ben, but before three words were out the general whispered to his lieutenant. Lieutenant Zemskov, in turn, interrupted the sergeant, speaking in Russian with the utter and demeaning arrogance of the czar's hussars. The sergeant, understanding and deferential, turned red, threw a salute so emphatically obedient that it threatened to displace some vertebrae, and marched his men off smartly. The general smiled, Zemskov returned a bland eye to the forest, and Sam, inquiring in German, learned that the sergeant had been threatened with Siberia for interfering with a Russian general on his way to town for vacation supplies. Lieutenant Zemskov was as satisfied with the episode as was Ben.

FOURTEEN

As the jeep purred along the dusty forest trail, crossing old log bridges of streams tributary to the Cerna, Ben began to feel euphoric. Perhaps they would pull it off. The general's whistling—he had an array of tunes to best a mockingbird—was infectious. Barrel chested, no neck at all, and—when his outrageous floppy straw hat came off—as bald as a gooney bird, General Myagkov was, as Europeans say, "an unusual." They could not, of course, speak English as long as Zemskov was around. Sam's German was the joining language now.

The jeep arrived at the gypsy camp about 7:00. The gypsies gave no sign of recognition to Ben and Sam. Cool players, thought Ben, how can they be sure who these Russians are? Ben went to find Zanko. The *voivode* was depressed—speech slowed, head down, listless.

"It was a terrible thing that happened last night," said Ben.

Zanko stared at him. "My Zorka, my fiancée, the man raped her. You saw that." His voice was flat.

"Yes."

"And you saved my life. Maybe you will save all our lives if they don't find out that you and I killed their soldiers."

"I'll try."

"But it's too late to save Zorka from shame. She was no

virgin, that is not our custom, but to have been debased by
a swine, an ugly thing . . ."

"Zanko, help her to feel better and then you will marry
her." Ben was afraid it might not be so.

Zanko raised his head. "Of course. What do you think I
am, a beast myself to reject her? I am not like that."

"I was sure of that," said Ben, reassured.

"But enough of Zorka's sorrow, my sorrow. What are we
to do? I can hide one Russian, but you have brought me
two. I have papers for only one. And the jeep. It must go. It
has the stink of death on it."

"Yes, the jeep must go. As for the Russian lieutenant,
why not do this? You give the general presents: wine,
bread, berries, meat, cabbage, a heavy load. I'll pay you for
it, naturally. Invite the general to stay in your camp for
music tonight. He can tell his lieutenant that the girls will
dance for him because he is the first Russian general to
come to your camp. The gypsy girls will honor him. The
general will send the aide back to the fishing camp carrying
your gifts and tell him to wait there. It will be a long walk
back to camp with that load, and the aide will expect the
general to get drunk here and sleep with the girls. He won't
expect him until tomorrow night, or perhaps even the next
day. By the time the lieutenant knows something is wrong,
we should be across the Danube."

"Good for you, yes, but not for us," said Zanko. "When
the Russian is found gone, the authorities will question us.
Torture is not pleasant. No, the lieutenant must see you
drive the general away from camp, toward town. Let him
tell the authorities that the general had gone from our
camp. Look, we will have a feast now, some music,
dancing, and vodka. Let the general get drunk, or appear
to do so. You two also appear drunk and drive the general
away in the jeep. We will all watch you go. Be sure you

drive badly. A few miles down from here the Cerna goes
through a steep canyon, the river is narrow and deep there
and the road—not the one we have taken but the west
fork—goes close to the cliffs. Push the jeep over the edge,
walk eastward through the forest for two miles to find the
dirt road on which we travel back toward Baile Herculane,
hide until you hear our caravans, and we will pick you up.
When the authorities find the jeep, they must consider the
possibility that you were drunk and drove it over the side
and your bodies washed downstream. It solves two
mysteries, what happened to two Roumanian soldiers, and
what happened to a Russian general."

"That's a workable plan, Zanko. But there were five
soldiers in the jeep; two dead still not accounted for by the
jeep accident, and then there's the fellow you whipped.
Where is he, by the way?"

"Ayeee," wailed Zanko softly, "Melalo got him. We sat
the man down next to the forest and Melalo came. Ayeee."

"Who's Melalo? Where did he take him?"

"Melalo is the worst demon in the world. He has two
heads. Melalo brings murder. He is a bloody demon, that
one."

Ben remembered with a start where he'd heard the
name—the old gypsy woman at the airport park in Zagreb.
And again, the *phari dai* as she looked at him, just after
he'd killed the soldiers.

"That Melalo," whispered Ben softly, "the one who sits
on shoulders?"

Zanko looked at Ben. "You know that? Those whom he
adopts he will possess if he can. They can hear him screech
like the owl, they can hear the beating of his wings in their
ears."

"I heard the screech before the shooting, Zanko, but it
was sure as hell an owl, no Melalo."

Zanko drew back. "There are no screech owls in this part of the mountains. None." Zanko scrutinized Ben. "Perhaps Melalo sits on your shoulder, my friend. If so, take care. If so, we too must take care."

Ben, not believing but upset nevertheless, changed the subject.

"We were talking about the missing soldier. What you mean to tell me is that he is dead, isn't that it?"

Zanko shrugged his shoulders. "It must be supposed. Melalo may leave the body with the others for the wolves to find. Soldiers who search for them will find white bone strewn about. They will believe the men got lost and were eaten by wolves."

"Maybe," said Ben. " Convenient if they do." His mind was on the injured man whom "Melalo" had gotten. It was a practical solution, but it was also cold-blooded murder. Ben hadn't been willing to do it himself. He realized he'd lied to himself when he gave the man over to the gypsies, deluding himself that they would not kill him when they must do so to protect themselves.

Ben was becoming a kind of Melalo himself.

"Well, there's nothing for it. Your plan's best," he agreed. "But can't we at least have the party off in the woods somewhere? Get us and the damn jeep out of sight in case anybody else comes wandering down this trail?"

Zanko shrugged. "Sure. We'll take one wagon with the dancing girl and the musicians down the path into the woods. You follow with the jeep. No one will come."

"Good. It will be a breather, at least. We're sitting on dynamite, you know."

"I know," said Zanko, "and all that because your general enjoys a servant. You will, I think, not find him so easy a man to deal with."

Zanko's words were prophetic. Ben and Sam surveyed the twisted frame of the jeep lying against a boulder in the Cerna some hundred and fifty feet below. They had just buried their own Roumanian uniforms, undressed the general, and done what they could to rig him in his gypsy clothes. Not easy, for General Myagkov had not played at getting drunk, he had done it good and proper. Singing along with the gypsy fiddlers in a gravelly baritone, hands on the dancing girl's fanny, and on her breasts when he lunged fast enough, and thence, smiling, to sleep in the jeep's back seat. Zemskov, burdened like a mule, had sadly watched his frivolous, sodden general leave the gypsy camp, driven by two wobbling, vodka-soused soldiers. The tale ought to stand up.

It was hot and heavy work dragging the drunken Myagkov across country to meet the gypsy train. The only trail was one made by goats and deer. They made contact with the gypsies about four in the afternoon, and the general was made up properly and stowed away to sleep in a wobbling wagon. They both breathed more easily. They were still near the Cerna, still above Baile Herculane, some miles from the car and a long way from Belgrade, but so far so good. By midnight they should reach the Mercedes.

They were stretched out on the swaying cots in the rear of Zanko's wagon. Ben was saying, "This has been nothing but close calls. The rhubarb with the patrol, the general's butler, the general drunk—I thought you guys in the Agency planned your operations."

"Not me, 'they.' And they do, on paper back home, with lots of committee meetings. We plan things here, too, but Headquarters always knows better. It doesn't matter. No one can plan the rare case. When it happens it happens, and you do your best. They ought to call our group CI for 'Crisis Improvisation.' That and filling out papers, that's what my job is all about. You're good at the crisis part, but I won't suggest you join the Agency unless you love bureaucracy better. If you live through this, you'll find that's what intelligence is mostly about."

The caravan went through three border patrol points, each one asking for papers, each time the soldiers sloppily bellicose. Stained dark as a berry, his eyebrows shaved while he slept beside the dark woman posing as his wife—who handed his papers to the soldiers—Myagkov snored through it all.

The closer the caravans came to the car, the more nervous Ben became. It was dark. The wagons, each with a rear lantern as a running light, jogged along. Ben took a swig of vodka, then another. Sam, watching him, said,

"Nerves getting you?"

"Will if they can," said Ben. "Like standing on a ladder sharpening a guillotine blade from the under-side. And I know the rope is frayed."

"Like you say, nerves."

The gypsy train reached the woods. They disembarked and hiked to the hayfield.

Zanko was the first to see the figure, dark, shadowy against a haystack near the one under which the car had been buried. He cautioned the other three—the general was now sullenly awake—to stop.

"I see only one," said Zanko. "Looks asleep. I find out." Before they could stop him, Zanko had thrown a stone near the figure. The figure disappeared behind the haystack.

"It's alive anyway," said Sam.

"I'll circle the field and work my way around the back of the stack, maybe see if there are any others," Ben said and crept off, blending with the night.

The others waited five minutes. Ten. No sounds came, except for nightbirds and a breeze in the leaves.

Sam and Zanko started as they heard the footfall behind them. Their eyes had been intent on the field. Sam's hand scurried for the butt of a pistol inside his jacket. Zanko's was reaching for his knife.

The voice behind them was a southern American drawl. "Just Joe here. Don't shoot the help; good help's hard to get these days."

"You scared me shitless." Sam's voice quivered.

Both men laughed. Zanko smiled, easing his over-worked knife back into its sheath.

"Where's the chargé?" asked Joe.

"Out there, fixing up a surprise for you Indian style behind your haystack," smiled Sam.

"Finders keepers." From the woods behind them came Ben's voice. Joe, startled, cried out irritably, "Jesus, man, what in hell are you doin'?"

"When I didn't find anyone at the haystack I had to check the field. Nothing there, so I figured whoever it was had come over here. I had in mind that if we were lucky it would be you, Joe. I'm . . ." he paused, remembering he was never Ben in Roumania, ". . . I'm Markus Adolphson."

The two shook hands.

"Time to go," Zanko ordered abruptly, back to his commanding manner.

"Right," agreed Ben, and reaching into a cigarette pack in his pocket, he brought out a roll of Roumanian bills. "For all the goodies you gave to Lieutenant Zemskov."

Zanko pushed back the money. "No. No money from the man who saved my life, maybe my tribe. Better we are brothers not doing with money."

"Brothers," said Ben, reaching out his hand to clasp Zanko's, "but as for the money, it's not mine. It comes from the government. Take it."

"No. I am no *ciora*."

"*Ciora?*" asked Ben.

"Magpie, a stealing bird. It is the gypsy way, but not from a brother."

"I understand," Ben said. "Sam, take this money, give it to the general, let him pay for the food. It went to his fishing camp, after all."

The general, sleepy-eyed and ill-tempered, did as he was told. Zanko, honor and pocketbook assuaged, moved out to the haystack to free the car. The others busied themselves rubbing off the gypsy grease with cold cream. Then they changed clothes. Sam and Ben into the diplomatic casuals that had been resting under the caravan's floor, the general into a civilian suit Zanko had given him.

Joe had spent a worried but dull four days; the party was, after all, twenty-four hours overdue. No one, he told them, had come near the car or the field. The hay would be another week drying before that happened. Zanko had been sure of the farmer's schedule; the farmer's helper was a settled gypsy, a cousin to Zanko.

Zanko labored by himself an hour to free the car, cleaning it free of dust and stalks, and then showed them the trail to the road. He advised sleeping in the car in the woods, except for Joe, who was to return to his camp near the highway. If they left at dawn they would join the early tourist and truck traffic on the main road.

The general's perch was under the car's rear seat, a mechanical arrangement Joe had seen to while the car was in its Belgrade garage. It was a tight squeeze for the heavy man, his ox-like muscles gone to fat, and the drive to Belgrade was no pleasure. Now Ben understood why the rear seat was high and hard, with only four-inch coils for springs.

No check point flagged them along the Danube. Joe,

traveling behind them, might as well have been a tourist. The border was again a file of waiting cars. In contrast to the Roumanians, the Yugoslav guards seemed cheery. There was no search. The papers were checked perfunctorily. Only Ben, elegant in his white turtleneck and black coat, was alert to the wheezing general in that compartment beneath the seat.

Ben caught a fitful catnap and dreamed of birds—birds which sat on his shoulder, birds which screeched softly in his ear . . . the screech of tires awakened him.

They reached Belgrade that evening without incident. Sam drove them to a safe house, a small cottage behind a large house in a suburban district. Joe left them as the car entered a side alley. Inside the attached garage they extracted Myagkov and helped him—he could hardly walk, so stiff he was—up the steps into the house. The general looked around approvingly. The place was tastefully elegant: thick carpets, heavy draperies, velvet-covered furniture. He plopped onto the sofa and, for the first time, spoke in English.

"Thank you, Comrades. Now if you will, please, food and vodka, then tell me where I am and who you are." It was courteous but no less a command. The general was used to having his way.

"I know where things are," Sam said, "I'll get some food for all of us. We can celebrate. You like champagne, General Myagkov?"

The general nodded, his round face cherubic without those lobster-claw eyebrows.

"Champagne, by all means. But don't forget the vodka."

They were eating slowly and drinking rapidly, as men do when tensions ease in situations which nevertheless remain dangerous.

"So we are in Belgrade, eh? The bridge between East

and West, as the Yugoslavs like to say. Well, let us hope the bridge is solid and our passage unobstructed. They wouldn't, of course, let me out if they knew I was here. I am too much a card for bargaining."

They agreed.

"And who are you? Both CIA? Or Defense Intelligence? In Russia, the GRU would like to attend such functions as this one."

"CIA," said Sam. Ben was about to enter a disclaimer. He was, after all, only a volunteer.

"Yes," smiled the general, "very well done, I must say. You know, when you met me fishing I had strong doubts about that situation. Roumanian soldiers looking as you did?" He shook his head. "CIA looking like you did? No, not that either. Frankly," the general nodded to Ben, "if you hadn't been knowledgeable about my sister Anna, I would have been suspicious. I don't trust these code identifications. Too easily broken, codes, even when my computer makes them. No, a real Russian trusts only family ties, and not all of those. Anna, you see, had described you to me, young man. That red hair under your cap, the scar on your neck, your build, eyes, voice, all in her letter. The American she hopes her niece will marry."

Ben looked up, chagrined.

Myagkov smiled. "Well, old ladies look out for their nieces, and I was watching for you while I was fishing. Tell your general that he was very clever to put you next to my sister so soon after she knew I would defect. I've been curious about that. I know the Americans are very good, but frankly, this intelligence about my own intentions, that was remarkable. And that story of my niece, Valeria, as your friend. Did Valeria agree to that charade or was she persuaded?" The last word was full of ugly meanings.

Ben realized that General Myagkov had not the

slightest understanding of the West. The man actually believed the whole operation had been planned. Ben wondered if they dare disillusion him.

Why not? The general might as well begin learning now.

"General, you misunderstand," said Ben. "I do know Valeria. My visiting Anna had nothing to do with you. It was sheer accident I learned of your intentions. And I damn near couldn't persuade the CIA to help get you out. As it is, I'm not CIA, just a private citizen volunteering because I know Anna and she asked me to help."

"Oh." The general chug-a-lugged another vodka. He wore a knowing smile. "And you have heard nothing of WALTZ? And you bought the Roumanian uniforms in a theatrical supply store. Is that it, eh?" He was beaming.

Ben replied, "We only know of WALTZ what you told Anna."

The general nodded. "Comrades, this is very rich. Ah, what a pleasure to be dealing with an efficient country where people like their work enough to joke about it. Our KGB never make jokes, the GRU are worse—they never have heard a joke. Well, I do congratulate your general on his excellent organization. You are, I suppose, both of military rank? Shall I guess? Lieutenant colonels, perhaps, or colonels? After all, this would be the most important assignment in the CIA, unless Strizhenko himself is planning some westward tourism about which he hasn't informed me." The general chuckled. "No, I should say colonels. Am I right, Comrades?"

Sam, a GS-14, and Ben, an Oregon art dealer, looked at each other helplessly.

General Myagkov downed another three vodkas, devoured a pound and a half of roast beef, dill pickles, salad, and brown bread, and, belching happily, fell asleep on the couch.

In the kitchen, cleaning up the dishes, Ben asked Sam.
"Whose house is this, anyway? Another rented safe house,
or did you lean on another one of your poker-playing
friends?"

"Ben, you stayed before in the only paid-for safe house
in town. If our station budget was any lower, we'd use a
youth hostel. I didn't find this one, Luke Franklin did.
Sneaked money out of the general fund. Luke told the
Japanese ambassador—that's his house up front behind the
trees—that he was in love and wanted a place for his
girlfriend. Luke and the ambassador are close, the
Japanese are very big here in Yugoslavia. Bingo. Luke gets
one of the unused guest houses. The ambassador takes it
back when he needs it."

"And Luke's wife? I mean, in a little diplomatic
community like this, doesn't she hear about this mistress
business?" Ben was concerned.

"Oh yeah, she might, but Luke's up to it. He sneaks his
wife in here once in a while. They have dinner and stay
overnight. The Japanese think Franklin is having a big
time. A Chief of Station has to be crafty to stay afloat these
days. I don't know whether the KGB, Congress, or our
own Director hates the Agency most."

"How long can we stay here?" Ben asked.

"As long as we need to. You stay with the general
because you've got no place else to go. And he needs
looking after. I'll go downtown tomorrow with the car and
check in at the station to learn how we're getting Myagkov
to the U.S. The Yugoslavs have an open border. We can
drive him out as soon as he's ready to travel, with a phony
passport. Two days, and we should be home free. Maybe
tomorrow night you can put on your Irish animal lover
costume and get out. Potter ought to be well now. He can
spell you here."

"Think it's all right if I call Anna Oposevic, tell her that I'm okay? Nothing else."

"Why not? Can't see any harm in it," said Sam.

"What about Steffie? I don't suppose an Irishman having dinner with her will get picked up, do you?"

"Don't telephone her. But you could pay a call at the airport and talk to her over the counter, but only as the Irishman. That should avoid trouble."

Flushed with liquor and success, they slept that night as soundly as the general.

FIFTEEN

Sam had left the house at dawn. Ben got up at seven to make breakfast. Soon after, he heard the general stir on the couch. Ben walked in to him carrying a cup of coffee. The general, rumpled but refreshed, was cheery.

"There are fresh clothes for you, General, in your bedroom. The bathroom has razor, toothbrush, and the rest. If you need anything, let me know."

The general nodded, heaved himself up, padded off down the hall in his stockinged feet. Last night Sam had taken his shoes off and covered him with a blanket. When he reappeared, showered, shaved, and in a new suit—there had been several sizes in the closet—he looked like a bull outfitted at Brooks Brothers. And he was angry.

"Where are my eyebrows, Comrade Colonel?"

Good Lord, thought Ben, what next? "The gypsy woman shaved you, sir. It was necessary for your disguise while we were traveling with the caravan."

"Necessary? I saw no need for it."

"We were stopped several times, sir. You were asleep. If they'd seen those eyebrows of yours . . ."

The general interrupted. "I liked my eyebrows, Comrade Colonel."

"Yes, sir, so did I like them. But they'll grow back. If not, the Agency can get you some false ones."

"False ones?" The general was outraged. "That would be decadent, Colonel. Effete!"

Ben was not going to put up with a temper tantrum. "General," he said, "remember you're out and alive. I suggest you concentrate on staying that way until you're out of Yugoslavia. Your eyebrows can wait."

The general, to Ben's surprise, subsided immediately at this cold-water dose of authority.

"More ham and eggs, General?" Ben spoke good-naturedly.

"Why yes, Comrade. Thank you."

He ate his second helping with gusto. "Now, Comrade Colonel, let us get acquainted, eh? You know my sister, you know my niece, you know Yugoslavia. What do you know of Russia?"

"Very little," said Ben.

"Modestly said," nodded the general, wiping his lips. "Well, I shall tell you. In the first place, we are a tyranny run by fools, thieves and jackals. We are a people who must have certainty, but we are uncertain as to which certainty we should have. We have, therefore, let the fools decide. Lenin was such a one. Wiser men reject such absolutism. Do you understand?"

Ben nodded. What else was he to do?

"Good. Now the present regime believes in nothing. Absolutely nothing. They have failed to find truth. Do you know why?"

Ben raised his eyebrows in a question.

"Because the leaders have not suffered enough. They climbed on the backs of others who suffered, the Russian people, but they themselves, no. Can tyrants know the truth? No. So they create artificialities; the laws, they call them, of Marxist-Leninism. Trash. The leadership would collapse but for one thing. They are clever. Stalin borrowed from Lenin the instruments of terror and passed them on. The class struggle, the administration, the police, my own beloved army, all instruments of repression. These jackals will keep themselves in power at home with terror. They will keep the capitalists from toppling them from abroad with the same terror. War is coercion. That is what their nuclear game is all about. You are taught to understand that much in War College, Colonel?"

"I've never heard it so clearly, General." Again Ben asked himself, what else could he say?

"Thank you. You see then, the fools in the Kremlin must be thrown down. They pervert reality, distort its principles. Is that not so?" The general was leaning across the table, intent.

"It may be, General. I have not thought it through."

"Few people do. Yet there is either truth or there is no truth. If there is no truth, then there is no way to order values; it is only each man and his truth against the other. That is intolerable. It creates a society of anarchists and opportunists or, if the society is more highly evolved, a collectivity which agrees to abide by rules that are arbitrary. That is the essence of an evolved capitalistic society, for it has no faith. The irony is that Russia today is a mirror of that, for since the Marxist-Leninist line is also wrong, and the wolves in Moscow know that as well as I do, then the rules in the USSR are also arbitrary. The difference is that the rules are imposed from on top, by terror, whereas in the West you agree among yourselves to live without faith, without certainty, but in a comfortable— however hypocritical—illusion; a pragmatic illusion insofar as it provides the authority of rules. Do you think that is so, Comrade Colonel?"

The general reached across the table, gripping Ben's

arm. His eyes stared into Ben's, searching for response.

My God, Ben realized, this man actually wants to know what I think. Ben was ashamed. He'd not been listening; the old man's tirade, a Russian's passion for talk. But the general had been thinking and it mattered to him, my God yes, Ben realized how much it mattered. Maybe for all these years the general had been thinking only to himself, and now at last, what defection meant was a chance to exchange ideas. Two days ago Ben had been surprised to find himself a killer. Now he was shocked to realize he was, intellectually, a fool. Ironically he, who enjoyed freedom without cost, had not used it to think at all; the Russian, who had never enjoyed freedom, had kept himself free nevertheless by working his brain.

Ben, becoming used to deception, lied, taking up the final words he recalled.

"No, sir, we're not always agreeable, and only sometimes hypocritical."

"Ah," the general almost shouted, "so you admit it, do you? That America is without faith. Yet maybe," the general's eyes were dancing, "maybe faith is slowly created out of the one fact that you Americans care so much about, that it *works*. What a paradox! Out of pragmatism comes faith." The general was gleeful.

Cornelius, Ben thought, you are one dumb bastard. At least, stop lying! He blurted out unhappily, "General Myagkov, I'm in over my head. I'm not worthy of this conversation. I'd have to start it all over and think it through. Forgive me, General. If you'll be patient, I'd be pleased to go at it again. Back home will be best, when we really have time." It was a humiliating admission, and Ben meant every word of it.

The general gripped his arm. "Colonel, you do me a great honor. You see, never before, or at least not for many years, have I talked like this. I've been in a prison, don't you see? I wondered if perhaps I had gone mad. Talking like this, testing my words, I had to see if I was sane. You are the diagnostician. You may think me a foolish old man—oh yes, I am getting old—but you respect what I think! Not even Anna respects that; she is afraid to think. This, too, is dictatorship here. To talk to someone seriously, freely, with respect, that is the reason I defect." The general paused. "You know something, Colonel?"

"What, sir?" Ben was moved.

"If you had said I was crazy, I would have believed you. I would have gone into the kitchen and blown my brains out. What an irony, eh?"

Ben shook his head. A month of sweat and being hunted, lives at stake, five dead Roumanians, and he, Benjamin, could have blown it all if some sweet whisper of honesty hadn't possessed him over breakfast.

General Valentin Petrovich Pavlichenko was looking at the ceiling in his office. Given the choice, were he to look for intelligence in the three faces in front of him or the ceiling, he told himself, it would be up there.

"Fools!" he yelled. "Fools!"

"Yes, Comrade General," agreed Komiakov. His two deputies nodded. Lenev, quiet on the side wall sofa, pursed his lips.

"In the American press Mr. Josh Seymour announced to us days ago that a Soviet defector was coming across, right? Our own surveillance of the American embassy also announced it to us. Right? And you, Comrade Major Komiakov, you yourself found out who was in charge of this defection. The American, Cornelius, right?" Pavlichenko nodded yes to each of his own questions. "And now, Moscow also tells us they may all have been right. Lieutenant General Pyotr Myagkov, Commander of CPS—what they call the Forward God, the most advanced military intelligence unit in the entire Soviet Union, in the entire world—a commander privy to the innermost plans of the General Staff, the Politburo, the most important single figure in Soviet military intelligence, is missing in the Transylvanian Alps."

Three heads nodded.

The Resident went on. "Moscow Center has put us on red alert status. No KGB or GRU member leaves this building unless on my orders and on this business. The ambassador is under my orders, so are all the local resources. If it is determined that General Myagkov has, in fact, defected, or for that matter been kidnapped, the world stops until he is found. Do you understand that?"

The three nodded understanding. Komiakov put his hand to his mouth; he was beginning to have the hiccoughs.

"Get out you cocksuckers," the Resident yelled, "or I will kill you myself!"

Lenev watched the outburst and felt sick. It was all so Russian, so pointless. Wasted brutality, punishment for its own sake. Power and submission as ends in themselves. The Resident, when Komiakov and his deputies had left, put his head in his hands and groaned.

"Really, Yasha, I want to kill them," he said.

Blagoje Savic was listening to the morning reports, his chiefs filing in one by one. Things were not going too badly. Savic was in a good mood. He was still lucky.

"The Roumanians reported to the Soviets that they believe Soviet General Pyotr Myagkov, vacationing there with his aide de camp, Lieutenant Zemskov, has defected. Five Roumanian border patrol soldiers are missing, their jeep has been found in the Cerna." Potiorek was speaking.

"The one we've been waiting for, then?"

"It would appear so, Director."

"And?" Savic knew there would be more.

"It appears that the man who led the team in to get Myagkov is L-IMOT. This time he spoke perfect Roumanian. An entire platoon of soldiers witnessed it."

"And did nothing?"

"Reports vary, Director. He seems to have had them all covered by a machine gun."

"A whole platoon?"

"That is what our agent in Orsova reports, Director."

"And why would a KGB agent bring out an important Soviet general?"

"The American journalist reporting from Belgrade last week claimed it was an American stratagem to surface a false defector to poison relations between the U.S. and the USSR."

"But," Savic smiled grimly, "Myagkov would seem to be a very real Soviet general and a very real loss."

"I don't understand it, Director." Potiorek held his eyes on the floor.

"A provocation perhaps, a diversion, some subterranean Russian scheme. Who can say?"

"What do we do, Director?"

"Anticipate the worst, as always. Do what we can. Love your children, be kind to your wife, steal a little less from the expense account this month, if necessary prepare to die. How's that, old friend, for honest advice to people who live next door to the Soviet Union?"

Potiorek smiled wanly.

"It is very un-Russian for an intelligence officer to be quite so effective as L-IMOT," Savic said. "Maybe we're wrong. Perhaps he's MI6, or French Security, German . . ."

"CIA, Director?"

"Can turtles fly? Do sowbugs sing? Is there a CIA these days, Potiorek? We must ask L-IMOT if we ever find him, mustn't we?"

It was 4:00 p.m. No one on the twelfth floor of the Soviet Embassy would pay attention to the clock today. They would sleep here on the floor this night. Not the Resident, of course; his quarters had a bedroom and bath. At 4:02 the senior communications officer hurried into General Pavlichenko's outer office, saying only, "Emergency." He brushed past the stocky secretary and presented himself to the Resident. As usual, Colonel Lenev was with Pavlichenko.

Sometimes when they were drunk, the junior officers referred to that pair as the "czar and his bastard Yid child." That was as satisfactory an insult as might be conceived. When they were not drunk but very angry, Lenev was simply "that cocksucking circumcised Jew boy." But no matter how angry or drunk, no one spoke ill of the Resident. The new nobility in Russia, *dvoryanstvo*, "service nobility," has created a second serfdom. Lower-ranked KGB officers, no serfs but junior nobles, know it is in their interest not to entertain doubts about the patents of office, for by these patents they themselves rule.

The Resident read the cable the senior communications officer had handed him. He rang the buzzer on his desk, gave an order, pressed his lips, cracked his knuckles. To Lenev he said only, "Trouble."

Major Komiakov and his two deputies presented themselves. The Resident wasted no time.

"The defection is confirmed. Five Roumanian border patrol soldiers are missing, presumed dead. A foot patrol saw the general, his aide, and two soldiers. The description of one of them is remarkably like that of Cornelius. Speaks Roumanian, it appears. And he has done exactly what Mr. Seymour of the New York papers told us he would do, exactly what he himself warned he would do. A reliable fellow, and our entire KGB, not to mention the Roumanian Army, seems unable to stop him. In consequence he has brought into Yugoslavia—I rely now entirely on his kind advice to this effect—a general who knows as much of our military dispositions, policies, capabilities, intents, as any man save the Party Secretary or the General of the Armies. Now, Comrade Major, with the advantage of all this intelligence, what does your department propose to do?''

Komiakov, hangdog, replied, "All decisions are in your hands, Comrade General.''

To be abject is not to be inert. Komiakov was sly, the Resident knew. The scapegoat could, with cunning, sacrifice the high priest.

"Comrade Major, Moscow has designated this development as the 'Uncontrollable Element,' the greatest possible threat to the security of the Politburo's plans, to military stability, what we are all taught most to fear in strategic planning. They have given it code name ETHON. We are to stop at nothing to find Myagkov.''

"I understand, Comrade General.''

"We have only one link to Myagkov. That is Cornelius. We have only one link to Cornelius, that is the woman.''

"What woman, Comrade General?''

The Resident suppressed the urge to shout. "The airport woman, Comrade Major. Remember the one our man was arrested upon interviewing? The UDBA woman.''

Komiakov recalled.

"Kidnap her. Take her to a safe house and interrogate her until she tells you about Cornelius. Use any means at all. Do not be squeamish."

"Yes, Comrade General." The senior staff filed silently out of the room.

Lenev drew on his cigarette. He was an incessant smoker.

"Comrade General?"

"Yes, Yasha?"

The Resident's voice was tired, the mind forming the voice was entering the inner void. Such is the Russian syndrome of despair. Lenev had seen it too many times. In his own father—before Stalin had killed him; in Valentin Petrovich here. Lenev reviled the Russian character.

"Will that be wise, Valentin Petrovich, kidnapping a UDBA woman? Cornelius will have told her nothing. Is it not just more trouble?" Lenev's voice was soft, the caress of a hand on the brow of a fevered man.

The Resident's voice was flat, his words slow. "Yes, Yasha. Unwise, as you say. But I have no time for wisdom. My career is at stake, yours too. If I fail, you fail. You fail badly, do you comprehend that? It is not a good time for a Jew to return to Russia."

Yasha's eyes narrowed, but his voice was unperturbed.

"There has never been a good time for a Jew to be in Russia, Valentin Petrovich."

The Resident stared at his adjutant. "Colonel, you supervise Komiakov. This time I don't want anything to go wrong. See to it." The Resident was suddenly furious with him.

SIXTEEN

Sam returned to the secluded Japanese Embassy guest house that afternoon, bringing with him a welcome change of clothes and instructions for Ben. Jim Potter, the other CIA station man, at last recovered from mumps, was with him. Ben and General Myagkov were talking animatedly over tea. Ben acknowledged their entrance. The general did not, for he was holding forth.

"You must understand, Colonel, that the Russian character demands faith. It is a sin to be without faith. In the old days faith in God, nowadays faith without God. One is 'obliged' by the Party and the *aparatchiks*, and by the soul's own compulsion to be faithful when there is nothing inspiring it. Temporal power must create dogma, so that the faith which pre-exists can have definition.

"If it is a sin not to be faithful to one's religion, then the same Russian character, as it comes modern, converts sin into its modern form, disease. Lack of faith is a sickness You think it is an accident that dissenters are put in psychiatric hospitals by the KGB, to be tortured by drugs and humiliation? Not at all. It is based on conviction. Only a diseased mind dissents."

The general frowned. "When Solzhenitsyn defected, did he simply denounce? Oh yes, he did that, beautifully, bravely. But denunciation was not enough. He was empty if all that was within him was criticism, renunciation. No, his soul refused to be empty, and so look at him now, a Christian, a fanatic Christian you might say. For Russians, it is the *idea* that we commit ourselves to.

"So, Colonel, can you imagine what it has been for me, a typical Russian, having no church, no faith in the Marxist-Leninist line? I have to ask myself, am I a sinner? Yes I am, I answer. Is my mind sick? I have to confess that, too. Does a sane man desert power? Can he abandon glory? Does he leave Mother Russia? When he knows he will be branded a traitor, can he come to the Capitalists whispering treason? Only a madman does that, Colonel. A pervasive sickness has turned me away from Russia.

"Thank God, like Solzhenitsyn, I am a believer in God. But only monks can appreciate God in solitude. Russians are social, Colonel, we are not like Hebrew prophets flowering alone in the desert. So you see, I must come to America to be a congregation. In the meantime, brooding like some Raskolnikov, admitting a diseased mind, I have become a desperate man. I drink too much. I think of killing myself. I have longed for someone to speak to honestly. I watched others speak out and wondered whether I would be so brave. I was not, and so I defect first and then make my public stand."

Ben replied. "I understand, General, but I disagree. It takes immense courage to do what you've done."

"Courage is a word used after the fact. So is cowardice. It is like a battle; you act. Afterwards others give you a medal for bravery or shoot you for running away. History is the science of judgments made by people who were not there."

Ben pursued a question. "So your decision to come West, General, really had to do with ideology, not so much with WALTZ?"

The general raised his hand, palm forward.

"If a man has an ideology, Colonel, everything is judged in its light. It is not situational. The principles are applied to the situation; the situation does not determine the principles. WALTZ is not separate. If I had not concluded that the Kremlin wolves were in error, I would have seen WALTZ as correct. As it is, my principles compel me to revolt, and WALTZ made it urgent."

Sam and Potter, a pasty-faced, chubby man, had been listening politely, surprised by how intent a listener Ben had been, but this Russian speechmaking could go on, Sam feared, for hours.

"General Myagkov," he interjected, "may I have a word with you?"

"Of course." The general was more genial than Sam had yet seen him. Obviously he was getting along famously with Ben.

"Unfortunately, General," Sam told him, "my chief has not yet returned from Washington. I've been ordered, since I'm acting chief, that you be kept here in Belgrade until certain decisions are made back in Headquarters. That will be a delay of several days. I am sorry but those are my orders. Naturally we shall do all we can to keep you safe and comfortable here."

"You're going to leave him here in Belgrade like a sitting duck when you could drive him or fly him out tonight instead?" Ben was shocked. "Hell's bells, Sam, anything can happen here."

Sam colored defensively. He was angry. "Look, I only take orders. What Headquarters wants, I do. Anyway, you've done your part. I'm in charge now."

"You officious son of a bitch," Ben said, rising from his chair.

"Fuck off, civilian." Sam stood up.

Potter began to move between them.

"Comrades," Myagkov said, "this is a tense time for us all. Let us not make it worse. Sit down, please."

They obeyed, and the general smiled. "This is all very refreshing," he said. "In the KGB such disputes are conducted behind backs and in personnel files."

"I apologize, General," said Sam. "I lost my temper."

"He really is in charge," Ben said. "I am a civilian, not Agency. I got into all of this by accident, crazy as it sounds."

The general didn't believe a word.

"Come," he said to Ben. "Let us make some tea. What is your name, if you are not to be a colonel?"

Ben told him. He followed the general into the kitchen and sat while Myagkov made tea.

"Tell me Ben—let us use first names since we are friends, I am Pyotr—tell me, do you comprehend how an old man like me, very powerful, very spoiled, must leave a corrupt ideal to seek a pure one? Oh, there are many who emigrate without that, normal people wanting freedom or money, but to defect as I do, it is a religious devotion, a kind of martyrdom."

The general shrugged and poured tea. "I don't know. Perhaps I shall be disappointed, diverted or corrupted. Perhaps I shall be miserable in America."

"I hope not. Come to Oregon. Live near me. We can fish together; you can farm and write."

"That is an intelligent idea. But would your friends welcome me?"

"Of course. Why not?" Ben was puzzled.

"Because I am a traitor."

"Not as far as my neighbors are concerned. All our ancestors came from somewhere else, rejected some homeland. No treason in that."

"I come bearing secrets entrusted to me, betraying

comrades, breaking laws, violating a trust. Is that no
treason?"

"You rebel, Pyotr, against tyranny. That's right to do."

"You invoke the natural law, eh? The right of the
tyrannicide. Good. I invoke it too."

But he did not seem reassured. After a moment, he said,
"Ben, let me test you on that. Swear to me you will give me
an honest answer."

"I'll try," Ben said.

"In the deep insight of your heart, do you think of me as a
traitor?"

Ben thought for a moment. "Well, not really . . ."

Pyotr interrupted, almost shouting. "The truth. You
promised the truth."

Ben's voice was low. "Yes, what you do is treason, but
no, I don't think of you, personally, as a traitor."

The general sat down at the kitchen table, his head in his
hands. He was sobbing.

Ben felt an immense sympathy for this bull-chested,
self-doubting, fanatic hero of a man. He walked over to
him, gripped the general's arm.

"You'll feel better once we're fishing in Oregon."

The general brought his great fist crashing down on the
table. He got up, went to the cupboard, brought out a
bottle of vodka, took one great gulp, and shook his bull
head from side to side. Tears were pouring out as he said,

"You are a good friend, but even fishing cannot repair a
flawed destiny, Russia's or my own."

SEVENTEEN

Ben, outfitted as Patrick Brown, Irishman, walked jauntily through the front doors of the busy airport building. It was 5:15 p.m. He knew that Steffie worked until 6:00. She was there, idle, at the tourist aid counter, absentmindedly leafing through a pamphlet. How very pretty she was, with a gray skirt, lavender blouse, rose scarf, and a flower in her hair.

"Care to have dinner?" he asked, making his voice mellifluous, practicing a brogue he'd heard from old O'Shaughnessy, who had a cabin near his grandfather's place.

She looked at the stranger, annoyed.

"I'm sorry, that's impossible."

"But you promised me dinner at your sister's place." The Irishman was smiling broadly behind the curly beard.

She stiffened in annoyance. Then, pausing, she looked again at the impertinent, handsome fellow leaning toward her.

"Who are you?" Her voice was suspicious.

"Santa Claus?" The voice was now all Ben.

Her eyes went wide. "Is it you?"

"Your dinner date, if you'll have me."

She worked fiercely to control her emotion. She would have, if she dared, embraced him wildly. She looked down at the counter for caution's sake. "Are you sure it's safe? The KGB is looking for you too, you know."

Patrick Brown tilted his head in surprise. "Well, that's interesting. Recently?"

"No, a few days ago, just after you'd left town. I'll tell you all about it this evening when we're safe."

"O.K. I'll wait for you to get off work. You take your bus and I'll get on the same one. I'll keep just behind you, don't worry. Don't show that you know me. Okay?"

It was okay. "I'll be at the bus stand outside at six. I'll call home and tell them I'll be late," she said. "My sister's still on vacation but I'm sure there's food in the apartment. Oh I'm so glad you're safe! Let's be careful, please."

At 5:50 Ben passed Steffie at the counter and went outside. He leaned against the airport building near the bus stand. The sidewalk was crowded, the buses modern and frequent. Cars and taxis discharging and loading passengers lined the curb. At 6:00 Steffie came through the lobby door, carefully nonchalant.

She was nearly abreast of him when the two men, both wearing sport shirts, moved in behind her. The rear door of a large blue sedan waiting at the curb opened and a third man, this one in suit and tie, got out. He had a sweater over his right arm, covering his hand. The men behind Steffie each grabbed an arm and one clasped his hand over her mouth. She managed a startled scream. The crowd—there must have been fifty people within fifteen feet of the spot—turned to look. The two men, running now, were rushing her—Steffie's kicking feet didn't touch the ground—toward the open door of the sedan.

Ben was running toward them, his hand reaching for the .38, before he was even aware he'd made the decision to run. He saw the man with the coat and tie swing that right arm slowly up toward him. The sweater fell off. A gun was in the hand. Ben's hand was already out of his tweedy jacket, his thumb pushing the safety. He fired at Suit-and-Tie. The man stumbled, then collapsed. The sound of a second shot cracked in Ben's ears. Chips of pavement flew up at his feet. Suit-and-Tie had missed. People were screaming, running. Ben kept running toward Steffie. The door of another sedan opened, behind the first. Three men, it seemed in slow motion, were lumbering toward him, toward Steffie. The same sport shirts and dark slacks as the two carrying Steffie. Ben swivelled his pistol but didn't fire; none of the five had guns in their hands.

From the airport lobby another man came running toward Steffie. Red shirt, pink pants. He was intercepted by the three from the second car. Like Ben, the newcomer had been reaching for a gun. Unlike Ben, his didn't reach firing position. There was a collision of bodies, like linemen in a football game. Red Shirt, the gun clattering from his hand, had wrestled—partly by momentum—two of the three into the back seat of the car from which they'd come, its door standing open. Ben saw the ugly, hard face of the man at the wheel. The driver turned on the tumble of bodies in the back and, swinging something, brought it down hard.

Then the door of the second car closed. A screech of tires and it was out on the street, sideswiping a bus lumbering innocently toward the bus stop. The car careered drunkenly.

Ben had reached the first car, reached the men abducting Steffie, had stepped over the body of Suit-and-Tie sprawling like a rag doll in a spreading red puddle on the sidewalk. Ben jabbed his gun into the ribs of one of the thugs pushing Steffie into the back seat. Her skirt had billowed high around her blouse; she was wearing pantyhose. She was kicking.

Ben pushed the gun hard into flesh. He pulled the angry trigger and felt the hot burn on his hand. Sport Shirt grunted, snarled, wheezed, shuddered, and fell on the back seat.

Ben propelled himself against the other man, Steffie beneath them now, a windmill of flailing arms and legs; the smell of sweat; Slavic curses; Steffie screaming full blast now that the hand came off her mouth. And behind Ben someone else, the third man from the other car. Shit, thought Ben, and began to move his body around to face outward, for he was now well inside the car. With one arm he struggled with the man, while with the other—the gun arm—he tried to turn his twisting body to face the sidewalk. He felt the pain of metal against his skull, and felt, not heard, the crunching sound vibrating forward, the pain radiating out, the blackness immersing him. He was dimly aware, only for a moment, that the car was speeding away from the curb.

Noise. Bumping. Sticky lips tasting of salt. Pain. Blackness. Throbs. Humming sounds. Toes wiggle. Fingers move. Head hurts. Eyes open. Car moving. Woman's legs next to me. That's it, Steffie. I'm on the floor of the back seat. Heavy load on top would be the other guy. Dead I bet. Hope so, the son of a bitch. No hurry. No strength. Ben lapsed back into unconsciousness.

The car had stopped. Someone was dragging the body off him, the feet flopping, bumping. Ben's trousers were sticky wet, becoming stiff. Patrick Brown would have been dragged out the same way if he hadn't made signs of getting up on his own. As he began to move he felt Steffie's hand stroking his head. She was whispering to him, something nice, he couldn't hear the words.

They were hustled out of the car along a narrow alley, high buildings on both sides. A rundown industrial area, inactive at this hour. There were two other cars, the sedan he'd seen at the airport and a VW beetle. Two men dragged him into a dilapidated, windowless wooden shed. It had once been a machine shop; he saw a rusty drill press, turret lathe, oily work benches. One driver prodded Steffie in at gunpoint, the other driver dragged, pulling and tugging, the unconscious body of Red Shirt, whoever he might be.

A dapper, black-haired man, short, thin, cold-eyed, sat on a wooden chair smoking a cigarette. Standing next to him, a square-faced fellow in a baggy brown suit. Square Face had gray eyes and sallow skin. Dapper had a darker complexion. Square Face barked in Russian, Dapper was disdainfully silent. Dapper was the superior. They did not appear friends. Square Face turned to Patrick Brown, tied now in a chair. Thank God, thought Ben, that damn false beard and wig had stuck. The wig had saved his skull. Square Face, a vein pumping at his temples, spoke in Russian. Patrick shrugged. Square Face tried German, French, then English.

"Who are you?"

"Patrick Brown. Irish. I've got papers in my wallet. Look and see." Ben's head must be better. He said it fliply.

Square Face pulled out the wallet, leafed through papers, and threw it on the floor. He also unbuckled Ben's shoulder holster and dropped it. Was his look disgust? Or fear?

"You have killed two of my men."

"Really? You should train them to be more polite."

Square Face hit Brown across the face. The pain in his head ventilated itself, like a steam tank valve bursting inside, down to his toes, Ben reminded Brown to be less flippant.

"Do Irish tourists always involve themselves in others' business? Carry guns?"

"If they are IRA, they might. They don't take lightly to abusing women, they don't." It was, Ben thought, a stroke of genius. Brown let the brogue curl over his tongue as he spoke.

Dapper explained to Square Face, "IRA, Comrade Major, the Irish terrorists. One expects nonsense from them."

Square Face answered, "This one must be a madman."

"Chivalrous," Patrick Brown corrected, "and if you were half the revolutionaries you claim, you Russians would be on our side fighting the British and Orangemen, not beating up women."

Komiakov looked at Lenev and then turned again to Brown. "You are a romantic as well as a fool."

"I'm a patriot and a gentleman."

Komiakov shook his head. Lenev ignored him, turning his eyes on Red Shirt slowly coming to on the floor.

"Who's this one, Comrade Major?"

"Part of the plague," sighed Komiakov. "Perhaps another Irishman. He too intervened at the airport with a gun."

"Check his papers," Lenev ordered.

Komiakov checked.

"He is UDBA, Comrade Colonel."

"Quite a haul, Comrade Komiakov. One self-confessed IRA terrorist, one UDBA officer, two of our own dead, and, it would seem almost by chance, the woman. Is it the right woman, Comrade, or is your disaster complete?"

Komiakov dared be snide to this Jew colonel. "Unquestionably the right woman, Comrade, and, as the Resident commanded, at all costs."

Lenev ignored the insolent tone and turned to Steffie. "Now, my dear, we seem to have gone to a great deal of trouble to bring you here. Please make it worth our while.

And yours. Our request is simple. I shall be completely honest with you. We have lost a very important general. An American agent, a man called Cornelius, appears to have taken the general from us, out of Roumania. We want the general back. We are indifferent to Mr. Cornelius who is, we believe, a particular friend of yours. The easy way for you and your friend is to tell us what you know about Cornelius so we may find him and, through him, our wayward general. Make it a bit harder and you will learn much suffering. That suffering we would also bring upon Cornelius. It is an economic matter; the more you cost us, the more we charge you. Do you understand?"

Steffie had been tied to a straight-back chair. Her skirt was rumpled, her blouse torn now, and dirty from the ropes.

"Go to the devil," she hissed at the Soviet colonel.

Lenev sighed. "Please, no histrionics. As I told you, this matter is entirely economic. You will tell us. We will learn. I am, out of distaste for pain, trying to short circuit that ugliness. In the end it is the same, except . . ." he paused, "except there will be very little of you left to appreciate the truth in what I have said. And less of Cornelius. As for the defector, Myagkov, I am honest. There is nothing anyone can do to save him. He will die."

Steffie, her eyes flashing, said nothing. Lenev turned to Komiakov.

"She shall be yours in a minute, Comrade Major. What a shame that the presence of fools makes for a general indignity."

"Will you observe?" asked Komiakov. "Most do not wish to watch, not after the first few minutes, which can be, for newcomers and with a young woman to work on, titillating."

"I have seen it all before, Comrade Major." His tone was

one of insufferable boredom.

Komiakov nodded and spoke to one of the drivers in Russian. The man trotted out toward the cars.

Steffie squirmed, so did Ben. Lenev was biting his lips. On the floor, Red Shirt, the UDBA man—Ben wondered if it was the same airport fellow Steffie had spoken of—groaned under his truss of ropes.

Lenev turned to Steffie. "Truly, you force us to regress to savagery. Will you be better for electric shock to your genitals? Without fingernails? With teeth pulled? Blinded perhaps? Acid where your nipples were? Really, is that what you seek? We must do it, you see. The defector Myagkov must be found. There is no alternative. Your Cornelius is the path."

Steffie was pale as a ghost. She was quivering. The driver brought in a box and began to unpack. It was a collection of medieval horrors to delight the Marquis de Sade. The Russians were not bluffing.

The first item that the driver assembled was a cattle prod connected to a six-volt battery and a variable transformer; the stock-in-trade since World War II for shocking genitals from Argentina to Vietnam. One of the men walked over to Steffie, tightened her gag, and tilted her back on her chair. The other, another driver, walked slowly toward her, his tongue darting over his lips like a lizard near the fly. He moved slowly, deliberately, obviously savoring his fantasies. Ben saw a lump in his trousers; the bastard was getting an erection. The man had reached Steffie and began to pull off her skirt.

"You bastards, leave her alone!" Ben cried. "I can help you."

Lieutenant Colonel Lenev turned those expressionless black eyes on the Irishman. "Oh?"

"For a consideration." Brown's brogue curled over his

tongue like a leaf of fresh cabbage, rough and pleasant.

"And that is?" Lenev gazed with studied calm.

"You stop behaving like zoo animals and leave the lady alone."

The man tugging at Steffie's skirt had it off now. He was pulling down on her pantyhose. She was writhing, trying to kick. He was moving in between her legs.

"Stop it!" the Irishman shouted.

Colonel Lenev gave a command in Russian. The man stopped, his fingers twitching. He kept his hands on Steffie's exposed outer thighs.

"I can find Cornelius for you."

"How?" The cigarette smoke curled idly. The man's fingers kneaded Steffie's white skin.

"Get the animal away from the lady," ordered Brown.

Lenev spoke to the man. The animal got up and walked away, unable to conceal the full erection. The man behind Steffie, still clutching her shoulders, looked at his colleague and grinned. He was enjoying the view of her breasts, partly exposed by the torn blouse.

The Irishman went on, "He's the redhead working for the Americans, right?"

Colonel Lenev nodded.

"One of my colleagues knows him. We were thinking about hiring him for a job with the IRA, a penetration of British military intelligence in London."

"You would hire a CIA man to work for the IRA?" Major Komiakov said sarcastically.

Brown frowned at the Soviets. "He's not CIA, you people know that. He's a freelance, private agent. He'll work for anybody for a price. He's a businessman."

Red Shirt on the floor, the UDBA body, was now fully conscious, taking it all in.

"Could be," he said, his voice slow and thick. "Our

Director has him on the list as identified, but without known affiliations."

Ben was grateful to the UDBA man. He too was doing his best to divert attention from Steffie. They would work in tandem now.

"And do you know," said Lenev sarcastically, "why the CIA paid a freelance agent to bring a Soviet general out of Roumania?"

"Maybe they wanted to protect their own people," said the UDBA man, "sacrifice an agent if it went sour."

"Maybe," said Brown, "or perhaps the Americans really weren't sure they wanted him out. What if he were a soft priority—some sort of dissident like General Grigorenko? Throw him back. Claim the operation had been blown. Less embarrassing if it's not attributable to the CIA. What kind of public relations is that for the next defector they *do* want? All the brass in Russia who are thinking about jumping ship would give it up if they thought the CIA couldn't be trusted to get them out."

Komiakov fumed, "There are no defectors among the Party in the homeland."

"Sure," said Brown sarcastically, "I bet if I had a ticket West on me today you'd buy it."

Komiakov began to move toward Ben. Lenev put up his hand. "It's childish, Comrade Major. Ignore it."

Ben, seeing he'd pushed his luck, let his mind race. Anything to keep them off balance.

He said, "There's another possibility. Maybe Moscow wants your defector out. A plant. Things like that happen, you know. Maybe Cornelius has the same boss back in Center that you do. That would sure as hell account for his success so far. One man getting a general out of Roumania? Ridiculous! They let it happen. And if that's it, they might not want you stopping him. If that's it, I wouldn't want to be the man who brings in your defector before he's over in America getting cozy and telling them blarney. Wheels within wheels. That's the way this business works. It's not for me to tell you that."

Lenev's mind went back to his earlier conversation with the Resident. The same idea . . . yet the Resident had sent him, Lenev, to assure Komiakov's success in bringing in the woman. Hadn't that same Resident told him he intended to sacrifice Komiakov? As this dubious Irishman had said, "wheels within wheels." Lenev's face was grim. He did not like what he was thinking. Annoyed, he said,

"Fanciful, and a waste of our time. More practically, since you are so chivalrous, how do you propose to find us Cornelius and our defecting General Myagkov? We are impatient." He spoke in Russian to the sadist with the torture devices.

The man smiled a crooked smile and connected the shock stick to the battery. In the man's crotch, Ben saw that hard lump appear. To Ben it seemed that time had run out. He was about to say that Cornelius was here at hand when they all heard the ululating claxon, that strident bray of an electric mule, that is the European police car siren. It was in the alleyway just outside.

"They're tearing the city apart looking for us, for those cars of yours, you know," said Ben.

The UDBA man tied so uncomfortably on the floor agreed.

"Every police unit, the army, all of UDBA, they will be searching every square inch of Belgrade to find you. I think your time is running out."

Komiakov, head tilted, ears cocked, said nervously, "He's right. We can only drive in your Volkswagen, Colonel Lenev. Our cars are sure to be spotted. There will be no room for any of these." His eyes were on the prisoners. "We can kill them and get out."

"And kill our only hope of finding Myagkov?" asked Lenev. "Comrade Major, you are a fool."

The major cursed him in Russian. Soon these barracudas would be at each other.

"I do not," said Komiakov, "take orders from you, Comrade Colonel. General Pavlichenko commands my department. I will check with him what is to be done. There is a radio telephone in my car." Furious, frightened, the major ran out into the enclosed yard of the old machine shop to his car. A few moments later he returned, saying, "Comrade Colonel, General Pavlichenko is already on his way here."

Komiakov was now more upset than before. He was lighting a cigarette when the shed door opened. Four men, three dressed in badly pressed trousers and cheap sport shirts, the fourth impeccable in a light gray summer jacket, entered the room. The well-dressed one was eminently in command. Those in the shed arose quickly, standing at attention.

"Comrade General Pavlichenko," said Komiakov, "you see I have captured the woman as you ordered."

The Resident gazed with crocodile eyes at the three prisoners, the UDBA man trussed on the floor, Ben tied to a chair, Steffie, her blouse torn, skirt off, pantyhose pulled low down around her lower abdomen, bound, gagged, and squirming.

"So I have heard. The Belgrade police radio is full of your airport triumph. Two of our men dead, a UDBA man, Bora something-or-other, kidnapped along with a civilian and the girl. Now Belgrade is crawling with troops and police, all looking for our KGB autos, Major. They have traced the plates. You realize, Comrade Major, that you have generated a catastrophe." His tone was searing.

Komiakov looked at the floor.

"And as for you," the Resident turned to Lenev, "you were to supervise a kidnapping, not a civil war."

"I left Komiakov at the airport, Comrade General, before the shooting started. I came here to be sure this building was prepared and safe. I believe I did my part. No one could have stopped this bungler once he was in action." Lenev spoke calmly enough, but Ben saw that his fingers trembled.

"And have you learned where Cornelius or Myagkov are?" The Resident's tone was sharp frost in the air.

"We have only been here a few minutes," Komiakov protested, "and already this one here," he pointed to Brown, "says he knows where Cornelius is. This one says he is IRA. They were interested in hiring Cornelius for some contract work."

"Really?" The Resident was skeptical. "And what do his papers tell you?"

"That he is Irish, has a cover, nothing more."

"Which is to say, nothing at all. Was it intuitive wisdom that made you kidnap him as well? The same wisdom that led you to kidnap a UDBA officer?"

"They interfered, Comrade General, tried to save the woman, killed my men. What was I to do?" Komiakov was close to whining.

"Leave them at the airport, you idiot. What did you think you were doing? Running a bus service?" Pavlichenko's eyes were blazing.

"I call to the General's attention that the one with Irish papers says he can get us to Cornelius." Komiakov's manner was hurt, sullen.

"And how will any of you get to Cornelius or anyone else past the hornets' nest out there? Don't you understand, Major . . ." his voice was rising. "with this UDBA man on our hands we are in terrible trouble."

Ben realized that the Resident, too, was near the breaking point. In this crisis, if Ben could show them a way out, he would have a kind of control. It was worth a try. He spoke calmly, slowly. He must convey confidence at all costs.

"I think I can help you, Comrade General Pavlichenko."

Pavlichenko turned toward Brown with interested disbelief.

"Who are you? Not IRA, I'm sure of that."

"Not IRA," replied Brown. "I am here, however, on an IRA-related matter. Carlos, the Arab-paid terrorist leader who killed the OPEC ministers in Vienna, moves in and out of Belgrade, as you know. We believe he is in contact with the IRA. I'm here on Her Majesty's Service, for the Foreign Office, trying to persuade the Yugoslavs not to allow Belgrade to be used as a sanctuary where Carlos and the IRA can plan more trouble for Northern Ireland. I travel as Brown because it is a delicate negotiation. But that is beside the point. You must take certain steps if you are not to embroil the Soviet Union in a major and portentous incident with Yugoslavia. I'm sure you agree that you are at very high risk of doing just that."

Pavlichenko nodded. Brown went on.

"You recognize that you cannot harm either Bora there or the girl, since the Yugoslavs know that it was the KGB that kidnapped them. Harm them and face a break in diplomatic relations between the two countries, even a Yugoslav entry into NATO. You must nip this in the bud before anything gets into the newspapers, before the government here is committed to an irrevocable collision course with the USSR. I don't need to tell you that if that happens, General Pavlichenko, you will either have to defect yourself or return to Russia."

Pavlichenko let go his resolve, slipping once again into
that despondency which Lenev recognised so well. He
stood passive, listening. Ben talked on.

"The Yugoslavs will not want this incident. That is your
salvation. It is as damaging to them as to Russia. You are in
a position to create a circumstance which allows it to be
reinterpreted and buried."

"How?" Pavlichenko's voice was flat.

"We," Ben was tying Pavlichenko to him, "we will
release the UDBA man and the girl here . . ."

Komiakov interrupted. "She is UDBA too."

"Shut up!" said Pavlichenko, his eyes not moving from
Brown.

"I will stay with you. There can be a hostage exchange,
me for your defector. Further, we must neutralize the
airport fiasco. There is only one way to do that."

Lenev tried to interrupt, but before the words came out
another police siren blasted down the alley outside. Ben
waited for it to pass and went on.

"You, General, and the Soviet Embassy, must be
disassociated from the airport incident. As I see it, your
Major Komiakov was fully responsible for that catastrophe." Ben paused. "Before I go on, I suggest you take
away the major's weapon. He's not fit to carry it."

The general narrowed his eyelids and held out his hand
to the major. The major looked apprehensive.

"Your gun," demanded Pavlichenko.

Komiakov handed a 9 mm Stechkin to him. The sheep
had not yet recognized the wolf which would devour him.

"And the other three who were with him as well," said
Ben, his voice firm. "None of them are fit to carry
weapons. They've demonstrated that!"

Pavlichenko spoke in Russian to the men who had been
with Komiakov at the airport. The three hesitated,

suspicious, balky.

"General, if I were you I would see to it that you maintain command here." It was a critical moment. Ben spoke as matter-of-factly as he could.

Pavlichenko spoke again in Russian, this time to the three heavies who had accompanied him, men who until now had been standing listlessly, not understanding English, near the shed door. Four automatics appeared in their hands, the weapons trained on their colleagues. Komiakov's thugs, sullen, confused, but not yet comprehending for they spoke no English either, gave over their weapons to the general's men.

"Good," said Ben. "Now untie me and loosen the ropes on the girl and the UDBA man. You needn't untie them completely. Keep a weapon trained on me if you like, but understand that if we, General, are to get out of this mess successfully, we will have to cooperate on a more civilized level."

General Pavlichenko hesitated, doubt in his eyes. Lenev watched suspiciously.

"General," said Ben, "we can still save the situation— get Myagkov too—but you must hurry. Come now, do as I say before those police outside come swarming in here."

Pavlichenko looked at Lenev questioningly. The colonel shrugged assent. What did it matter? the colonel asked himself. What did anything matter? If it did matter, what was to be done? It was a question Russians had asked for centuries.

EIGHTEEN

Bora and Steffie, her skirt mercifully back on, were seated on a rickety bench along the old shop wall. Steffie's mouth, no longer gagged, was now a rose badly bruised. Ben dare not let himself think about what had almost happened to her, what still might happen. General Pavlichenko stood, arms folded, waiting. Lenev, seated, smoked a cigarette. Komiakov was obviously shaken by events and stared at the floor. The two drivers and the other disarmed man were in a sullen cluster. Pavlichenko's men kept their guns in hand, letting them droop, not knowing for the moment who was the enemy.

Ben turned to the UDBA man, Bora. He was watchful, reading Ben like a trapeze artist calculating the arc of his partner's swing.

Ben said to Bora, "Tell me if anything I outline is unreasonable. I want you to represent us to your government when you're released. In the meantime, you will have to speak for your Ministry as best you can. We must have agreement here among us." Ben was surprised by the easy command in his voice, by the acquiescence of the others. A tightrope walk. Any breeze could bring him down.

Bora nodded. "I will do that."

"And you, Miss." Ben addressed Steffie. "Tell us if there's anything you do not agree to." Slowly he was shifting power, making them participants, creating a group; each sentence a step further away from their place as victims awaiting the hangman.

Steffie nodded assent. She was immensely proud of Ben. Nodding was easy, speaking would be difficult; she was still jelly inside. And boiling hate.

"It is my view, General Pavlichenko, that Komiakov and his men acted without any knowledge or consent from you or any Soviet official. It is my view that Komiakov acted entirely on his own. Colonel Lenev played no part. After all, he was here when we arrived. Do you two agree?"

Bora and Steffie nodded agreement.

Ben went on, "It is remotely possible that the CIA paid Komiakov to pull this stunt in order to create a major incident between the USSR and Yugoslavia. On the other hand, it is much more likely that they are common thieves and that they were embezzling money from the Soviet Embassy's general fund. What do you think, Comrade General?"

Pavlichenko, his head at an angle, studied Patrick Brown, and then Lenev and Komiakov. He blinked his eyes as though awakening, slow to come out of his mood of despair.

"But why?" He was puzzled.

"Because," said Brown, "in either case this is a criminal rather than a diplomatic matter. The Yugoslav press, like that in Russia, is totally controlled. If we can agree that this is indeed what occurred, if the Yugoslav government can concur that only a common criminal act occurred and orders the press to print that, we have gone a long way in neutralizing this situation."

The general began to see.

"And so," Brown went on, "we understand what really happened. Assume Komiakov was a thief, assume Soviet

Embassy officials had found that out; naturally he would flee. That is why he went to the airport. Now, without visas they couldn't fly commercially, so they had no choice. Komiakov intended to hijack an airplane. That has to be the explanation."

The general was thinking. Komiakov had turned pale. He looked as though he had seen himself hanging from the gibbet.

"Comrade General," Komiakov shouted, "this is insane. This man will say anything to escape us. How can you listen to him? How can you even think of betraying us like that? We acted on your orders, you know that." Komiakov was shouting at the top of his voice. "Give me my gun, Comrade General. I will kill this scheming bastard myself."

"Shut up," said the general, and to Brown, "Go on."

"Komiakov intended to hijack an airplane. He parked his cars directly in front of the airport building. Bora and the young woman here, both UDBA, as Komiakov himself has said, naturally concern themselves with unusual people, unusual movements. No doubt they saw that these thugs were armed. They understood immediately what was happening. Like policemen they drew their weapons to stop them, but Komiakov would not be stopped. His men opened fire. Bora here, possibly the girl, fired back. They were the better shots. They killed two of the hijackers and pursued the others. That's when they themselves were overcome by Komiakov's men as they fled, escaping like common thieves to hide out here. Everything that happened at the airport can be explained just this way. No eyewitness there will dispute it. After all, who can know just who shot first? I will insist that I was only an innocent bystander that Komiakov took as a hostage. A tourist. My own government, the Yugoslavs, will be happy to agree. I am positive that it happened this way. Bora? Miss? Don't you agree?"

"That is exactly what happened," said Bora. Inside he was thinking of the medal Savic would pin on him for all that fine defensive shooting he'd done. This Brown deserved a hero medal himself if he could sell this story.

Steffie, trying hard to maintain her composure, nodded. If she weren't so frightened, she realized, she'd want to clap her hands at this audacious performance. This lovely man was miscast as an art dealer. Surely he'd once been an actor.

"You agree, then," asked Ben of Bora, "that in the interests of justice and of fraternal relations between socialist states, that you will tell your chief and your Minister that events are best explained just as we have outlined here?"

"Certainly," said Bora, "but it means we shall have to arrest Komiakov and these others. If the Russians protest, that is still a big problem."

Ben nodded vigorously. "I agree absolutely. But there's a solution." He paused to let the sound of a nearby police siren die out. "I believe Komiakov and his scoundrels must be brought in this evening by the two of you. No doubt about it."

General Pavlichenko cleared his throat, speaking first in Russian to his bully-boys, who levelled their weapons on Komiakov's crew. "I agree," said Pavlichenko. "Embezzlement in the USSR is only sometimes a capital crime, whereas hijacking here in Yugoslavia, and in Russia too, of course, is inevitably a capital offense. I think I can guarantee that my ambassador will convey our most sincere apologies for this affront to the Yugoslav people. We will not seek extradition, and we shall revoke diplomatic immunity for such common criminals. Under these circumstances I am sure that the trial of these hijackers can be abbreviated and be, I trust, closed to the public?"

"My government exercises that option frequently," said Bora.

"But you can provide evidence for the embezzlement of the funds to help the prosecution establish motive and character, can you not?" asked Brown.

"By all means." Pavlichenko smiled as he said it.

"Bora? Miss? Is there anything else?"

"My name is Steffie," she interposed. "No, I think everything is very clear."

"And so," the general was speaking, "we now make a delivery, eh? A band of thieves and the public servants who apprehended them. I like it." Pavlichenko grinned.

Komiakov tried to speak but only rasping sounds came from his parched throat. He was terrified. At the Resident's orders, the sacrificial lambs were gagged and tied, and bundled through the dark into Lenev's unidentifiable VW. Next to it stood the large black Mercedes in which the Resident had driven. With two of his men in the VW, there were seven in this large car: Brown, Steffie, Bora, and one gun-toting thug in the back; the driver, Lenev and Pavlichenko in front. The driver opened the squeaking wooden gate to the machine-shop yard.

Steffie finally had herself in hand.

"You understand, General Pavlichenko," she said, "that my government will be most concerned about the safety of Mr. Brown here. We will want to convey our assurances to our Ministry that he will be well treated by you. This time there can be no question as to who is responsible for him. I would like him to join my Director later this evening. If that does not occur, serious difficulties will arise."

"You have my personal assurances," said Pavlichenko

suavely, "offered in the same spirit of socialist trust that moves me to rely on your assurances as to your government's handling of the unfortunate events at the airport today."

Ben saw that the Russians would hold him hostage until they were certain everything had worked itself out. As Brown, a British diplomat, or suspected MI 6 officer, it was to the Russians' advantage to keep him. The potential of an incident involving Britain would further force the Yugoslav agreement with the Russians along the lines he'd proposed. On the other hand, if the Russians found out he was Cornelius, not only would they have no leverage with the Yugoslavs, but they would have in the hand the very bird they wanted.

Steffie, too, understood. What could she do? Nothing at all for the moment. Bora would see to it that UDBA would do everything it could to get Ben released. But she also realized that if Pavlichenko knew who Brown really was, the stakes were so high that one couldn't anticipate what might happen.

Major Komiakov and his three helpers were delivered as damaged goods. Bound hand and foot, they were pushed out of the moving VW as it passed the Interior Ministry. Bora and Steffie were graciously released, unharmed, near their trophies. The Mercedes sped off.

The yegg in the back seat had not, for one second, taken his gun or his eyes away from Ben. The 9 mm Makaraov SL is a blunt, unesthetic automatic, its muzzle end as attractive to the viewer as a cobra. There was nothing further Ben could do. He was exhausted. He let himself slump back on the soft seats, dozing off. Russian conversation in the front seat was held low.

The Resident's voice intruded itself. "I want to congratulate you on your performance back there. But I fear you cannot sleep on your laurels yet. Remember, you promised Colonel Lenev here to retrieve our wayward General Myagkov."

Ben roused himself. What the hell. There was no more bluff to play.

"So I did," he said, his voice heavy with fatigue.

"Surely that should not be so difficult for you?"

Was there mockery in the voice? Ben replied, "It seems harder now."

"You disappoint me, Mr. Cornelius. I had expected another bravura display. Well, well, I suppose we all tire, do we not?"

Ben heard, understood, and didn't care. Had the bastard known all along, or just now figured it out? Or was he playing games?

"Brown," he insisted quietly.

"We are all tired, Mr. Cornelius. Let us play no more. I credit you with intelligence. Please credit me at least with common sense."

"Okay," said Ben. "How'd you know?"

"I didn't until recently. I should have suspected the heroics, but really, it was your wig. You see, when you were hit you bled a little. Ordinarily a head wound bleeds into the hair, but yours bled under it, a little trickle out from under the hairpiece, down the back of your neck. Not very evident, but telltale. It made no difference. Your proposals for the UDBA people were fine. As it is now, they think I believe you are MI 6 and they do not worry. I'd have to release you. The same if you were a CIA officer. But you've convinced me you're not. You are a contract agent and, as your employer, Mr. Franklin, knows as well as I do, you're expendable. It's the way the business works, is it not?"

Ben nodded. He was too tired to care.

"You can save yourself, however."

How syrupy the Resident's voice now, how warm those crocodile eyes, thought Ben. He didn't bother to reply.

"If you lead us to Myagkov, we would show our appreciation."

"Only if you figured I could do you no damage," retorted Ben.

"How could you damage us?" inquired the Resident.

"How indeed!" snorted Ben.

The Resident was coy. "Well, I admit if I believed the defector had told you his story, yes, you'd have to go. Indeed, if he's told it to anyone, it might be too late for us, unless we could silence them as well. Has he told you?" So innocent that voice, so softly curious.

"Hell no, he hasn't told me. Why should he spill anything to anyone until he's safe in the U.S.? If he talks here, what more does he have to sell? The CIA could throw him back and avoid the diplomatic protests."

"Would they do a thing like that, those honorable men? Throw a Russian major general back to the sharks simply because he'd told them everything here in Belgrade? No, you can't be serious." The Resident was enjoying himself.

"You're right. They wouldn't." Ben believed that himself.

The Resident, who had turned around to face Ben slumped in the back, drummed his fingers on the seat top.

"Mr. Cornelius, you jest. Of course they would do it if it suited them. Think of the allies the CIA abandoned in Vietnam, in Angola, in Cuba, in Hungary. Your Mr. Kissinger once said at a CIA meeting, 'You must not confuse the intelligence business with missionary work.' It is not a nice business. Further, you're at the wrong end of it. Don't fool yourself. They will betray you just as they would betray Myagkov."

"As you did Major Komiakov," Ben noted.

"Exactly. We are *all* expedients. Given the position you're in, if you hope to stay alive, you must also be."

Ben grunted disagreement, saying only, "Don't wake me up. I'm tired."

Astonishment covered the Resident's face. Lenev, also watching, was thoughtful. Ben slept until the car reached the dark building on Birskaninova Street. It slid behind the electronic steel garage doors of the KGB utility house.

They had been inside a few minutes, Ben seated on a hard chair and covered by a gunman, the others lounging, eyeing him hostilely, speculatively.

"You will not call your people then, to ask for an exchange? Your life for Myagkov?"

"No."

"We will torture you, learn where Myagkov is," affirmed the Resident.

"Why bother? If I tell you now there's nothing you can do about it, not unless you've got a tank brigade handy."

"We'll decide that. Tell us where he is."

Ben decided on the bluff, basing it on something Potter had idly said during a conversation—no secret, it was in the local papers.

"The Yugoslav Air Force is taking delivery of twenty-five American F1-11 fighter planes this month," Ben began. "They're being ferried in to Vukasin Air Base outside of Belgrade. I'm sure you know that. The U.S. Air Force has an advisory group helping the Yugoslavs check the planes out. They've been given an office at the air base. A small contingent of American airmen, manufacturer's engineers, and so forth are working there. There's a duty officer and a couple of bunks for the fellows checking out the night flying. What could be simpler? The Agency's dressed Myagkov as an Air Force sergeant. There he is, safe behind a perimeter protected by the Yugoslav military. You'd have to go to war to get him out."

"I don't believe the CIA would take the chance," insisted the Resident. "The risk if the Yugoslavs found out. They'd have Myagkov and there'd be a terrible protest."

"Who's going to bother him? One more sergeant pushing a typewriter in the office," said Ben.

Lenev spoke. "It's very clever, Comrade General. I don't see why they wouldn't do it. They can fly him out from there on one of the planes taking ferry pilots back to the U.S. Quite clever. And Cornelius is right. We cannot get to him."

Pavlichenko was biting his lip. "We've got to do something. We'll call Franklin and tell him we've got Cornelius, want Myagkov, and will throw in Smith and Jones from Moscow."

Lenev looked puzzled. "Smith and Jones?"

"The names don't matter. We'll ask Center to arrest two Americans in Russia tonight. Get them out of bed and down to Lubyanka Prison, charge them with something serious, make a fuss. They can get the U.S. ambassador out of bed tonight and deliver a protest about this American crime wave. That gives us three warm bodies to bargain for Myagkov. So far the Americans have always fallen for it. They will again. After all, until Myagkov tells them his story, they can't comprehend who he really is and how important his information. Lenev, cable an IMMEDIATE to Moscow suggesting the arrests. In the meantime, call Mr. Franklin and tell him I want to set up a meeting to talk about the exchange. Six a.m. will be good. By then we'll know if Moscow has made the arrests. So will Franklin. Tell him we'll bring Cornelius if they'll bring Myagkov. Propose we meet on neutral ground, say the Swedish Embassy."

"I wouldn't expect them, Comrade General

Pavlichenko, to bring Myagkov. That would be insane, breaking security. Frankly, I don't expect them to agree to the meeting at all. Why should they? What have they to gain?"

"Nothing, Lenev, nothing, unless Moscow scoops up a very big Mr. Smith and a very big Mr. Jones. When the stronger man speaks, the weaker man listens. I believe the Americans understand that they are now weaker than we are. We intend to continue to intimidate them."

Ben, listening, was depressed that it might well be true. The last thing he saw as he drifted off to sleep again was the muzzle of the automatic pointed at him. The gunman, a square-built man with a black stubble on his crude-featured face, eyes set back and deep-shadowed like a skull, was grinning. Ben felt the man was looking forward to killing him.

NINETEEN

It had been a good day, thought Savic. Even Potiorek, his face ordinarily a stone griffin, was smiling. Bora and the woman had been thoroughly debriefed. L-IMOT was out of Savic's hair. He was not KGB after all, not Irish as he had briefly claimed, not British at all—a check with the Yugoslav Foreign Ministry established that—and so he was indeed American. And he seemed only a contract agent at that, a fly to be swatted by anyone, with no repercussions. Soon to be squashed, if Pavlichenko were true to form, and Savic had no doubts he would be.

The girl had admitted lying when Bora had shown her L-IMOT's photo at the airport. Stupid women and their infatuations, but hardly consequential. Things had turned out too well to chastise the girl. Yugoslavia would go along with the Russian request that the whole affair be handled as proposed. Bora would get a medal for shooting the would-be hijackers. It was publicly embarrassing to the Russians, and the Yugoslavs had the upper hand. An agreeable conspiracy. Yes, Savic was pleased.

The defector Myagkov was still in Belgrade somewhere. Savic might still find him. What a coup. If the Americans debriefed the defector, they would only tell the Yugoslavs what they wanted to about Soviet military intentions. Yugoslav-U.S. relations were too uncertain to encourage full disclosure. On the other hand, if Savic got to Myagkov, tore his story out of him, they could bargain with NATO for money and arms in trade. The Soviets, thanks to the airport escapade, had no grounds for protest no matter what Yugoslavia might do about Myagkov. All the mud was on Russian faces.

If only Savic could find Myagkov.

The committee meeting was being held in the American ambassador's bubble, that inflated air chamber secure against audio surveillance. The plane from Washington had brought in the Inspector General's chief deputy, Squires—a senior counterintelligence officer—plus the square-faced young naval commander representing the Director, also Derek Rylander and Luke Franklin. Others had tagged along as well. The Washington people traveled under false names but with the usual diplomatic passports. Yugoslav immigration had paid them no heed.

At Headquarters, the leak to Josh Seymour had all but been forgotten as the dispute between Rylander and Franklin was taken up by many others for their own political reasons. State intervened, shrill as an old maid, fretful about chilling detente. The CI, always paranoid, bought, on principle, Derek Rylander's pitch that Cornelius was KGB. The Director himself looked toward the White House. His posture to the internal affairs for which he was presumably responsible was simple: if it's doubtful, don't do it, for Congress and the President may be looking. The defector scared him. Only Barbour, the Soviet Bloc chief, had any interest in what the defector might have to say. The Defense Intelligence Agency was certain, in advance of all facts, that General Myagkov was the shot in the arm needed to get the Defense budget through the House Armed Services Committee.

No one at Headquarters had the guts to call the tune: was Myagkov another Penkovskii, or was this, in its own way, a budding Bay of Pigs? The committee concluded it couldn't conclude. The committee would reassemble in Belgrade. There, they decided, they could reach a decision by evaluating Myagkov themselves. If Myagkov were there. They'd evaluate Cornelius too, they said. If they could find him.

Franklin, using language they were not accustomed to these days, added, "And if you can get your heads out of your ass." He reminded them he was quitting. He'd already told them that but they had not comprehended it. He would go back to Belgrade with the committee because he had to pack. Besides, Cornelius, if he was alive, and Myagkov, if he had gotten out of Roumania, were still on the hot seat. Someone had to care.

The message from Belgrade that Myagkov was there reached Headquarters as the plane carrying the committee took off from Dulles Airport. They traveled, as they had debated, in ignorance.

In Belgrade, the young commander chaired the meeting in the bubble. Saunders, as the ambassador's representative, sat to his right. Smug. The Director's puppy had hardly cleared his clean-cut throat before there was an interruption. A nubile brunette secretary came in. The message she brought was marked CRITICAL. It was for the Chief of Station. Its author, Munson, stood in humble agitation outside the ambassador's offices.

Franklin read slowly, for at 2:00 a.m. he was, like the rest of them, exhausted. The meeting had been called as they arrived, when they learned that Myagkov was in Belgrade. Now this, the KGB calling to say they had Cornelius and wanted a 6:00 a.m. exchange session.

The duty officer came in with an IMMEDIATE from

Moscow. The American ambassador in Moscow had been routed out of bed to be told that Aronson Whitecliff III, onetime ambassador to France, advisor to the Republican National Committee, now touring Russia, had been arrested, charged with espionage. So, too, had one "Collie" Dunefield, traveling near Kiev. A Harvard professor, senior staff member of the Council on Foreign Relations, sometime State Department advisor. "Capital offenses," the Russian Foreign Ministry protest had read. "Further arrests might follow."

The group in the bubble were stunned. "Dirty bastards," Franklin growled. The naval commander wondered what it all meant. Franklin told him. The Soviets meant to get Myagkov back.

"The proposed meeting is an ambush," Squires from CI said dogmatically.

Rylander agreed. "Cornelius is setting us up."

"We have Myagkov," said the man from Soviet Bloc. "The hell with meeting Pavlichenko. Let Cornelius hang and Washington worry about the others. We've done our job."

"Which one of you," asked Franklin angrily, "did any job?"

They gave him dirty looks and agreed, lest further developments overtake them, that Myagkov should be interviewed immediately. If what he had to say about WALTZ was convincing, they would authorize his urgent evacuation stateside.

There is a rule that defectors in transit do not set foot in U.S. embassies abroad, lest there be repercussions. Besides, one might want to throw them back. One slaughters one's goats in the abattoir, and does not invite them to the living room.

The three-car convoy arrived at 3.00 a.m. via the back

drive at the Japanese guest house. The house guests had been alerted by phone. The lights were on. Potter was entertaining the general at chess; Potter had lost the first game in five moves. The general, as the committee came in, lowered his head like a bull ready to charge. His wrestler's torso was muscling beneath the jacket; one could see the sleeves crawl up his arm. He looked every bit a general. The Agency commander was respectful, introducing the group, lamely trying to explain why they were all here in Belgrade rather than interviewing Myagkov in the U.S. The general cut him short.

"Because you wish further to examine my bona fides."

Saunders fancied himself tough. "General," he said, "there are doubts as to whether the best interests of the United States are served by your entry at this time. On the other hand, if your material is indisputably vital to NATO interests, we can be persuaded."

"I see," said the general, scowling.

The Soviet Bloc deputy sought to soften the remark. "I would not put it so harshly, General. We are, in fact, immensely pleased you wish to come West. However, I'm sure you understand that we must evaluate your information prior to making a decision. It is . . ."

The general interrupted.

"You evaluated the documents I submitted earlier. On the basis of those you have gone to considerable trouble to arrange my escape from the Bloc. I appreciate caution, but I disdain lies. I have had too many of them in my time. What, exactly, is troubling you?"

Rylander spoke emotionally. "We do not wish to be duped, Comrade. There are some doubts as to your purpose in coming over."

"What reassurances do you want?" asked the general.

The commander was respectful. "Not reassurances,

General, but at least some outlines of WALTZ, its elements. I would presume you brought along in support further documentary details of WALTZ, whatever that may be."

The general glowered. "Is this some joke?"

Rylander answered hostilely, elevating his chin. "This is a serious matter."

The defector spoke firmly. "I have told your Colonel Cornelius about WALTZ. He knows its elements. As for documents, yes, I have them, but I have put them away. After your announcement the other evening," he waved his finger at Sam Munson, "when it became clear that you were all putting me in jeopardy, I decided at least to secure the documents, even if I could not secure myself. You will have the documents when I am convinced you deserve them. You see, gentlemen, trust goes both ways. So does distrust. Now it seems we must distrust each other." The general sat down heavily, leaned back in the deep-cushioned sofa, closed his eyes, and appeared to go to sleep.

The SB deputy, almost on tiptoe, moved closer to General Myagkov. He spoke softly. "Sir?"

The general was asleep.

Squires from CI had never faced so diabolical a plot. An enemy sleeping. To the CI mind, enemies never sleep, ipso facto, this man could be no enemy. Then his enemies were enemies, this man victim of a plot. Squires looked again at Rylander, who had accused Cornelius, at Saunders, who opposed accepting the defector. Of course! The enemies were where they must be, within.

Squires shook the general gently by the shoulder, saying, "I understand, sir."

The general came awake and looked at him with one suspicious eye, asking only, "Where is Colonel

Cornelius?"

"Mister Cornelius," corrected the SB deputy.

The general made a wry face and waited.

No one answered.

"I order you to tell me!" It was the blast of a bull horn. The young commander was compelled to obedience, the general outranked them one and all.

"We have reason to believe that he is being held by the KGB. They called demanding we bring you to a meeting to which they would bring him. Neutral ground, General. The Swedish Embassy."

"And?" the general bellowed.

"The committee decided that there was nothing to be done, sir. We have you and thereby the WALTZ plans. We can't negotiate your return. It is, no doubt, a trap. Cornelius will simply have to take his lumps. That is what the committee has decided, General."

General Myagkov rose from the couch. His hands reached upward from immense shoulders as though he would pick up the commander child by the armpits.

"You are a military officer?" asked the general.

"Yes, sir."

"And you say Cornelius is a civilian?"

"Yes, sir."

"But Cornelius led the team that got me out, and he killed Roumanian soldiers to do it, whereas you sit in a chair and say you will not fight to assist this man?"

The naval officer blushed. "It's a committee matter, General."

"Well," said the general in a positive tone, "you do not have WALTZ unless you have Cornelius. You do not have me unless you agree to the meeting. That is my committee's decision."

"This has become a State Department matter,"

Saunders observed with haughty craft. "The General himself acknowledges the possibility of a meeting with the Soviets. Let us be realistic. We could negotiate this man's return for Cornelius. If Cornelius knows WALTZ, if the WALTZ documents are hidden near here—they must be, after all—we can find them. I accept the general's implications. There need be no defection. U.S.-Soviet relations in this delicate period will be undisturbed."

"They will not give you Cornelius, even for me, if they know he knows WALTZ," the general reminded them. "You must all agree to deceive on that score."

The commander said, "I will have to cable Headquarters for instructions."

"I will suggest to my ambassador that he cable Washington demanding this entire matter be put under State's jurisdiction," said Saunders.

The committee and its assistants began to file out toward the car, all but Franklin.

"Are you not coming along?" they asked him.

"I'm going to keep the general company," said Franklin. "Go send your cables. Tell Headquarters that, as of now, I have retired."

The general sat down beside him. "So," he said, "you, too, are tired of it all."

"Yes. Very tired. It doesn't work any more. Time was when I was proud of it. No longer. Look at them: pansies. Can't take a crap without cabling Headquarters. Potter, go make us a drink. Bring some sandwiches."

Potter, tired and sullen, walked to the kitchen far down the hall.

"Mr. Franklin," the general said, "can you imagine how one feels in my position?"

"I can imagine," said Franklin. "Like I do myself. Disgusted."

"That, yes, but worse. I fear it is a typically Russian feeling. I feel debased. I loathe my own baseness. I long for purity, to be reconstituted pure. Do you understand?"

"My mind doesn't run along those lines."

"No?" The general was pensive. "I talked to Cornelius for some time. He is understanding. This problem of baseness, for example, we agreed it is an error of character, perhaps of the soul. Cornelius has his own experience with it. There is a gypsy bird, a demon, Melalo. The gypsies say it brings rage, madness, murder, rape. Cornelius was told by a gypsy woman that the bird circles him. He has felt it on his shoulder, heard its wings in his ear. I can imagine it easily myself."

Franklin shrugged. "A manner of speaking, perhaps."

"No. Demons are real, just as ideas are. The idea of baseness, for example. I defected thinking I would renounce that in me, become purified. That was very important to me."

"Was?" asked Franklin, not comprehending.

"The striving for purity by coming West, yes, that is over now. Another error. As Hegel would say, I had not resolved the contradictions."

"And so?"

"The higher plane of resolution evades me. Yet, fanatic that I am, I must still seek it out. It is salvation one seeks."

"I can understand that," said Franklin.

"I thought you might. A man who has spent his life in your business might, I should think, contemplate baseness and purity."

Franklin pondered that. "He might," he acknowledged.

"Yes," said the general. "So perhaps, the two of us, we might reach some understanding?"

"What do you have in mind, General?"

Myagkov told him. After some talk, Franklin made two

telephone calls.

When Potter returned with the drinks, it was in time to hear Franklin's car drive off. Misled by the low music coming from the general's bedroom, Potter didn't realize that Myagkov was in it, concealed on the floor of the back seat.

As the car left the alley, an auto that had been parked by the curb pulled out. As the tail car turned on its lights, Franklin jerked his thumb backwards.

"Company."

"Russian?" asked the general.

"Nope. Yugoslav. I saw them tail us from our embassy. They've got something up their sleeve. Stay hidden until we get to the Swedish compound, then sit up, let Savic take a look at you. That will get things moving."

"Savic?"

"The boss at UDBA. I know his plates. It's his car that's tailing us. He's not going to go anywhere tonight without a brigade following him."

"Will they try to stop us on the way in?" asked the general.

"I doubt it. They'll want to be sure it's you. They'd expect us to send in several cars as decoys; they won't know which is which. Wouldn't be smart to blow it before the prize comes in the doorway."

"You've a cool brain."

"'Hardface' they call me in the Agency."

"In *Eugene Onegin*, Pushkin wrote, 'The mind's cold observations are the bitter insights of the heart.'"

Franklin nodded. Pushkin understood how one became a hardface.

"Tell me, do you think I am a traitor to defect?" asked Myagkov.

Franklin answered slowly. "I think you're a brave man,

General, and that the world will owe much to you, if we squeak by this last round."

"You haven't answered me, Mr. Franklin. Am I a traitor to Russia nevertheless?"

There was a long pause. "Yes," said Franklin.

"Does God forgive traitors?"

"I don't know, General. I imagine they have a hard time forgiving themselves."

They drove up the circular drive of the Swedish Embassy, an aristocrat's house from the days of King Peter. The outside lights were on. Two Swedish officials—Franklin recognized them from the cocktail party circuit—were outside. They looked glum.

Markus Adolphson, stern and formal, dressed in undertaker's black, ushered them into a book-lined study. A late September chill was in the air. The room felt clammy.

"Have the others arrived?" asked the general.

"Yes. They are with my ambassador," replied Adolphson. "It is highly irregular, all of this, but in the interests of world peace, Sweden will do what it can." Markus Adolphson was a stuffed shirt. One would never have guessed he had a light-hearted mistress and gambled, but Franklin had ceased to be surprised by any man, least of all himself.

The door opened. The Swedish ambassador entered, accompanied by Pavlichenko, Lenev, and a surly brute of a KGB aide. Cornelius was with them. Ben was as himself, no wig, no moustache. His hair had been washed, and it shone in the study light. There were introductions all around. Stiff strangers gathering to discuss a corporate takeover, thought Ben.

Both the station chiefs, KGB and CIA, knew each other. It was a small town and both, accredited as high embassy officials, met at major receptions. Curious, thought Ben, how men in their business could be so civil in the drawing room. Lenev, beads of sweat on his forehead, rocked on his feet nervously.

The Swedish ambassador, as if this were a cordial social occasion, had a servant bring in drinks. No one touched them. There was silence as the men appraised each other. Lieutenant Colonel Lenev continued to sweat. Ben's heart was pounding, the air was electric. Myagkov sat down, leaned back in his chair, and closed his eyes. General Pavlichenko stood erect. Silence. The Swedish ambassador realized that his was an encumbering presence. He excused himself. Lenev circled, as a dog does before a fight.

The Resident broke the silence, asking General Myagkov if he had left Roumania of his own free will. He had. More silence. Franklin asked Ben how he was doing. He was doing as well as could be expected. How easy it would be, thought Ben, just to stay here, refuse to leave. But the gentleman's agreement, made when Franklin called Pavlichenko, when Pavlichenko called the Swedes, was that they would not embarrass the Swedes. Diplomatic niceties, like the truce talks under a white flag beneath the cannon. No violence in the drawing room. That would be delayed until they left. Ben had seen the KGB cars take up stations around the embassy as Pavlichenko had brought him over.

"Would you," the Resident inquired of Franklin, "consider an exchange of Myagkov for Cornelius?"

Franklin would not. Myagkov interrupted.

"I will consider it," he said.

The Resident, Lenev, raised their eyebrows.

"We offer you a safe return," said Pavlichenko. "No retribution."

General Myagkov nodded. "Of course." Mature men do not protest the grossest of lies.

"Assuming," said the Resident, pro forma, "that you have turned nothing of value over to NATO."

"You know how these things are done," said Myagkov. "I would not have done so as yet."

Not that it mattered to Pavlichenko. If he returned Myagkov to Russia, his own career was saved. Let Moscow concern itself with what the traitor had revealed.

"You are sure you wish to return?" asked Franklin.

"I am sure."

Ben looked at Myagkov. He was powerfully moved. Here was courage. To save him, Myagkov would go back.

Ben said softly, "Don't do it for my sake, General. I am content with my fate."

"As you know," Myagkov replied, "I am not content with mine. There is no salvation in geography. I will not depart one error for another, exchanging sicknesses. The higher resolution is not environmental, it is within."

"I understand," said Ben.

The defector smiled. It was important that his friend understand.

"You agree not to hinder Cornelius's departure with us?" asked Franklin.

"Certainly not," protested Pavlichenko. "We have reached an agreement. There is nothing more. Shall we inform the ambassador of this happy outcome? Perhaps he can arrange some vodka." The Resident turned cheerily toward the door, beckoning Franklin to come along. Two old boys would celebrate with the third old boy, the ambassador. The serfs could cool their heels. "Comrade Colonel Lenev, you stay with Myagkov."

Ben noted that Myagkov had, with one word, been stripped of title and social rank. Franklin, joining the Swedish ambassador, left the library with the Resident.

TWENTY

"Vasilie speaks no English," Lenev said when the senior officers had left the room. He was referring to the thug sitting alert in a chair.

As if Ben cared. Myagkov did not look at the KGB colonel. All KGB were despicable in the view of Soviet military men. Lenev was agitated; there was a nerve working in his right cheek, twitching wildly.

"Mr. Cornelius," Lenev went on, "I have something very important to tell you."

"Which is?" Ben felt no interest in this thin, hostile man.

"It is not General Pavlichenko's intention to let you leave this area alive. You are to be assassinated as your car reaches the corner. The Chief of Station will not be harmed if it can be helped."

Ben felt the vibration in his left ear; Melalo. Jesus, he said to himself, will it never end?

"I can help you, if you will help me." Lenev's voice was low and tense.

"How?" asked Ben. Myagkov watched Lenev suspiciously. Vasilie ignored the conversation he could not understand.

"I want to defect."

Ben and Myagkov looked at him in astonishment. The Russian spoke rapidly, almost in a whisper.

"You saw what happened today to Comrade Komiakov. If anything goes wrong with this exchange, I will be blamed. I assume that something will go wrong. Your men will somehow keep Comrade Myagkov from going with us, is that not your plan?" He looked at Myagkov for confirmation.

"That is not the plan," said Myagkov. "I am returning because I wish to return."

"I don't understand," said Lenev. "You are close to freedom. You know we will kill you when you come back to Russia. You are lying."

"Comrade Colonel, you are too used to lies; for you there are no other words. I will not bother to explain. But there is no plan to save me. I do not wish it."

Lenev shook his head. "Insanity," he said. "You are a traitor, you will be shot."

"I am a traitor if I leave, not if I return," said Myagkov.

"A fine distinction, not to be made by your firing squad," said Lenev.

"It is my distinction. That is why I return. It is a sin even to betray the devil, that much I have learned about myself; a sin not against the devil, but against God. I have had enough treachery. I renounce it, my own included. Therefore I return."

Lenev stared at him, astonished.

"Nevertheless, I want to defect," insisted Lenev to Ben.

"I would expect as much," said the general with distaste.

"Will you help me?" Lenev beseeched Ben.

"Do help him," said Myagkov irritably. "He can go in my stead."

There was nothing Ben could say to Lenev. He let the man twitch.

When Franklin returned, Pavlichenko and the ambassador with him, all smiling good will, Ben took him aside to a corner of the library. Whispering, he told Franklin what Lenev had said.

Franklin was not surprised about the ambush. "Par for the course," he said.

"Well?" asked Ben. "I'm not entirely indifferent to it. Do I embarrass the Swedes by hiding in the pantry? Or do I just go bravely forth to be shot?"

"Can't let you get shot," said Franklin. "You're the only one who knows about WALTZ. Why else would we agree to the trade? I plan to get you out of this. I took a precautionary step before we came."

"Like getting Agency backup, I hope?"

Franklin looked sour. "When you see a herd of flying hippopotamuses, the CIA backup will not be far behind. No, we're going to have to rely on the locals."

"UDBA?"

"Yep. They're tailing us all anyway. This time I didn't try to shake them. I called up Savic instead from the guest house. Told him Myagkov was being brought over here by the Swedes, that you'd be here, big trade in the offing, I told him. They'll want Myagkov for themselves. I told them they could have him if they kept the Russians off our backs on our way in and out of here. By now the KGB boys Lenev told you about will be outnumbered ten to one by UDBA. The Russians won't be shooting anybody. Any of them carrying a gun is going to get sent back home persona non grata on the night plane. Poor Pavlichenko! He'll have an empty store tomorrow morning: no thugs, no Myagkov, no Cornelius. Maybe he'll want to come crying over with Lenev."

"You mean you'd betray Myagkov? He wants to go back. You know that. He's set on martyrdom."

"But I ain't," Franklin said, "and neither are you. We need you, and the rest follows. UDBA gets the defector, we get you and the WALTZ plans, and Pavlichenko gets to eat crow."

"Myagkov told you I know about WALTZ?"

"Yes. It's true, isn't it?"

"It's true," Ben said. "Maybe that's why he told me, so he could go back. He hates being a traitor, and I don't think he's pleased with what he's seen of the West."

"Can't blame him," said Franklin. "Not with our station handling him. Maybe he'd like it better once he got stateside. Well, we'll never know. He made his choice. Damn lucky one as far as you're concerned."

"Can't we do anything to save him?" Ben asked.

Franklin shook his head. "He told me he was saving himself by going back. The old boy has guts, honor. They don't make them like that any more."

"Nothing at all we can do, then?"

"Screw them before they screw you." Franklin meant it. There was no use arguing, Ben saw that.

"What about Lenev?" Ben asked. "Will you take him?"

"Don't see how I can. He isn't much use to us anyway. All he'd know would be Soviet—Yugoslav operations."

"You don't care about that?"

"As God cares about every sparrow's feather, but no more than that. Besides, I don't see what we can do."

Ben was thoughtful. "I have an idea."

"What?"

"Let the Yugoslavs have Lenev. With his information, they could roll up the Soviet nets here."

"Sure, but Lenev isn't going to tell that to the Yugoslavs when they stop the cars leaving here. How's he going to know they'll take him without some prior negotiation? Besides, Pavlichenko would have him shot before he got out the car door."

"But how are they going to take Myagkov?" Ben asked.

"The same thing will happen."

"I told Savic's people over the phone that Myagkov would identify himself when the car with him in it was stopped," Franklin replied. "He's to say, 'Let us pass. I am General Pyotr Myagkov of the KGB.' That's the signal for Savic's boys to cover everybody in that auto with orders to shoot anyone who says 'boo.' That includes Pavlichenko, if he's dumb enough to make a move. Tonight, old chum, is a night when everybody is playing for keeps."

Melalo screeched in Ben's ear. Ben couldn't help himself; he felt the bird's excitement.

It was a cordial group that thanked the Swedish ambassador. Except for the hour, it might have been the breakup of any intimate embassy reception. The pre-dawn night was quiet except for crickets and night birds.

Franklin's car, an Audi, was first to leave. Franklin wanted to get by the expected UDBA blockades before Pavlichenko reached them. Pavlichenko, his own plans in mind, held back, glad to let the Americans be well ahead.

They were not thirty feet along the driveway before they heard shooting up the tree-lined, badly illumined street. Short bursts and single shots ravished the night in this sedate residential diplomatic neighborhood. The headlights of a car beamed for a moment and then went out suddenly with the shattering of glass.

"UDBA," said Ben, "doesn't quite seem to have the situation in hand."

"The Balkans," Franklin was cursing. "Nothing ever right, nothing ever on time. Look at 'em, just coming in now."

Headlights from several more cars swept down the street, catching flowering bushes in their beam. At the intersection, under the streetlight, they saw three cars parked barricade style, men on this side of them firing at the vehicles coming at them from farther away. To their right, at the other intersection, a firefight erupted. By the dim street lamps, it was a war of shadows. Behind the Audi, Ben heard the engine of Pavlichenko's car, moving down the driveway toward them.

"Pavlichenko behind us," Ben shouted.

His words were punctuated by four shots coming from the driveway. The front and rear glass of the Audi shattered. Ben felt a hot iron slice into his upper arm.

"Stay low and jump clear of the car once I get it moving down the street," yelled Franklin, as he gunned the motor. The Audi jumped out of the driveway and headed to the left toward the firefight. Ben opened his door, leaped out, fell as he hit the pavement, rolled, hit the curb with his wounded arm, felt the searing pain, ignored it, and went into a crouching run, sprinting to the shelter of thick bushes.

From behind the bushes Ben saw the Audi move unguided, steadily down the center of the street toward the blockade. Two men crouching behind a parked car were caught in its lights. One stood up to leap out of the way. He jerked wildly, a spastic puppet, as a volley of bullets hit him. The other man moved slowly sideways, keeping low behind the car, firing outward toward the intersection. The driverless Audi, as if intent, turned toward him and, before he dared leap into the open field of fire beneath the streetlight, hit him, grinding him against the parked car. The crash was accompanied by the staccato shriek of the man crushed by steel against steel. The intensity of fire increased as more cars arrived at the streetcorners and more UDBA men peppered the Russian cars.

In the street in front of him, Ben, his eyes accommodating to the night, saw Pavlichenko's car jerk to a stop in the relative darkness of mid-block. The doors opened. From the front seat the driver and Lenev bolted for the cover of the gardens, Lenev heading directly toward Ben's hidingplace. The driver disappeared. From the rear, Pavlichenko and his Neanderthal companion prodded Myagkov at gunpoint behind a clump of trees on the front lawn of a mansion.

Panting, an automatic in his hand, Lenev stopped in a lilac cluster about ten feet in front of Ben. On his knees, he peered out at the firefight. Ben, doing his best to ignore the pain in his useless left arm, crept toward him, slowly, over the soft garden earth.

With a final leap, he kneed Lenev in the kidney while his right arm hooked the thin man's throat. He squeezed as Lenev sagged sideways, gasping, onto his belly, his feet kicking, his gun hand striving upward. Ben threw his considerably greater weight on top of the Russian, bearing him flat down on the ground, pulling up on his neck in a binding throttle. The gun arm flailed wildly.

"Drop the gun," Ben ordered.

The gun fell from Lenev's hand.

Ben withdrew his arm from the man's neck and quickly grabbed the fallen pistol.

"Okay, you can turn over. Face me."

Lenev didn't move. Ben was not sure the man was breathing. Had he broken Lenev's neck? He probed Lenev's body with his foot, not daring yet to put the gun down. Nothing. He pushed again. A groan. Thank God, Ben thought.

As best he could Ben, using his own belt and Lenev's, tied the man's hands behind his back. Taking his shirt off, he knotted Lenev's ankles together. It would have to do, with one-armed trussing and no rope. Slowly, Lenev was coming around, his breath rasping.

"Take it easy," said Ben.

Lenev turned his face toward him, confused, sick, angry. "Still want to defect?"

Lenev was trying to collect himself. He moved his head slightly, "Yes."

"Okay. Then just sit tight. Escape if you want, but keep in mind the homecoming Pavlichenko has for you. Stay here and I'll see what I can do to save your ass. Mine too." Ben slipped out of the bushes, heading to the darkest portion of the street, his eye on the trees where Pavlichenko had disappeared. Franklin must be somewhere in that same area.

Ben darted across the street, expecting but receiving no fire. He held Lenev's gun at the ready. At both ends of the block the gunfire continued only sporadically. From the direction of it, a few KGB had made it from the barricades to the trees and bushes of the gardens. It was Indian fighting now. At each intersection, an army truck had pulled up with searchlights illuminating the cars and bodies there. Figures darted in and out, obviously afraid of collecting fire.

Ben made his way through the shadows toward the tree clump, keeping well into bushes in front of the houses. Wisely, their inhabitants had not turned on their lights. Yugoslavs have a natural understanding of guerrilla warfare. Ben pressed close to the housefronts as he moved.

Close ahead of him, Ben saw a single figure pressed against a tree, warily scanning the street and lawns. It should be Luke, but Ben could take no chances.

"Put your hands up," he commanded.

The figure, startled, made as if to slip protectively behind the tree.

"Up in the air or I kill you," said Ben softly.

The hands went up in the air. Ben came closer. It was Franklin.

"You son of a bitch!" he hissed.

"Lucky it was only me," said Ben.

"I guess," said Luke, cooling down. "Where'd you get the gun?"

"Lenev lent it to me. Did you see any sign of Pavlichenko and the general?"

"I think so. The three of them ought to be holed up in the bushes over there." Luke pointed to a clump of heavy shrubbery two houses down.

"Let's take them," said Ben. "I'll go around the house and come up around the corner at the far side. You move in on them from here. When I get to the corner I'll throw a shot above them. Tell them to surrender. They won't, of course, but you keep moving in behind them. With any luck you'll get the drop on them while they're banging away at me. I'll be okay around the corner and they're exposed in the bushes. I think we can do it."

Franklin thought about it. "We could wait it out," he said. "UDBA will clean this mess up in a little while. Safer that way."

"No," said Ben curtly. "UDBA would get Myagkov if they do the cleanup on this block."

"That's the way it was going to go anyway," said Franklin.

"That was your way, Luke, and maybe Myagkov's. Not mine. Take it or leave it. I'm going after Pavlichenko. You coming or not?"

Franklin shrugged. "Why not?" he said.

As Ben disappeared, Luke realized he'd been too long at a desk, presiding over other people's risks. He began to creep slowly along the housefronts, low behind the bushes, aware that he was afraid. That was the way it should be. It had been a long time since people in the Company had been rightfully, manfully afraid.

It was a piece of cake. Ben fired a round high in the air from behind the corner near Pavlichenko's shrubbery and yelled for him to give up. Pavlichenko and his caveman shot back wildly. Ben pumped a few more shots above them; he could take no chance on hitting Myagkov. Pavlichenko and the other never noticed Franklin until he was close enough to scratch their backs. He would have done that with lead had they not responded to his compelling invitation to put down their weapons. Pavlichenko was in the fore. A man with a diplomatic passport need not get hurt. General Myagkov, his hands tied to a small tree with his own belt, was grinning as Ben untied him.

"These comrades here," he joked to Ben, "are better at firing memos."

Ben turned to Franklin. "Do me a favor, will you Luke?"

"What is it?"

"Keep Pavlichenko and this turkey company while Pyotr and I go get Lenev, if he's still there."

"Pyotr?"

The general nodded. "For friends, first names."

Ben and Pyotr ran across the street. There had been no firing for some minutes.

Lenev was waiting patiently. He'd made no effort to loose himself from the unsure bonds that held him.

"Pyotr, I want you to meet General Myagkov," said Ben, pointing to Lenev.

Pyotr shook his head. "I don't understand." Lenev was likewise puzzled.

"You don't mind living in Yugoslavia, Lenev?" asked Ben.

Lenev shrugged assent.

"Good. You are now General Myagkov. Got that? Come on." Ben untied Lenev's ankles, helped him to his feet, and freed his hands. "Let's go."

"Where?" asked the colonel.

"I'm turning you over to UDBA." He pointed toward the crowd of men at the now-quiet barricade. "Unless, of course, you want to go back to Pavlichenko."

"Yugoslavia," insisted Lenev.

Myagkov protested. "But they'll recognise him as Lenev as soon as they check."

"Sure they will," said Ben, "but not tonight. Lenev won't say it, I will. When UDBA finds they've got Lenev, they'll be unhappy but not miserable. It is a victory for them to close down a local Soviet operation."

At the corner, hostile weapons were lowered as Ben showed his American passport. The UDBA officer happily accepted Lenev as Myagkov. Every man there had been told that the general was the objective. Ben returned to the Audi where he'd left Pyotr. Pyotr, settled down on the back seat, was sleeping soundly.

Luke joined them shortly. Tiring of babysitting the two Russians, he had turned them loose, weaponless.

"Why not?" he told Ben. "Diplomatic passports. Pavlichenko will be on the cocktail circuit again next week. Lenev's defection was his miracle. He'll say it's proof that Lenev had conspired all along with CIA, UDBA, and Myagkov. The enemy within, you know, just where everyone has suspected. It was a beautiful idea you had, Ben. Pavlichenko will hire you as fast as the Agency. You saved his ass."

"No thanks!"

"What about Myagkov?" asked Luke. "Does he still want to go back to Russia?"

A sleepy voice from the back seat broke in.

"Of course I want to go back."

"But Ben is safe. You don't have to do it," said Luke. "I agreed to your scheme to save Ben when we planned this back at the guest house, because it made sense then, but now it's crazy."

"I want to go back to Russia," Pyotr insisted. "Purity comes only with repentance."

"So you've repented," said Luke sharply.

The general sighed. "Words, only words," he said. "Like the rest of the Russians, I only talk."

"Be practical," Ben said. "Just think fish, Pyotr. Go home and try fishing from under a tombstone."

The general groaned. "Why is life so difficult?"

However sorry he was feeling for himself, his hearty voice suggested that the old boy's spirits were rising.

Ben persevered. "Pyotr, if you go back, you get shot. And that firing squad won't even care that you die nobly, heroically repentant. One giant good deed ought to do; you've helped the world by defecting. I'm not religious, Pyotr, but I'm sure God doesn't want blood sacrifices. Why spoil things for everyone? Don't kill yourself."

"Kill myself?" Pyotr was suddenly outraged. "After all this? Certainly not!"

"Good. Then you've no choice."

Pyotr grunted, a rumbling echo, a bear with his head stuck in a cavernous honeypot. "All right," he said, "if that is my fate. But I will die in bed, crying."

The big man fell silent. Ben, worried, peered at him through the dark. He was asleep.

TWENTY-ONE

They were seated in the ambassador's bubble. The four-star general from the Pentagon had landed just an hour before. He had two aides, both generals, both carrying notebooks. The Under Secretary of State was also there, and so was the Deputy Director of the Agency. The debriefing might have taken place in Washington, except that Ben had refused to leave Belgrade. He had promised Steffie dinner and meant to do better than his word. That morning over the telephone he had promised her two dinners as soon as his chores were done. Then he'd slept the day through. But dinner this evening had been with the brass, a flattering event, but a bore.

The Chief of Station was at the table; Rylander and Saunders were not. No one was buying their story now that the Russians had gone to such trouble to get Myagkov back. Seven dead KGB in the gunfight the night before along with the two Ben had killed at the airport; Lenev's frightened defection—these events spelled no Soviet disinformation operation. Myagkov was real. WALTZ would be too.

The ambassador called the meeting to order. "I will turn the meeting over to you, Mr. Cornelius, since General Myagkov is adamantly silent and has appointed you to represent him, including this briefing on WALTZ."

Ben looked at the long notes before him, his outline. He had Myagkov's documents too, but these, written in Russian, told him nothing. Myagkov had told Ben, however, what they contained.

"Before I begin, Mr. Ambassador, Mr. Secretary, General, Director, Gentlemen," Ben wanted to get the protocol right, "I want to confirm with you all the agreements we have come to concerning General Myagkov. He is to be resettled in the U.S., in a place of his own choosing, with an identity satisfactory to him. He is to receive a resettlement allowance sufficient to maintain a decent standard of living. Until such time as he revokes the appointment, I am to represent him in dealings with the U.S. government. For legal matters, the general will be represented by an attorney. His plan now is to settle on a farm near Hillsboro, Oregon, near lands owned by my relatives. The government will advance a lump sum for that purchase, on the order of four hundred thousand dollars. That is my understanding."

The Deputy Director of the CIA agreed. "Yes, that is the arrangement. As the general's agent, you drive a hard bargain." There was disapproval in the voice, hostility in the tense lines of the man's face. "I wish you had represented the interests of the United States as well."

Ben felt the old anger come crashing over him.

"You and your tinhorn Agency!" he exploded. "You screw General Myagkov ten ways, you leave your own station chief hanging, coddle that little prick, Rylander, whose self-righteous stupidity damn near cost everybody their lives, and then you have the gall to insult me! Who the hell risked his ass through this whole thing?"

Franklin was dumb with admiration. Never had an ambassadorial meeting been treated, at least in his presence, to such an unloading of honest anger. Luke struggled to avoid a loud guffaw. Finally, he couldn't control it. He burst out laughing.

The group at the table polarized spontaneously into two camps. One set of men were pale, aghast, furious; the other, like Luke, were trying hard, or not so hard, to turn back laughter. The ambassador was one of the pale ones.

"Gentlemen," he said reproachfully, "let us return to business." The ambassador looked at Ben, an appeal on his face.

Ben's face was still flushed.

"When this man apologizes, then we'll get down to business."

"When *he* apologizes?" The ambassador could not believe he heard right.

"That's it." Ben's face was murderous.

Those present knew their committee lessons well. When power wounds the weaker of two men, the other fish make of him a meal. Today Cornelius was clout, the Agency man the meal. Quietly, reluctantly, the Agency brass hat apologized.

Ben nodded and began matter-of-factly.

"Now for WALTZ. I'll begin with the troop dispositions. These can be verified through normal military intelligence. I focus on Poland and East Germany, for these are the pertinent armies. The First Guards Tank Army—I'll pass around a list of the rifle and tank divisions involved and their locations—is being reinforced. So is the Third Shock Army which is north at Magdeburg. Naturally there are tactical nuclear weapons in each army's artillery. The forward deployments are poised to move through the Fulda Gap and Hof Corridors to the west. If WALTZ goes well, they won't have to move."

Ben continued. "WALTZ has already begun: in Strasbourg, seat of the Council of Europe. Over the last several years, Department S of the KGB First Directorate has been dispatching illegals there. It has recruited East German agents and documented them as West German workers. Since no visas are required for Common Market migrating labor, they have settled without question. Some are now re-papered as French citizens.

"WALTZ is really a number of isolated, carefully planned occurrences, set up to look like a chain reaction. A serious incident will occur in Strasbourg; a bomb will explode in the town hall during the council meeting. Most elected officials will be killed. A fictitious right-wing German nationalist group will claim credit. The bombing will be portrayed as a German reaction against further European internationalism. The assassinations will require that a new election be held; all Europe's attention will be on the city.

"There is a strong Communist Party in Strasbourg. Eurocommunists, independent—they say—of the Russian line. That party will win the election. Through bribery, fraud, intimidation, Department S's agents will see to that.

"That Communist victory will be followed by a conservative reaction in the whole province of the Alsace. Department S will also be behind that. Riots, violence, finally a bloody massacre of the newly elected Strasbourg Communist city government. Moscow will kill the expendables just elected.

"Department A, the propaganda unit, uses this as a point of departure for a global campaign against reactionaries—those who assassinated the Strasbourg officials. The Nazi ghost is to be invoked worldwide. Communist parties in France, Italy, Spain and Greece call general strikes. Eurocommunists become martyrs and heroes. Ordinary people around the world become fearful about a reactionary threat to the European Economic Community, shocked at the Nazi revival in Germany. Department A of the KGB will orchestrate it all.

"The next phase is linked to the upcoming French general elections. Department S, with more illegals, more money, and with the all-out help of Comintern elements in the French Communist Party, will disrupt the election. Intimidation at the polls, violence, accusations of false ballot counts; the election results will be in doubt but the Communists will claim a victory, will claim that the Right is trying to deny them office. The Red press will print the phony vote counts. The Reds will occupy the presidential palace by force, will claim they are the rightful government."

Ben shuffled his notes. The room was deathly still. He went on.

"The socialists, center, and right-wing parties will no doubt begin violence of their own. If not, Department S will ensure it. The result? The so-called legitimately elected government of Eurocommunists will be in jeopardy of violent overthrow. They will claim they cannot maintain their constitutional right to govern without outside military aid. General strikes around the world will be generated in support of democratic 'legitimacy,' against the 'terrorist right wing camp.'

"The new French Eurocommunist government will then uncover a plot showing that Bonn has provided weapons to the 'terrorists,' that is, the rightist opposition parties. Department A provides the phony documents, the seized weapons, all of the theater. France's NATO and EEC partner, Germany, will stand accused of subverting a legitimate and presumably non-Soviet NATO government. More Department A documents, and neo-Nazis are shown to be behind it all.

"The French then request military assistance to oust the

mythical German-backed right wing as civil war threatens. The request is made to the Soviet Union. Any government has the right to request help from anybody it wants to. And France requests its NATO partner Germany to allow safe passage of Soviet airlifted troops over Germany. The German people are in an uproar, some believing the Nazi imputations, some trusting the Eurocommunists, some insisting on France's legal right, but most of them, of course, saying *nein* to overflights."

Ben continued. "Then the French Communist government makes a formal request to the Soviets to enforce overflight 'rights.' In the meantime, the Soviets have already sent troops in to France the long way around, overflying the Baltic and Denmark and the Mediterranean. The Soviets purposely tested that capability in 1978 in the Ethiopian-Eritrean conflict, illegally overflying Turkey and Greece with no one able to do anything about it. Five airborne divisions will be in France before anybody knows what's happening. The command of the French Army is in the hands of the Communists. The French Army dissolves, repeating their World War II collapse. A pincer against Germany exists.

"Now, as the USSR again demands overflight rights over Germany, the crunch is on. If the Germans say *nein* the USSR attacks through the Fulda Gap, the Hof Corridor, where the two armies I mentioned stand ready. That would have been Myagkov's war: Germany attacked on two fronts, NATO troops in Germany in the pincers, Soviet divisions moving from the western border. The Americans are denied landing or overflight rights by the French. Germany will fight, of course, but can't last long. The UK is a base, but this isn't World War II, with time for planning an invasion. The U.S. must decide immediately whether to commit itself to nuclear war. Why bother? Soviet cities will have been evacuated; American cities are sitting ducks. The calculations are twenty to thirty million Soviet dead if war goes nuclear, ninety to a hundred and twenty million American dead.

"According to Soviet calculations, WALTZ wins them Europe, possibly at no cost if Germany allows the overflights, and at low cost if it is a war with an unreinforceable NATO army. NATO disappears. The U.S. stands alone against the entire Soviet-dominated world. The U.S. simply does not have the resources, even if it had the will—which it does not—to win."

Ben put down his notes. "That is WALTZ; the kind of music the Soviet Union expects the world to dance to. I have here the documents detailing Soviet military plans under the three contingencies: no German reaction, NATO non-nuclear response, NATO nuclear response. General Myagkov's underground CPS is the monitoring and feedback point for all Soviet military moves on the NATO eastern frontier."

The eleven men around the table were silent. They had listened to the natural evolution of Soviet policy as the Soviets entered an epoch where the West was the weaker. Each of these men was a Soviet expert, each understood that this was a predictable development, each in his own way had warned of such eventualities should NATO weaken. Yet here in a Belgrade conference room each was shocked, disbelieving. As Western men, each had, beneath his hawkish cries, been personally sure it could never happen.

"Thank you, Mr. Cornelius," said the four-star general gravely. "We will see what we can do to prevent this."

Luke Franklin walked out the door with Ben. Munson appeared with another message. Director Savic of UDBA would like, it said, the pleasure of meeting Mr. Cornelius at lunch, if he would be so kind.

"Safe to go?" asked Ben.

"Sure," said Franklin. "The game's over. You're kind of official now, by virtue of what's happened. See Savic if you like. He's an interesting fellow."

The next morning, after a good night's sleep as Luke's house guest—what a relief it was to have a night free of strain and fear—Ben had breakfast with Anna Oposevic. She'd come up from Split in hopes of seeing her brother. They'd talked on the phone the evening before, with Pyotr on the line, a secure connection that Franklin had set up. Anna had complained at first, but now understood that as Pyotr's sister she could not possibly visit him, since UDBA would inevitably be following her.

"You'll just have to come visit us in Oregon, Anna," Ben said. "See Valeria, Pyotr, enjoy yourself. By the way, have you heard from Valeria?"

"Oh yes," said Anna. "She's just fine. Your art shipment is due in soon. She says she's looking forward to seeing the ikons but not nearly as much as to seeing you. She was worried terribly all the time. I'll cable her now that everything is fine."

"How could she have been worried, Anna? Since none of us wrote, she couldn't have known about any of this."

Anna fiddled with her spoon. "Well, she may have had a hint of it. You see, when she has been here before, we talked a lot about Pyotr. I knew he was in danger. We wondered then if there weren't some way of his getting out, if it came to that. When she wrote that she had talked you into coming over, she mentioned maybe you were the one to help her family. She meant Pyotr, of course."

"You mean she talked me into coming here for reasons other than the art work?"

"Oh, I'd rather say she may have. Valeria had an

intuition, so to speak, Ben. You were the only one that either of us could turn to. And we were right." Anna reached across the table, took Ben's cheeks in her hands, and leaned across to kiss him.

"Intuition?" Ben was suspicious. "Do either of you have any more 'intuitions' that I ought to be warned about?"

"Just a little familial intuition, Ben, that's all. A man of your age, one who's done so much, ought to think about settling down, having children. Isn't that so?"

With such gentleness, Ben realized, the women of this world do plan the lives of men.

TWENTY-TWO

After breakfast with Anna, Ben sat down with Luke Franklin in his office. Franklin had been persuaded not to resign. Headquarters, he said, was going to give him a medal instead. He chuckled. The medal might, he said, be boobytrapped. In the meantime, what the hell, a little leverage, a little grace, but something would soon come up to turn it sour.

"You're seeing Savic at lunch?" Luke asked.

"Yes."

"It'll be fun. You'll eat well and he'll say thanks and mean it."

"That will be it, do you think?" Ben inquired.

"Oh, I doubt that. My bet is he'll try to recruit you. Why not? It would be a good move."

"Over my dead body. I'm going home to Oregon. I've had enough."

"Oh, I wouldn't be so quick to decide if I were you." Luke was leaning back in his chair, looking contemplative. "You could do worse and, of course, if you do it, why we'd have to keep you on our payroll. Double you."

"Double me?"

"You'd be a double agent, both sides witting. A little game. You work for them, but tell us what you learn. But naturally you don't tell them anything about us."

"And the Agency doesn't mind that kind of treachery?"

"Hardly. It's one of the oldest games in town. Fact is, when we heard Savic asked you to lunch I cabled Headquarters. They asked me to ask you to accept if he did make an offer. Bridge to the Yugoslavs so to speak. Our liaison up to now hasn't been all that hot. Besides, it keeps you on the Agency's leash; you take money and you have to be a little bit politic. You're good, Ben, and this way they keep you on board in case better things come up."

"You're kidding."

"Not a bit."

"Well, it's not for me. I don't like anything I've seen either of the Agency or of UDBA. I'm going home to fish with Pyotr."

"It's part time. Plenty of time to fish and sell antiques. Give us an excuse to get together here and there on the taxpayer's ticket. Think about it."

"I don't think so," said Ben.

"No hurry," said Franklin. "Talk to me after you see Savic. Think about it after you've been home for a while. It's open-ended."

As he left the CIA station, Ben thought he heard, in the distance, the shrill cry of a bird.

"Yes, sir!" Blagoje Savic received royal treatment in the elegant dining room of the Moskva Hotel. Savic was all smiles, a happy cobra over the first-course caviar.

"You can't imagine how much I've looked forward to meeting you," the UDBA chief said suavely.

"I bet," said Ben.

Savic grinned. "All's well that ends well. I confess I was a little put out that the Myagkov you gave me was an imposter, but he did prove useful. You knew that would be the case, I imagine?"

"I figured you wouldn't object to rolling up the Soviet agent networks around here. Lenev should have seen to that for you."

"Oh yes, that and more. Lots of little mysteries solved and of course some new ones raised. It keeps the work interesting. In any event, you've done a great service to Yugoslavia. My Minister asks you to accept this." He handed a small case to Ben. Inside was a medal resting on red satin. "You understand, we'd rather not have a public ceremony. It's better if we take the credit for Lenev and the rollup. As you would say, public relations. But we Yugoslavs, for all the fault you may find in us, do remember our friends and we're grateful. That comes from the heart, Mr. Cornelius, not PR."

"Thank you." Whatever his reputation for kidnapping and murder, Ben acknowledged that Savic was sincere. The medal pleased Ben more than he could have imagined.

"Tell me, do you like intelligence work?" Savic asked with a disarming smile.

Ben had to think about it. "I'm not sure. So far it's not been boring, but there are some drawbacks. From what I've seen of the organizational side, I'd say that is no plus."

Savic nodded. "It takes patience in any bureaucracy; one must tolerate fools and rascals."

"Patience isn't my strong point."

"So we have heard. Still, there's always room in this world for men of action, the ones who save the drowning child while the lifeguard is filling out forms. Our own partisans were like that. I was once like that, but you know how it is, the paper work, the meetings, they take their toll of character."

"So I've seen."

"As I was saying," Savic continued, "there is always room for independent people. Any organization which is facing real crises has to rely on them for creative solutions."

"I suppose." Ben wondered if Savic meant it? There was hardly much creativity in a Communist bureaucracy.

"You for example, UDBA could use a man like yourself. Oh, not regularly you understand." Savic was speaking quickly now. "And please appreciate that I'm not suggesting you would work against the U.S. or any NATO ally; after all, that's not in our interest either. But from time to time we do have special problems with the Soviets, or the Bulgarians, or Croats, problems in South America, Asia, northern Europe. It would be helpful if we had someone like you to play a key role in such operations." Savic paused, looking at Ben. "You're clever, Mr. Cornelius, and tough. You don't shy away from killing and even in this business a good mechanic is a rarity. What's more, you can be trusted."

"You're really asking me to work for UDBA?" Ben didn't try to hide his astonishment.

"Why not? I have no objection if you keep your own CIA informed; indeed, implicit in what I'm proposing is that we improve our liaison with your people. You can be part of that bridge. We pay well, very well, and there are amenities, lovely amenities . . ." Savic let his voice trail off, the tone suggesting whatever fancy might wish.

"This is hard to believe," said Ben.

"Think about it. As you've seen, we have our attractions here, certainly your Steffie is one. And I assume the CIA will continue to pay you. In other words, we do not object to your being a double agent as long as you get our work done. What do you think? It will be a great deal of money, Mr. Cornelius; travel, an expense account, and you would continue to have your fine cover, that antiquities business back home. By the way, did the ikons arrive safely? We did our best to expedite them."

"You did what?"

"Oh think nothing of it. A small service. Whatever we could do to help." There was humor in those cold eyes.

Ben paused, trying to sort things out. How could UDBA have been involved with the Oposevics? Was this not simply Savic pretending omniscience? Ben realized it would have been easy by now, long after the fact, for Savic to have checked Ben's activities in Split. He'd certainly have done that before offering Ben a job. But was there a touch of blackmail here? The bastard. Would he blackmail Ben using the safety of Anna and Edvard? As he thought about it, Ben felt his blood come up. He leaned across the table menacingly.

"What are you telling me, Savic?"

"Nothing at all," replied the other urbanely. "What you and your Valeria's uncle and aunt did was perfectly fine. Did we object? No. Really, you have no reason to be concerned. You love them, we love them. Don't worry." A soothing voice, but behind it, innuendo?

Ben looked him in the eye, speaking in a hard, knife-edged voice. "If you so much as look sideways at Anna or Edvard, I will personally kill you. Do you understand that?"

Savic smiled at him from across the table, his eyes impenetrable. "That is exactly what I like about you, you are loyal, you are tough, you are not afraid, and you are not entirely realistic as to the odds. Nevertheless, Mr. Cornelius, your friends have nothing to fear." He grinned broadly. "I take it that I may relax for my own safety? As head of UDBA I simply can't afford to have anyone else looking for my head." Savic laughed heartily.

Ben, cooling, wondered if he should feel chagrined, but only for an instant. This bastard, however much he'd been bluffing about his knowledge of the ikon exports, had most certainly been probing, looking for weakness. He would have blackmailed Ben if Ben had shown himself vulnerable.

"But now, do assure me that you will think about my offer. Shall I say, since I seem to have offended you, please?"

Ben, about to say "no" found himself reconsidering. After all, the Agency had encouraged him, and the rest of one's life spent only in Portland might, after this, be a bit dull. Ben twirled the wine glass in his fingers.

"Well, Mr. Cornelius?" Savic was pouring the dessert wine into both their glasses, waving off the hovering waiter; Savic, the attentive perfect host.

"Well," said Ben, "let's wait and see."

The two parted cordially, certainly not as friends, but as appreciative acquaintances who understood each other very well.

Dinner with Steffie at last. For old times' sake, he took her to the Metropole. They were not entirely alone; Savic— was it a token of esteem?—provided them with an escort: Bora. Steffie was furious, turning on Bora and telling him to leave the two of them alone. Bora, embarrassed, told them he had no choice. Director Savic wanted to be sure their country's honored guest was safe. He, Bora, apologized for the intrusion on their privacy. Steffie should know, he said, that he would never intentionally do her anything but kindness.

The way the poor devil looked at her, Ben realized it was so. Even Steffie softened.

"What we do," she said quietly, "is our business."

Bora, suffering envy's worst, agreed unhappily that yes, it certainly was their affair.

Dinner and dancing, elation, relief, and frivolity. Ben could fall for this lovely girl. It seemed to go both ways.

Then Valeria came to his mind. What a richness of choice. Was he fated to fall only for Yugoslav women?

"Will you come home with me?" Steffie asked over the wine. "My sister is still away. I have the keys to the apartment."

She was so direct. The liberated woman. Ben looked into warm eyes, followed the curves of firm breasts, imagined the warmth of thighs. How could a gentleman refuse a lady's bed? They took a cab to the apartment, poor Bora following in another cab behind.

Sex was absolutely delightful. So, too, was Steffie, every laughing, passionate, tender, thrusting, yielding inch of her. That wondrous selfishness, which weighs each one's pleasure by the joy of the other.

They talked that first night, as lovers do, of the future. They would dine again tomorrow, in the apartment, in bed perhaps. Yet the longer term was clearly set. Steffie had no interest in returning to America. Yugoslavia was her home. Would Ben return? He didn't know. Roots matter. So does work—he did not tell her of Luke's advice, Savic's offer, or of Valeria. He did say he'd promised to be Pyotr's fishing companion.

They laughed some, cried some, made much love. Blessed, thought Ben, are those who enjoy, without regret, the good that is. He kissed her again, put his lips to her nipples, felt the surging desire. It was one hell of a fine way to say goodbye. It might not even be goodbye. If there was a bird on his shoulder these days and nights, it was only a nightingale.

Over breakfast the morning of the day they had agreed would be the last, Ben, full of love, felt a small devil in him. A man does, after all, want to hear of his own importance.

"I know we've agreed it's over, Steffie, sensible adults and all that, but you must admit, we have been something special to each other."

"Very special, Ben."

"But you wouldn't consider even visiting me in America?"

Steffie smiled. "You're testing me, Ben. You know how I feel. No, we've made our agreement. I plan to stay here."

"If I came back here?" As he said it, Ben wondered why he was skating so close to the edge of the nuptial precipice.

"Who can say, Ben? I'll go my way, you'll go yours. One can't predict the future. Perhaps I'll be married, fat, and have three children by then. My husband would be jealous."

Ben felt hurt. What he wanted to hear was what every man does; how each of his loves loves him only and forever.

"Look Steffie, mind you now I'm not serious, but shouldn't we even consider the possibility of getting married?" Ben knew he was crazy to ask, opening floodgates, complicating life. After all, didn't he want to marry Valeria instead? Or both of them? Or neither? How does a man really know?

"Ben, it's better not to talk about that." She spoke tenderly, but was unsmiling.

He looked at her: a diaphanous nightgown over peach-brown skin; her breasts small melons, the nipples pert and pink. Damn it, he wanted something more than realism from her.

"You wouldn't even consider marrying me?" Ben was astonished, for such is the vanity of lovers.

"I love you, Ben, in my way. You are a lovely man. But no, I don't think we should marry."

He could see it pained her to say it. It pained him to hear it. "I'll be damned," he said.

"Take no offense, my darling. I just think it wouldn't work."

"But why not?"

Her gray eyes surveyed him. "I told you it was better not to pursue this. But since you insist, I'll tell you." She was annoyed. "You're not the one I want for my husband, nor to father my children. Don't be hurt. A woman has to decide these things sensibly in spite of how she feels. I admit I've thought about it myself a great deal. But over these last few days we have gotten to know each other . . ."

"Intimately," Ben interrupted.

"As you say, intimately." She went on. "You're not the naive young American I met that day at the airport. These last weeks have hardened you, Ben, perhaps a necessary hardness—after all, you saved my life, saved your general, and helped both our countries immeasurably. You are really a hero. But you pay a price for being able to be one. Not quite brutality, but you're not too far from it. And I'm afraid of you in a way. I don't want a warrior in the house, Ben, nor such a good liar as I've watched you be. There's a cunning in you, Ben. I see that is what some men must be, spies, for instance. But that's not for me. I don't like blood, nor plots, nor cunning."

She was right, Ben didn't want to hear it. What was worse, he knew it was true.

Steffie saw how hurt he was. She got up, walked around the table and held his head in her arms.

"Do you understand, Ben? I do love you, but not what you're becoming. I can't help that. Kiss and make up? Bed?"

Ben smiled at her. He realized this was one special woman.

"Bed," he said, "where I shall forget my sorrows between your thighs." But he knew he would not.

"Forget your sorrows," she said as they walked toward the bedroom. "But don't forget me. Not to marry isn't the same as not to remember." She pulled him toward the bed. "After all," she said, giving herself to him, "you can't have everything."

As he plunged himself into her, he felt she was very near to being wrong. He'd already forgotten to be sad.

The ambassador, Luke, hangers-on, Bora, all said goodbye to Ben at the airport. The VIP lounge was courtesy of the Interior Minister, a reminder of those amenities awaiting him if he accepted Savic's offer. His first-class ticket home was on the American taxpayer. Pyotr had left several days before, muttering, for being a moustachioed, heavy-haired Dutch tulip grower had been an affront to his image.

Luke was shaking his hand. "The Director wants me to be sure you understand you have a job with the Agency. Full time if you want, or beginning the way we talked about the other day. If I were you I wouldn't touch it full time. You'd end up a hardface like me. What shall I tell him?"

"Tell him I just don't know. As I said, maybe, and thanks for the invitation."

"No hurry," said Luke, grasping his shoulder warmly. "There's time. I'll be in Oregon next summer to join you and Pyotr fishing."

Ben got on the plane, waving to them all.

He was riding in the upper cabin of the British Airways 747, sipping champagne. At London there had been the VIP courtesies again, this time thanks to a very proper and reserved fellow at Heathrow, a Franklin type in Savile Row MI 6 clothing. In flight now, Ben was glad to be on his way home at last. He was reading the *Herald Tribune*, the front page.

Paris, France (Agence France Presse). The French Sureté today announced the arrest of over 1200 illegal aliens in Strasbourg and surrounding Alsace-Lorraine. A large cache of arms, including automatic weapons and mortars, was uncovered. Printing presses with plates prepared for what French officials termed "incendiary" and "terrorist" propaganda were found, along with a large supply of currency and false documents. Highly placed sources indicated that there were plans for election manipulations, assassinations, and mass agitation. These same sources hinted that two unnamed "foreign powers" had been implicated. Official spokesmen stated that further arrests throughout France could be expected.

Paris (AP). The French capital today was shocked by the announcement that Paul Cloché and Jean Soulé, leaders of the pro-Soviet faction in the French Communist Party, had been arrested for plotting the overthrow of the government. Raids by French security forces throughout the capital and in major provincial cities had yielded arms, documents, and other materials which, said the official announcement, "clearly implicate foreign powers in an effort to destroy the French Republic through criminal election fraud and violence." Sources next to the highest levels of government said that France would tomorrow announce that it was re-establishing full ties with NATO.

London (Reuters). Commentators here quote Foreign Office officials as saying that an urgent meeting of heads of state from NATO countries, along with allies such as Japan, will be held very soon. "Non-aligned" nations may also be invited, among which Austria, Sweden, China and Yugoslavia were mentioned. Rumors have it that a major intelligence coup has revealed Soviet plans to precipitate a crisis through political destabilization of NATO countries and direct military threat. A source in the Foreign Office stated that, in the light of documentary evidence produced by American intelligence of a most serious threat to the free world, NATO military capabilities will be dramatically enhanced.

Moscow (Tass). The Soviet leadership today denounced the "slander and calumny" directed by the reactionary NATO leadership against the peace-loving socialist peoples. *Izvestia*, in a front-page editorial, directly accused the French government of precipitating a crisis in the movement toward peace by encouraging right-wing agitators and their Nazi henchmen. The Soviet government takes the most serious possible view of the brutal repression of human rights in France, as evidenced in the arrest of peaceful German workers and the suppression of the political rights of arrested French Communist leaders.

Belgrade (UP). The Interior Ministry today confirmed speculations that a senior Soviet embassy official had defected to Belgrade. Widespread arrests in Yugoslavia, with public charges of "unspeakable" Soviet violations of Yugoslav friendship and integrity, had triggered these rumours. In an unprecedented off-the-record session, the Minister of the Interior acknowledged that a second defection, a senior Soviet general, had taken place. He credited UDBA with the intelligence coup.

New York, by Josh Seymour. My exclusive contacts in Belgrade and Washington have revealed that an American secret agent was responsible for engineering the escapes of two of the most important Soviet defectors in years. These sources claim that the CIA intentionally timed these defections to disrupt the normal evolution of peaceful relations between NATO and the Warsaw Pact. The saber-rattling in the Western capitals as a consequence of these defectors' claims is proof, if such is needed, that the CIA's clandestine activities have once again brought the world to the brink of war. Unsupervised, uncontrolled, these illegal wars—undeclared but fought by the CIA and its allied services in the UK, France, Germany, and even UDBA in Yugoslavia—represent the greatest threat to the security of America that can be imagined. When will these criminal CIA spies be put where they belong, in prison?

Washington (UP). The FBI today announced the arrest, on espionage charges, of Miles Saunders, a Foreign Service officer until recently stationed in Belgrade. An FBI spokesman said the arrest resulted from information provided to the U.S. by the Yugoslav government.

In his confession, Saunders admits to acting as a Russian "agent of influence," seeking to block the recent defection of an as-yet-unidentified Soviet major general. Saunders' confession describes how his repeated efforts to communicate with his Belgrade "handler," KGB Major Vladimerovich Komiakov, were frustrated by Komiakov's failure to service the dead drop, a clandestine message exchange center behind a statuary niche in the lobby of the Moskva Hotel. "Komiakov simply forgot to do it," lamented Saunders. Komiakov, Belgrade sources report, identified Saunders to Yugoslav authorities during interrogations following Komiakov's attempt to hijack an airplane in Belgrade. Authorities here agree that if the Soviets had received the information in Saunders' messages, the defection would have been blocked.

Washington (AP). The president at his news conference today refused comment on reports circulating in official Washington that the Soviet general defecting to the U.S., identified today by a CIA leak as General Pyotr Myagkov, had been recruited three years ago through his niece, Valeria Oposevic, a CIA contract agent. These reports claim that Miss Oposevic, of Yugoslav origin, worked through her aunt to "handle" the general, who was brought out of Russia only when he came into possession of plans showing that Soviet military moves against NATO were imminent. The American agent who brought both Myagkov and an unnamed KGB colonel into the West remains un-identified. CIA sources assert that the defection, the most significant intelligence coup since World War II, was a "routine operation in line with the Agency's mandate."

Ben finished his reading and asked the stewardess for more champagne. The woman sitting next to him on the lounge seat in this spacious stratospheric flying bar, a white-haired dowager, had been reading the *Herald Tribune* as Ben had held it in his lap.

"Isn't it a wonder," she said, "what goes on in the world? That spy business. You know, I travel a lot, but I've never met a spy. I bet I wouldn't know one if I saw one."

Ben smiled, handed her his copy of the *Herald Tribune*.

"Bet you wouldn't," he replied. "Same with me. Bet neither of us would."

He was thinking of the president's news conference. His Valeria had some tall explaining to do. But then, Ben knew, so might he.